A MESSAGE FROM CHICKEN HOUSE

My grandmother was Irish and she was always telling stories – these were often scandalous and sometimes cantankerous. So you'll soon see why I was drawn to Alvy Carragher's hilarious, poignant and irrepressibly wise story of growing up in a bonkers Irish household with more love than sense. Can our heroine sort out the mess that is her family – and save the chickens too? You'll laugh, cry and consider turning vegan . . . though not necessarily in that order!

BARRY CUNNINGHAM
Publisher
Chicken House

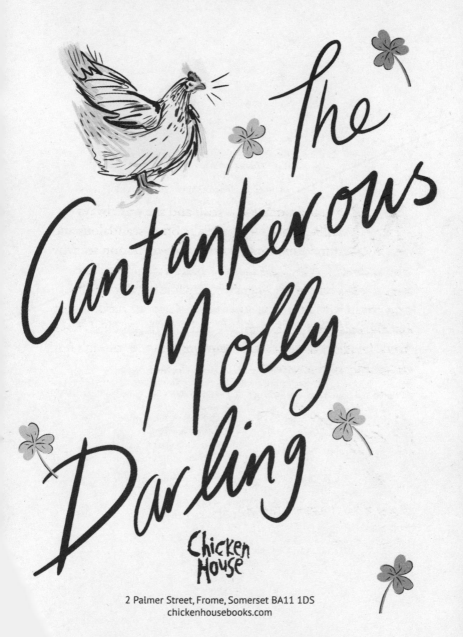

The Cantankerous Molly Darling

Chicken House

2 Palmer Street, Frome, Somerset BA11 1DS
chickenhousebooks.com

ALVY CARRAGHER

Text © Alvy Carragher 2019

First published in Great Britain in 2019
Chicken House
2 Palmer Street
Frome, Somerset BA11 1DS
United Kingdom
www.chickenhousebooks.com

Cover and interior design by Helen Crawford-White
Typeset by Dorchester Typesetting Group Ltd
Printed and bound in Great Britain by CPI Group (UK) Ltd, Croydon CR0 4YY

The paper used in this Chicken House book is made
from wood grown in sustainable forests.

1 3 5 7 9 10 8 6 4 2

British Library Cataloguing in Publication data available.

PB ISBN 978-1-911490-54-8
eISBN 978-1-912626-33-5

To Stephen Murphy, for always making me laugh
(even when I am mid-teary-cleaning-rampage).
Without you, I'd be far too stressed to write a novel.

I wake to Mum singing Dolly Parton in the attic, which is never a good sign.

I pull the duvet over my head and try to make a soundproof bed-cave but it's no use. Our old farmhouse intensifies noises. Between its groaning floorboards and moaning pipes, and Mum's tendency to break into song, there's never a quiet moment.

The stretched-out lyrics filter down through the floorboards as she croons about how to make a living.

Mum started to sing three days after Dad left, as part of her new arty persona, and I've learnt that the songs tend to *mean* something. Her performance is no doubt connected to the fact that it's the anniversary of Dad's departure – 365 days since he packed his bags and left behind a PowerPoint presentation entitled 'Data Supporting my Departure from Farming'. Mum pretended not to care, but if anyone ever bothers marrying me and then leaving me, I would like them to use proper stationery.

Mum interrupts my thoughts by switching song to 'I Will Always Love You'. As she strains for notes that don't exist, I roll out from under the duvet and sit on the edge of my bed, wiping the sleep from my eyes while I think about how to handle the day.

Luckily, Polly never came home last night, so that's one less piece of melodrama to worry about.

My room still looks as if a six-year-old sleeps here, with its sunshine-yellow walls, rainbow duvet cover, and an old doll's house that I store my knickers in. Aside from that, there's not much to it: a load of fairy lights criss-crossing over my double bed, a disgruntled pile of clothes, and a paint-faded wardrobe that still boasts my early crayon scribbles.

I pull on a fluffy, giant jumper over my pyjamas, and tie my long brown hair into its usual loose plait. It is my only noticeable feature – I'm the kind of girl who looks so ordinary strangers wave at me just in case. I stick my feet into the pair of green wellies that stand to attention beside my bed, having accepted the fate of wellies long ago. There's no point pretending we're going to wake to a life of glamour anytime soon.

'Here we go,' I say to the upstairs hall when I step outside my bedroom.

Leaving my room usually feels like it requires some type of armour, something to deflect the chaos that lurks in the rest of our house. As I pass the door to Polly's room, I pause and listen, but there's none of her usual shuffling and murmuring. She met BrainDrain's mother last night. Afterwards she texted me to say she was taking a long walk. Which most likely means they broke up. The time Dermot dumped her, she walked thirty kilometres across the fields and ended up three towns away.

There's a loud thump from the attic, followed by a drawn out *youuuuuuuuu* that sounds more like a wild cat in a death grip than a heartbreaking solo. I glance at the trapdoor to the attic but decide to avoid Mum for the moment.

Instead I make my way carefully down the stairs, my breath visible in the cold air. Morning light makes our house look shabby. The once-plush stair carpet is now muddied by time, as if the colour red is decomposing there. The actual stairs are rotting too, so Mum has stuck plastic glow-in-the-dark stars where it's safe to step, and there are buckling turrets of dusty books lining the bannisters. Most of the books are older than me and, according to Mum, have been sitting on our stairs since the beginning of books. We refer to it as the Great Wall of Books and we slot books in and out of it, treating it like a precarious game of Jenga. It is an unspoken house rule that one should never compromise its overall structure.

In the kitchen, the sink is crusted with food. Mum used the last of the oats in a flapjack binge last night. I'd found her spooning the gooey mixture straight into her mouth, without a thought for baking them into squares. She considers the final step (i.e. the baking) irrelevant. I'll have to fetch eggs from the shed for breakfast or try to locate bread that isn't sprouting fungus. Our larder is home to many foods; few of them are edible.

I scrape out the hardened oats and add them to the slops bucket, and think about washing up, but the water in the tap is icy and the kettle takes five minutes to wake up in the morning. The fire in the range is out. And the fuel box, a giant coffin-type chest that is about as big as the range, is empty.

'Typical,' I grumble. Feeding the chickens, I decide, is a much better option than deciphering Mum's Sunday-morning vocals or cleaning the kitchen or wondering where Polly ended up walking to last night.

Feeding our seven little cluckers has always been my responsibility. There have been two deaths over the years: old age and an unfortunate incident with a water pump that I won't go into. But other than that, this sisterhood of hens has served us well. Farmers aren't meant to name animals, but ours are rescue hens and I've carefully christened them all after literary characters: Mrs Danvers, Boo Radley, Scarlett O'Hara, Miss Trunchbull, The White Witch, Bellatrix and Lady Macbeth.

I stir the slops bucket to make sure it's full of the chicken's favourites: oat scrapings, carrot peelings, lumps of tuna and leftover baked beans. Not exactly appetizing, but the chickens aren't one bit fussy. They have been known to savage tiramisu. As chicken's lives go, they have pretty cushy ones. They sleep inside the shed at night, and all day they can choose between wandering the yard in search of meaning or heading back to bed if it all seems a bit too much. Dad had wanted to fence them in, but Mum tended to take charge when it came to the farm and said a chicken would never leave you if you treated it right. It's a pity she didn't extend the same logic to husbands.

Heaving the slops bucket with me, I walk out of the kitchen, through the small hall, past the stairs and out into the big hall. It is home to a banjaxed grandmother clock, a large flagstone floor, and a giant rug that has a path beaten into it from the front door towards the kitchen. I nod good morning at the Three Paddys – three snarling fox heads mounted on a plaque by the front door, an heirloom that remains despite Mum's best efforts to hack them off the wall.

Dad's old orange waterproof coat hangs on a hook beside the Three Paddys. Not that he wore it much; he was never prone to the outdoors. Sometimes he helped me feed the chickens, but he didn't like chaos or getting his hands dirty, so he'd stand nearby and tell me his latest notions. They were always new ways to revolutionize the farm, but never became more than just things for him to say while I fed the chickens. Sometimes I wonder if I should have encouraged him more.

The coat fitted him perfectly, but swamps me, skirting my knees. It is necessary, though, because we live, literally, on a big wet hill. That's what our farm name, Leitirmór, means: big wet hill.

I often think of our house as a place where clouds go to reproduce. The rest of the sky might be entirely blue, but there will always be a wisp of rain hovering over our hill. Today the red-and-green corrugated roofs and white walls of our patchwork of sheds are bright against the slate sky. Dark skies make the rest of the world look so much more vibrant. The splay of green fields that reach in every direction looks bright and inviting, although the reality is muck to the knees, and cowpats to the elbows.

I shuffle between the potholes and puddles, careful not to spill the slops down my pyjama leg – it has happened before. In the shed where I keep the chicken supplies, I stick my head in the grain sack and take a deep breath. There's nothing quite as lovely as the smell of chicken grain; it's the only part of a farm-morning worth inhaling. Then I dig in with the red enamel cup, scoop out the grain and mix it through the slops. I fill the watering can from the rusty old tap. The water is so I can top up the water trough in their shed and then indulge the chickens in a bit of a sprinkle.

I close the supply shed and go to unleash my beauties.

On a Sunday, the chickens are normally causing a ruckus. They're accustomed to being let out earlier on school mornings and have adjustment issues at the weekends. I've explained about teenagers needing to catch up on sleep, but, as with everything else I confide in the chickens, they don't appear to listen.

Today, though, the yard is strangely quiet. When I open the shed door, rather than the usual burst of feathers, clucking and general mayhem as the chickens make a beeline for the slops bucket, there is only silence.

My first thought is that a chicken has died, and the others are honouring their lost feathered friend. Since Dad left, my mind defaults to the worst-case scenario and then, after a deep breath, slowly allows room for more reasonable ideas to float to the surface.

My more reasonable thought is that they must be hiding.

'*Shuk, shuk, shuk,*' I call as I step into the dark shed. '*Shuk, shuk, shuk.*' Dad used to raise his eyebrows every time I did this. He said it was another of Mum's ridiculous inventions. And though I agreed, Mum was the authority on farming. She grew up at Leitirmór, and inherited the farm. She said chickens responded to this call and that it was passed down through the generations.

'*Shuk, shuk, shuk,*' I call again. And it feels meaningful, as if I come from a long line of chicken whisperers, rather than bog-standard Ballyfert farmers who happened to have chickens.

The shed has always been full of straw, shelves, old kitchen drawers and cupboards without doors for the chickens to make nests in, but as my eyes adjust to the gloom, I notice that the cupboard homes have been smashed up, the wood piled in the corner like fire-wood, and the floor has been swept clean of straw. Aside from a few feathers here and there, the place is empty.

My chickens are gone.

I stand completely still, letting their absence sink in. Mum has sold off every other animal since Dad's departure – the cow, the three goats, the fifty sheep, the six ducks (who might have left of their own accord) – but I'd petitioned hard for the chickens. They were the only piece of our old life left. If I kept them fat and happy, part of me felt like Dad would return and the farm would go back to normal. Mum said it was the dumbest thing she'd ever heard, considering Dad had about as much interest in farming as in toenail clippings. But we'd spoken about it and eventually she agreed to let me keep them. That was just last week.

And now they're gone.

Like Dad.

Here one day. Gone the next.

My life an endless series of disappearances.

Turning away from the empty shed, I march back up the yard, stamping right in the middle of any puddles, letting the muddy water splash my pyjama bottoms, kicking at pebbles and behaving in a generally rebellious manner, the anger gurgling away. Leitirmór House looms at the top of the hill. Even the ivy on its walls looks half-hearted, as if it knows by now that nobody will bother cutting it.

Mum's probably peeping out of the attic window. How dare she sit up there yodelling Dolly Parton tunes as if that was any way to warn me? My chickens aren't ordinary farm animals; nobody else will care for them like me.

Will anyone else bother to sit down and keep Mrs

Danvers company when she gets creepy? Or praise Boo Radley for the unexpected bottle caps she leaves amongst her eggs? Or put a mirror in the coop for Scarlett O'Hara? What about Miss Trunchbull? Who will hug her when she battle-rams walls?

For all I know, Mum has sent them to a farm where a bunch of philistines will fail to take care of their needs. Will they know to make a higher shelf for The White Witch, so she can nest above the others, ruffling her milk-coloured feathers with an air of cool detachment? They certainly won't understand that Bellatrix, my feathered nightmare, needs to be kept in isolation whenever she takes to pecking Lady Macbeth.

And as for Lady Macbeth. The most misunderstood of the bunch. What if the new owners force her to act like a rooster? Sure, she was born one, but she was so determined to be a hen that she learnt to cluck, build nests, and tries to lay eggs. Part of my daily routine is to slip a new egg into her bundle. Lady Macbeth guards these dormant treasures, strutting about with pride, nuzzling them while the other chickens are guzzling slops.

How can Mum upend their lives like this? As if it wasn't traumatic enough being rescue chickens the first time round.

My babies in a factory farm. How dare she!

I'll show her.

As I near the house, I kick an empty bean can that has fallen out of the recycling.

Yes, that's right, I'll show her exactly what I'm made of.

Why didn't she have the backbone to tell me herself? Did she sell my chickens to fund her stupid new art habit?

She's had her year of pretending we're fine, fine, fine, selling off the animals, spending all day in the attic, dating the insufferable Hulk, and ruining what's left of our lives.

My thoughts aren't this constructed, though, more a jumble of:

It's not fair, I hate the world, incoherent mind grumble, MY chickens, MINE.

2

I fling open the trapdoor to the attic, hoping to surprise Mum with the momentum of my anger. The attic is the length of the house and there are four large skylights, which allow the grey sky's light to filter into the room in a gloomy, romantic way. One half of the attic is stacked with bottles and jars full of jams and the remnants of Mum's pickling phase, from back when she was still pretending to be a fully functioning farmer. There are abandoned bottles of home-made wine and jars of questionable chutneys, including several miserable rows of her infamous Pickled Chilli Carrot Surprise.

The other half of the attic is now Mum's art studio. It's a mess of canvases covered in paint splats and half-made horse sculptures constructed from the recycling. Mum has a wiry build and a goat's tendency to perch in precarious places. She is sitting on a pile of wooden boxes puncturing a milk carton with a stapler. She is dressed in her art attire: a tunic that she splattered with paint to make it look authentic, a blue wig that she stapled flowers to and, of course, a pair of tights that depict the solar system. She has thankfully stopped singing.

'How could you?' I say. I try to look as powerful as possible but am aware that even a power stance can't detract from the pathetic nature of staging a confrontation in one's pyjama-welly ensemble. I make a mental note to assemble an emergency outfit for future arguments. Something I can whip on and off on a whim.

'Oh, Petal of the Earth, I knew you'd get upset. I can't afford them – I mean, have you any idea what it costs to feed those greedy peckers?' Mum says, without so much as glancing up from the milk carton. She bangs the stapler off it in vain.

'This isn't working,' she mumbles to herself. She drops the stapler and picks up a screwdriver, which she uses to violently dent the carton.

'Mum,' I try again, doing my best not to wince as she narrowly misses her hands, 'it's not fair. You said I could keep the chickens.'

'Well, Petal of the Sky, you can blame your father – we can't afford them now and that is that,' Mum says. I hate it when she calls me Petal of the Anything, but

I choose to ignore it.

'But I use my pocket money for the feed . . . they hardly cost you a thing.'

'Really? And where does this magical pocket money come from? Don't tell me – you've been culti-vating a rare money tree beneath the floorboards . . . or, wait . . . you've managed to fit in a job between mooning about after chickens and school?' Mum eyes me before returning to her milk carton. 'You're too old for chicken nonsense. It was cute when you were eight, but now it's just another luxury we can't afford.'

Mum loves to talk about luxuries we can't afford – they include everything from crunchy peanut butter to fancy soap. They always tend to be things she never had much time for in the first place, like *my* chickens.

As Mum batters the carton, I realize there is no way to explain what the chickens mean to me, even to myself. Is it familiarity? Or routine? I'm not sure. I know that Polly is too busy to notice me most of the time, Dad may have disappeared, and Mum might be reinventing herself in the attic, but the chickens remain constant. They need me in much the same way they always have.

'Well, at least tell me what you did with them,' I say.

'I sold them,' Mum says, 'and it doesn't matter who bought them, so don't ask.'

She looks up and gives me a half-smile. Mum rarely portrays the correct emotions.

'Who?' I say, knowing from her expression that I won't like the answer.

'Someone who can afford them, that's all you need to know,' she says, shrugging. 'They won't bother these people one bit.'

'Oh, I see, and when exactly did they bother you? Last time I checked I was the one who dedicated my life to minding them.'

'Minding them is one thing, Molly. Paying their bills is quite another. Look, these people have over three hundred chickens. And it wasn't even my idea – I'm struggling to make ends meet and Gary said I should sell off something valuable.'

'Three hundred chickens! Mum, they will end up in a skillet. And since when does the Hulk have any say in family matters?'

'Well, there's no use getting all high and mighty. I've never seen you turn down a chicken sandwich,' she says, placing her sculpture to one side and giving me a long, hard look. 'And I've asked you before to stop calling him the Hulk. Gary has a name, you need to respect that.'

Mum looks upset. Gary is a walking muscle that showed up with a shoulder to weep on a couple of months after Dad left. Not that Mum does any weeping; mostly the Hulk encourages the art habit and takes her out to dinner once a week. Whenever he knocks at the door, I make a point of answering it with contemptuous silence. Lately, Mum's been threatening to make us spend family time together. Which would not be ideal, as the Hulk's son, Fiachra, is in my year. The last thing I need is for him to witness this crumbling dump, complete with a mad mother in the attic.

'I don't need to respect the Hulk. You don't get to demand that.' I cross my arms and glower at her. She glares back, settling the milk carton on her lap and wrinkling her brow as she considers what to say next.

Suddenly, there is a loud crashing downstairs. We both glance at the floorboards as if it is possible to see through them.

'Did you hear that, Molly?' Mum asks, looking puzzled.

'I'm not deaf.' This is meant to be cutting, but it lands as a sulky flump. I am in no mood to be distracted from Mum's ultimate betrayal. Before I can muster any more chicken-related accusations, there is another loud bang in the hall.

'I wonder . . .' Mum says.

'Do you think?' I say, the chickens fading into the background.

We listen to the clattering downstairs, our hearts

in synch.

'He always was very clumsy, wasn't he?' Mum says.

'I suppose so,' I say. 'You don't really—'

'It's the anniversary,' Mum breathes, her voice tense. It is a relief to discover Mum has been counting the days too, to know I'm not the only one.

It isn't impossible. Maybe he hasn't abandoned us permanently. Perhaps it was simply one of those midlife crises that plague TV dads. It makes sense, kind of. There is a nice symmetry to it – a gap year. One of those run-of-the-mill breaks from reality. If he shows up now, we can forget all about it.

Mum has done a pretty convincing job of pretending she doesn't give a damn. She has spent an entire year reinventing her life and ignoring the Dad-shaped hole in it. The crashing sounds have changed that. I can see there is light in her eyes, the kind of light she usually reserves for triple-chocolate fudge cakes.

'Should we . . .' I suggest, because we are both frozen in place, listening carefully to him crashing about the kitchen.

'I didn't, oh God . . . you know . . . but I didn't really believe . . .' Mum says, getting up slowly from her project and dusting off her solar-system tights. She moves down the attic ladder dream-like. I almost tell her to take off the wig, but stop myself. It's about time Dad realized he isn't the only one who gave up another life to come and live on the farm. It's not as if Mum spent her childhood dreaming of polytunnels and manure.

I follow her through the upstairs hall, suddenly conscious of the state it is in. Coats, shoes, dust and a random teapot all lounge about, as if they had escaped in a hurry and had no idea what to do with their freedom. Mum practically floats down the stairs, her feet barely skimming the glow-in-the-dark stars. We are both trance-like as we approach the kitchen.

My heart thunders with hope. We are moments away from wrapping our arms around Dad's long thin frame, minutes from returning to a kind of normality. Mum reaches for the kitchen door, her hand resting on the knob.

There is another clatter and the sound of someone talking animatedly to themselves.

My heart sinks so heavily I'm not sure it will ever float again.

Dad rarely talks, let alone to himself. Mum turns from the door. Her tender, hopeful expression flickers to sadness, and then, as she draws herself into a firm line, disappears into something cold and removed.

There is only one person in our family who makes this kind of entrance. It is just like Polly to make a racket on the day Dad is most likely to return.

Mum slowly opens the door.

Polly cavorts around the kitchen with a dustpan brush in one hand and feather duster in the other. She swings them at cobwebs, keeping up a steady stream of comments about the absolute filth of the place.

There's a big bowl of suds and steaming water beside the semi-empty larder unit. Most of the larder's former contents have been emptied on to the kitchen floor. There's Weetabix which has escaped the package, mouldy bread huddled in a corner, and an assortment of sticky jars waiting to be scrubbed. We watch in disbelief as Polly deftly swipes the top shelf of the larder with the brush, sending a cloud of dust and some old pasta shells flying into the air. Her cheeks are pink and flushed from the cold, she's wearing a neat pair of kitten heels and a fitted navy dress, her dark hair pinned into a Dutch braid. I notice that her feet are caked in mud, as if she walked home barefoot through the fields. She looks equal parts dignified and crazy. Polly spins to face us, accidentally knocking a jar of spices from its shelf. It smashes on the ground, sending a cloud of cinnamon dust into the air.

'If it isn't my cantankerous darlings?' she laughs, coughing a little as the cinnamon cloud rises around her. 'And what are we doing on this, this most momentous of mornings?'

Anything else she is about to say catches in her throat. She doubles over, the cough worsening as the cinnamon makes its way into her system. Within seconds, she's crouching on the floor.

'Where were you last night?' Mum says, channelling the warmth and understanding of your standard doormat. 'You can't just disappear like that whenever you get your heart broken.'

Mum's tone, or the cinnamon, causes Polly to start crying. Judging by the state of the kitchen, she has been on the brink of crumbling from the moment she picked up the dustpan. Polly gets possessed by a frenzied housewife whenever she feels uncertain. Between the walking and the cleaning, she's quite useful in an emergency. Although it does make me worry about her; the last time she was this antsy it was after Dermot dumped her, and that took months to wear off. I hadn't thought she was overly attached to BrainDrain, but there must have been something about him I missed.

We stand stiffly, watching. Polly is an ugly crier. It's hard to know what to do. Sometimes she gets sad for days, but refuses to talk about it. When we were younger, she would curl up and let it all out, but the last year has just been tantrums followed by a dazzling smile and denial. Thinking about how to cope with Polly gives me a headache. She is this funny, bright creature that disappears all of a sudden into a cloud of gloom.

'You should have called,' Mum says, ignoring the state of her daughter. As if crying fits are by appointment only.

'That's not helping, Mum,' I say, because Polly isn't responsible for our disappointment. There is a stretchy silence. It goes on and on as I try to formulate a sentence that says, *Maybe you should try to be a mother for five minutes.* I can't figure out how to word it, though, so it is Mum that speaks first.

'I don't have time for all this nonsense. If it's not a weird chicken obsession, it's a kitchen rampage. You girls need to grow up and act like responsible teenagers.'

Mum brings up responsibility whenever Polly is in the room. Mostly because Polly failed the Leaving Cert after Dad left and her boyfriend dumped her in the same week. She is taking a year out. I thought that meant she would travel or get a job, but she's really only used it to date BrainDrain and bake cakes.

'Mum, would you ever shut up?' I say. Polly's crying has descended into soft hiccupping sobs.

'Oh, fine, of course, don't listen to the truth. I'll be in the attic when you figure out how to get your act together,' Mum says.

I follow her into the hall, hoping she might come to her senses. But Mum ascends the stairs in her blue wig, without glancing back.

'You two need to think about your behaviour,' she says as she goes. 'You're not children.'

I feel like pointing out that by law I am a child for several more years. But Mum isn't listening. I take a deep breath before turning to deal with the situation in the kitchen.

Polly is still crying, but has gathered up enough of her old self to be looking at the food on the floor with interest. Polly loves to cook; it's about the only time she ever behaves like a decent human.

'I should put some of this away,' she says, picking up a sticky jar reluctantly. She hauls herself on to all fours and stands up shakily.

'Is everything OK?' I say, belatedly.

'Oh, sure, right on track,' she laughs, her face contorting into a half-angry, half-sad shape.

'Don't you think we've enough to worry about without you acting like this?'

'What could you be worried about, Molly? Does some boy not want to kiss you back?'

'Some of us have more important things to worry about than boys. Toast?' I say, popping a stale piece of bread into the toaster.

'I don't even eat gluten. Do you know how bad gluten is?' Polly says, glaring at the toaster as if it has been sent to climb down her throat and pollute her bloodstream.

'Well, maybe you should get some sleep instead?'

Polly nods, shoulders sagging as she straightens up and wipes at her eyes, causing the leftover tears to smudge her mascara and leave dark streaks. She seems more upset than if it was a standard break-up. I can't help wondering if Dermot is back in town with a new girlfriend. Or if BrainDrain said something cruel as he was saying goodbye (although I'm not sure he's capable).

'What?' she asks, forcing a smile.

'Nothing.'

There's no point asking, I won't get any real answers.

We make our way soundlessly upstairs and settle ourselves on Polly's bed. She flops down with a sigh of relief, and I perch beside her, ready to flee if she takes another turn for the dramatic.

'You're so good to me, Molly, I should tell you my news,' Polly says. She props herself up with all the pillows on her bed, loosening her hair from its plait and letting it fall around her face in crinkled waves. Her big blue eyes are red-rimmed. She wiggles her bra out from under her dress, sighing with relief, before nestling back into the cushions.

'I'm getting married on Saturday evening, Molly,' she says, holding up her hand, and revealing a ring. 'Everything will be OK now.'

'Married . . . Dermot?' I'm baffled, Dermot left for South Korea ages ago, and there is no way she would end up with someone like BrainDrain – it wouldn't make any sense.

'No, not Dermot, Brian,' she says with a tinge of sadness.

'Brian?'

She yawns as I reach for her hand, holding the ring up to the light. It sparkles, looking incredibly out of place on her young hand. She isn't *that* much older than me. Maybe if there were ten years between us? But there are only four. Her hands are soft, her navy nail varnish chipped, and her nails all bitten. Surely people ready for marriage have French manicures.

We both gape at it, hypnotized by its life-changing twinkle.

'Brian says it was his Granny's,' she says. 'Brian Doran . . .' His name sounds uncertain on her lips, as if it is a trick she is playing on herself. She repeats it five times, before she falls asleep.

Brian Doran.

Surely not? It would make more sense for them to break up. They have nothing but their location in common. Just yesterday, Polly made some disparaging remark about his *mammy issues*. I was sure the all-night walk had been because dinner at their house had proven to be the last straw. Part of me imagined her despairing over a boring plate of bacon and cabbage and legging it before the dessert.

I sit beside her, stroking her dark hair, looking around the room. The walls are papered with band posters and old photos, and her clothes are heaped on every possible surface. Old schoolbooks and childhood dolls fight for dominance in one corner, and dream-catchers dangle from the ceiling. Her science phase is still visible on the now-abandoned desk. She sighs softly in her sleep, the ring glinting as her hand moves.

I stare at some of the photos of a younger, happier Polly, of Granny and Grandad when the farm was still theirs, of Mum and Dad with their faces pressed close together. I pick up the picture on her nightstand: it's all four of us outside the farm on the day we moved here. Back when Dad still thought it was possible to build a life with us. Polly is gazing straight at the camera, and she seems so certain of her happiness. Sometimes I hate Dad for leaving, because it feels like he took a chunk of each of us with him.

I tuck the duvet tighter around Polly, trying to imagine the kind of life promised by such a ludi-crously shiny rock.

After Polly drops off to sleep, I retreat to my room

and flop on to the bed. I roll over, counting the fairy lights that criss-cross above my head. Sometimes I focus on little rituals like this to push away my worries. It's almost a relief if I lose count and have to start again.

There's a battered old poetry book lounging beside my bed. I like to keep it there to read a few poems before I go to sleep. Our English teacher told us to read a poem every day if we wanted to learn compassion. Keeping it where I can see it is the only way to stop myself forgetting. I pick it up and try to force myself to focus on something meaningful, but my mind keeps wandering back to Polly. Her ring is massive. And Brian Doran? I try to picture Polly in a white dress, but the image is foggy, her face a mind-blur. BrainDrain made his first appearance about three months ago – Polly hauled him into the kitchen announcing proudly that he was an accountant, as if she was one-upping Mum by finding a man prone to responsibility.

Mum shudders at the mere mention of Brain-Drain. She won't handle the news well. In fact, she mightn't handle it at all. I can still hear her pottering about the attic. I envy her, innocently gluing milk cartons in place, unaware of Polly's plans.

Perhaps it is the fairy lights that make me think of Dad, or maybe it is because the day is so laden with his memory, but he seems like the only reasonable option I've left.

Dad of the endless answers. Dad who now spends his days solving complex equations for a fancy French corporation in Lyons. That's all Polly's situation is: a maths problem.

I'll call him. Except I'm only half-sure I remember the Skype address he included on the last slide of his PowerPoint. It was hard to focus at the time because I immediately flipped back to the start of the slideshow to try and find some love hidden between the graphs. I have been waiting for him to call me first and apologize. It's hard knowing I am part of an equation that results in his projected eternal boredom.

But Polly's problem is bigger than me. Dad could actually help. There's no harm in trying.

I heave myself up from the bed and traipse down-stairs, digging Mum's laptop out from a pile of old post and ratty receipts on the kitchen dresser. The laptop is a clodhopper of a machine, thick, black and prone to churning and crunching in its efforts to perform simple duties.

Two cups of tea later and the laptop finally chugs to life. As the main desktop loads, sweat begins to blossom, making my hand clammy.

What will I say to Dad?

Oh, hey there, remember me? No biggie, but I've got your

DNA coursing through my veins. I hate to interrupt your shiny new life but the family needs rewiring . . .

Should I ask why he left?

Although I know the answer to that: all he'll say is, *Please refer to slides 5, 9 and 10 of the presentation.*

I shake the thought from my head. All parents go through rough patches. This is a phase, a blip, a note in the margins. I'll tell him that life will be different when he returns. There will be no more fights. We can begin again, like the years before, when Mum's smile filled up all the rooms in his heart.

The icons flicker to life on the desktop, I hover the cursor over the blue Skype logo.

Maybe I'll focus on Polly. Yes, that's better. I'll say: *Dad, Polly is marrying the dullest man in Ballyfert and is ninety per cent of the way to becoming housewife of the year.* Surely he wouldn't want Polly to end up shackled to an oven?

I click the icon, my mouth dry. The app starts to load and as the blue circle whirls on screen, I panic.

Maybe Dad won't want to hear from me? It's not like he kept in touch. And what if the French seductress answers and I'm stuck making small talk with a pixelated version of sophistication. Worse, what if she doesn't know who I am?

I slam the laptop closed and fold my arms over it. This is a terrible idea, worse than the time Mum turned me into a living tinfoil horse sculpture for the farmer's market. I don't have the strength to call Dad. So I text Tess instead.

> Me: Tess, usual time, usual place? I have a chicken-related emergency.

> Tess: Look, babes, you're weird enough without being, like, a chicken freak. Why don't you just have a crush like a real person?

> Me: What if I said, the Great Chicken Disappearance?

> Tess: Um . . . reread that and think for a second, Molly. How is that any less like a chicken freak?

> Me: You're curious, though, right?

> Tess: Gurl, any excuse to get out of this house. The parentals are out of control with Netflix 'n' custard.

> Me: Custard?

> Tess: OMG, I explained Netflix 'n' chill, they substituted the chill with custard and have like a bowl EVERY night. They think it's the height of comedy.

> Me: It's better than the jokes about turning off their oxygen tank. See you tonight xxx

3

Tess prefers to operate under the cover of darkness, so I spend the rest of the day waiting for her grand arrival. I avoid contact with Mum and try to see if Polly wants to chat, but she just asks where the sewing machine is and then locks herself in her room with it.

To distract myself from Polly's imminent doom and the fate of my chickens, I spend an hour traipsing up and down from the fuel shed, refilling the coffin-like chest in the kitchen with turf and wood. It's rarely ever full, and used to be my favourite hiding place. I would climb in and pull the lid closed, breathing in its earthy smell, waiting to see how heartbroken the others would be when they realized I'd gone missing. I always gave up before anyone missed me. I'd probably still fit inside, it's that big, but I'm old enough now to know that nobody will notice my absence.

It takes a good hour to trudge back and forth with the wheelbarrow, but it's worth it. There's something comforting about a full fuel chest. All that promised warmth, stacked and ready for action. Or maybe the comfort is knowing a fire can be lit at night without an expedition down the yard with a torch. The fuel shed is a dark, mouldy-smelling pit that has the feel of rats about it. I always make a series of loud noises before opening the door, to give the rats plenty of time to scarper.

I mooch about for the rest of the day drinking tea, lying on my bed, flicking through a tattered copy of *Harry Potter and the Goblet of Fire* and rereading all the bits with Hermione and Ron. It's hard to lose myself in the world of Hogwarts when all I can think about is Polly and my missing chickens. Are they lonely? Are they thinking of me? Will they be shy around three hundred other hens? Is anyone going to bother singing to them before bed?

I watch the drizzle slide down the windows, obscuring the view of the garden. I think about school tomorrow. How easy it is to hide problems in the neat lines of the school uniform. It's as if it's designed to even us all out, soften the lumps and bumps of our lives. I'll slouch a little in my seat, answer questions, and lean on lockers in the halls joking with Tess.

Occasionally, I tiptoe out of my room, and listen outside Polly's, but there's only the sound of the sewing machine and I don't want to be roped into fashioning a wedding dress from old bed sheets.

I do keep her stocked up on mugs of tea, though, and slide a bowl of pasta sprinkled with garlic into the room at dinner time. When Polly has a project, she forgets humdrum activities like eating or sleeping. Mum's similar, but prefers to work through the hunger. Polly eats if I place food near her. Mum's more likely to throw it back at me and ask why I've had the audacity to interrupt the energy in the attic.

When I go to check on her, Polly's bowl is empty and sitting expectantly outside her door. I peek in to ask if she needs more food, but she has fallen asleep. She is curled up in the middle of her bed, her body gentle with sleep. The soft arcs of her eyelashes flickering, her cheeks a pinkish colour. Polly is one of those fortunate people that go pink in the appropriate places.

It is midnight when I finally hear a tap on my window. I put my book to one side and go to open it. Nobody would stop Tess using the front door, but she says it feels more clandestine to arrive through a window. Her description of the climb often includes ninja-like movements and the effort of an Olympian spy. It's not that dangerous. The downstairs bathroom was added as an extension by my grandparents; the roof is flat and situated directly under my window. All Tess does is scale the wheelie bins, pull herself on to the roof, and walk across to my window. When we don't want to be overheard, we stage our meetings on the bathroom roof. It offers a better quality of air, and the opportunity to make meaningful comments about the stars.

I open the window, and she bursts through with her usual energy.

'OK, so what's this nonsense about chickens? I'm after, like, snagging my tights on the bin, so this better be good.'

Tess throws her schoolbag on the floor. She usually sleeps here when she comes over, because she arrives way past a normal person's bedtime. On a good day Mum jokes she's like a third daughter, and on a bad day threatens to get rid of her, in much the same way as the chickens.

'So, enlighten me, Molly Darling?' Tess says, standing with her hands placed matter-of-factly on her hips. She is dressed in a black miniskirt and kitten heels; at four foot eight she insists on heels in every situation. All the girls at school would kill to have

Tess's brown almond-shaped eyes, tanned skin and shiny black hair. She is a complicated blend of America, Russia, Hawaii and China – that only Tess can explain. Even the teachers call her 'cute'. A label Tess tries to shirk by wearing a stuffed push-up bra and thigh-high boots with her uniform.

'Mum's after getting rid of the chickens,' I say.

'Your chickens?'

'What other chickens are there?'

'I suspect there are others . . . but I'll, like, google it if you need hardcore numbers.'

'You know what I mean,' I snap.

'Well, it's just – there was something else about chickens today,' she says, wrinkling her face up and pulling her phone out. I don't bother asking why. She's a Tinder fiend and all her boyfriends think she's eighteen. They are also all either secondary-school dropouts or young farmers with mother issues.

Instead of addressing the rudeness of Tess whipping out her phone amid my personal crisis, I collapse on to my bed, tugging the duvet around me and curling into a cocoon.

'And that's not all . . . Polly is getting married and I thought about calling Dad . . .' I gulp, I didn't mean to mention Dad at all. I guess part of me wants Tess to look at me instead of her phone.

'Hold up – that is a lot for one sentence. Polly's

getting married, and your dad, seriously?' she says, still thumbing through her phone with a fixated look. As she scrolls, she adjusts her skirt and kicks off her heels. 'Thank Christ, my feet are killing me.'

'Yeah,' I say, annoyed. I had anticipated a mild dose of sympathy.

'And . . .' She is cautious when it comes to the subject of Dad.

'I dunno,' I say, all cold and removed. Tess is barely paying me any attention.

'I KNEW IT,' she says, punching the air triumphantly and throwing her phone to me.

'I'm not really in the mood for social networking right now . . . in case you haven't noticed.'

My biggest failing as Tess's best friend is my lack of a smartphone – which is where she claims life happens. Mum will only let me have a crappy mobile because it is farm-proof and has *none of that internet nonsense* on it. Mum says technology only lures us into a false sense of security, which is also how she feels about stock photos, marriage and taking vitamins.

'Yeah, yeah, trust me on this one, Molly, you're going to want to watch that video. I mean, I saw it earlier and was all, like, WEIRD, I've seen that some-where before, but I didn't think anything of it, cos, well, it's Claire, and I couldn't care less what that hag does . . .'

This couldn't be further from the truth. Tess is locked in a battle for social media fame with a girl in our class, Claire Kelly. The only problem is, people actually like Claire's posts and nobody really notices Tess's. So, it's currently a one-way battle.

I fumble with the phone, unlocking the screen and staring at the video post. It has two thousand likes and even more views. The headline is 'CRAZY-ASS ROOSTER ATTEMPTS TO LAY AN EGG'.

'What the?' I click in, horror building. The camera jumps about at first, but as it focuses in on the rooster I can see two beady chicken eyes staring out at me in despair. I would know that face anywhere – the delicate beak, the bright red comb and wattle that make everyone assume *she* is really a *he*. It's Lady Macbeth. Whoever is videoing laughs shrilly in the background, and the camera swings to take in Claire Kelly. She sits near the chicken, her blonde straightened hair resting on her shoulders, her camogie-honed abs visible because she is wearing a pink belly-top.

'So, I literally got this new rooster, and it's so random cos it, like, thinks it's a chicken. Check this shizzle out . . .'

The camera cuts back to Lady Macbeth. She is rocking back and forth on a cushion, squeezing her eyes shut. She must be so overwhelmed; she hasn't twitched like that since we first adopted her.

The camera flicks back to Claire's smug smile, but before she can say anything else, I drop the phone.

'I can't watch, it's too much,' I say, burrowing further into my bed.

'So that *is* your chicken,' Tess says triumphantly, plucking the phone up and muting the video.

'You've met her like fifty times,' I say, annoyed that she can't remember a chicken as distinct and special as my Lady Macbeth.

'Well, yeah, but they all look like beak and feathers to me.' Tess shrugs, tapping her foot on the floor and considering me for a moment.

'I can't believe she would do this,' I say.

'That's what happens when the internet eats your soul,' Tess says. 'I mean, that video was so tacky.'

I can tell by the dreamlike look in her eyes that she is mentally reshooting the video, casting a more flattering light on Lady Macbeth and picturing herself as the presenter.

She eyes me.

'So, did you call me over here to stroke your hair or are we actually going to do something?'

This is why I love her. Tess completely ignores my defeated-blob status and instead insists on action. Her fake nails tap the screen of her phone.

'I'm not leaving, so you might as well come out of that weird cocoon. Either that, or you're just going to

37

have to accept the loss of the chickens,' Tess says, without missing a tap.

'Well, it's not like we can get them back,' I mumble from inside the duvet mound.

'And what, pray tell, is stopping us?' Tess jumps neatly on to the end of the bed, and settles into the lotus position, propping herself up with some cushions like she is queen of my bedroom.

'Eh, the law . . . common decency . . .'

'Oh, common decency . . . I've heard of that. Is that what Claire is doing by exploiting *your* rooster?'

'*Chicken*. Lady Macbeth does not identify as a rooster . . .' I cast aside the duvet and sit up to face her.

'All I know is, there are things you can't control, and there are things you can,' Tess says. 'There's not much you can do about Polly or your dad, but we can sure as hell steal back the chickens.'

'Grand Theft Chicken,' I say quietly.

'There's no need to get weird with it,' she says, blowing me a kiss.

'But how?' I ask.

Now that she has my full attention, Tess puts down her phone. She flexes her fingers and takes a folded sheet of paper and a pink fluffy pen from the pocket in her skirt. She scribbles furiously for ten minutes and then hands me the piece of paper.

'This is what we're going to need.'

4

*I*t is one in the morning by the time Tess is satisfied with our preparations. Although 'deems them passable' is more accurate; her standards are too high to ever really result in satisfaction. We have: a rope, chicken-catching bags, torches, and, for some reason, pliers. There are even snacks and water bottles in case we end up trapped in the wilderness. I explain that although it's a trek to Claire Kelly's farm, getting lost is a slim possibility.

'But still a possibility,' Tess says, slapping my hand every time I try to remove one of her 'necessities' from the bag. We have a long walk ahead of us and, knowing Tess, I'll be lugging the bag.

Claire lives about twelve fields away, right on the outskirts of town. It's safer to get there by going cross-country. There are roads connecting our houses, but it is a labyrinth of boreens, dead ends and potholes. And if one of the neighbours happens to spot us out after midnight, we'll be up in front of the principal first thing tomorrow for interfering with the school's reputation. News travels faster than people around here. Probably because Ballyfert and the surrounding area is a place where cows outnumber people ten to one.

We go through the fields. There is a lot of getting stuck in hedges, hiding behind stone walls to stare into fields before committing to them – making sure the shadows aren't lurking bulls – and whisper-squealing over stepping in cow dung. We are both wearing Mum's discarded farm gear: navy overalls that make us look more like plumbers than chicken thieves. Tess is not enjoying the overalls. She also vetoed wellies, so we are wearing some old runners that we found lurking under the stairs, and every bit of unexpected mud is dramatized. Tess is unfamiliar with the concept of wet feet.

'Oh my God, Molly, it's, like . . . oozing.

'It's freezing my toes off.

'There's, like, a creature moving in my shoe.

'What if we, like, die out here and people think we always smelt this way.'

By the time the farm is in sight, Tess is listing Instagram stars, so she won't forget where she comes from. I've given up talking and am fantasizing about the moment when Lady Macbeth, Scarlett O'Hara and

Bellatrix lunge towards me. I wonder if Boo Radley will be a reluctant follower. In my fantasy, I single each chicken out by name, giving it a comforting squeeze before confining it to the potato sacks we've brought along for chicken transportation.

The moon is high in the sky, and there is an eerie quality to the night. We reach a long hedge which borders the farm, and follow it until we find a gate. The gate has recently been painted, and though all it's doing is bordering an empty field, it seems to be intent on keeping up appearances. I think of our own farm and the series of rusting, crooked gates that struggle to stand up between our fields.

Tess crouches beside the gate and stares in. From here we can only see the back of Claire's house. It's massive, entirely too big for a family of three people. Even in the dark, there is a shiny white newness to it. The walls are neatly decorated with trellises, and each windowsill is home to a basket of flowers. During the day, these probably boast bright colours, but currently they look like black death bushels.

Luckily, the lights in the big farmhouse are off, and the yard is pristine and deserted. There are no visible cameras, dogs or alarms, no random bits of farm debris peppering the place. An impressive tractor gleams at one end, its claw reaching up into the night. There is a row of sheds, all neatly closed up for the night, and a huge green corrugated-iron building plonked right in the middle of the yard. I can't help feeling the sheds are hiding something.

Shrill squawking makes us both jump. As suddenly, it dies.

'That's one creepy-ass sound,' Tess whispers.

'It came from there,' I say, indicating the monster shed, which looks more like a prison than a home. There are no soft touches. I shudder at the thought of my chickens being kept in such a heartless structure.

'So, I guess this is it,' Tess whispers.

I gulp and look at the looming shed. If it had a voice, it would be cackling obscenely in our direction and goading us like a Bond villain. I shake my head; personifying the shed is not good for the nerves.

'This is it,' I say.

We climb over the gate as quietly as possible and then, for no reason other than it feels right, we tiptoe towards the shed. There isn't much noise coming from inside, which suggests chicken misery to me. There is a chain and padlock looped around the metal door.

'It's locked,' Tess says, dismayed.

'It just *looks* locked,' I say, reaching for the chain and tugging it. Sure enough, it unravels easily. The padlock is simply there for show. I feel like an unstoppable evil genius, but decide to exhibit humble dignity.

'Mum does the same thing,' I say with a shrug.

Slowly we open the doors. A horrible grating noise. We slip inside and wait until we are a few steps in before switching on our torches, pointing them towards the floor.

'I don't want to, like, step on a chicken brain,' Tess mutters. 'Can you smell that?'

'It smells like chickens,' I explain.

'Dead chickens maybe?' Tess says, pinching her nose in disgust.

I realize I've been holding my breath, so I've no real idea what it smells like. I take a deep breath and immediately regret it. The stink is something much more sinister than chickens. It is actually closer to rotting chicken faeces than anything else, or at least to how I imagine a pile of rotting chicken poo would smell.

I switch to breathing through my mouth. Unfortunately, the smell climbs in there too.

'This makes Claire constantly smelling like a bubblegum factory *très* disturbing,' Tess says, pinching her nose harder.

I point my torch's beam across the floor of the shed. Hundreds of chicken eyes glint back. The shed is one long sprawling slab of cement, covered in chickens and years and years of chicken poo.

I shiver. Some of the chickens are shrivelled and

missing patches of feathers, others are plump and fully feathered. One particularly scrawny bald bird stares at the light blankly, as if someone has exorcized the chicken soul from her little body. She opens her beak to squawk, but no sound comes out, so it seems to me that she is mouthing the word *help*.

'That is so freaking horror movie, I can't even,' Tess says, clutching my arm, as we stare into the abyss of chicken eyes. They are everywhere.

A faint clucking grows around us, and there is a flurry of movement as they begin ruffling their feathers and stalking towards us.

'I kind of felt that Lady Macbeth would stick out. How the hell are we meant to find any of your chickens in this mess?' Tess whispers.

'I'll know them when I see them,' I say, with a lot more confidence than I feel. Obviously I can rule out the scrawnier birds, but there are still about two hundred healthy hens strutting about. 'We just need to . . . um . . . systematically look them all in the eyes . . .'

'Any better ideas?' Tess asks. Her fingers are digging into my arm. There are chickens brushing off our legs now.

'No, I don't have any better ideas. I want *my* chickens, not some random chickens who've been conditioned to a life of confinement.'

'OK, well, what do *your* chickens look like? Oh, no, wait, let me guess . . . they're the image of all the other freaking chickens.'

'No, they're different . . . um . . . Mrs Danvers is black and probably skulking . . . Let me see, Bellatrix is sort of . . .'

'Are you seriously telling me you called a chicken Bellatrix?'

'Eh . . .'

'Whatever, Molly, let's hurry up and find them.'

We start in the left-hand corner of the shed. It is hard to tell if we've already examined a chicken, because they all keep moving. We walk up and down, shining the light in each chicken's face as I consider whether it is one of mine. Every now and then a chicken has the same reddish feathers as Boo Radley, or a beak that reminds me of Scarlett O'Hara, so I stare deeper into the black glinting circles of its eyes, looking for a recognizable soul. Tess gets hopeful the longer I stare.

'Is she one?'

'I don't think so, I mean, I don't feel anything.'

'OK, and what is it you expect to feel exactly?'

'Um . . . a knowing.'

'Oh, good! We're hinging this grand plan on your ability to have a hunch about a chicken. Don't they have like discernible features?'

'I mean, yeah, when there's seven of them.'

'I see.' Tess is trying not to sound angry, but she is hissing. I am getting panicky. None of the chickens seems familiar. They are just . . . chickens. The situation is made worse by the birds bumping against our legs, and pecking our ankles.

'I just need to close my eyes,' I say.

'Oh, great, we're going to go with the eyes-closed method of detection.'

'*Shuk, shuk, shuk, shuk, shuk, shuk, shuk,*' I murmur, standing stiffly in the middle of the shed, giving Mum's famous chicken-whisperer call one last chance to prove itself. '*Shuk, shuk, shuk, shuk . . .*'

'Something's happening,' Tess whispers. And she's right, I'm not sure whether it's because of the chicken-whisperer call or the fact that we're standing still, but the chickens have stopped bothering us. There are no more soft bodies brushing against our ankles or demented pecks at our feet. I try to breathe deeply and focus.

'Um . . .' Tess interrupts.

'What?'

'Molly . . .'

'*What?*'

'We forgot to close the door.'

I snap open my eyes and look to where Tess is focusing the beam of her torch. Sure enough, the door is ajar and the chickens have formed a steady stream out into the yard.

'They're escaping!'

'We need to do something,' Tess says, but she isn't moving. It is as if the strategic part of her brain is shutting down.

I don't bother waiting for her to react. I run towards the door and try to shut it, but the chickens are having none of it. There is no pause in the mass exodus and I don't want to squish them or hurt their tiny claws. Breaking and entering is one crime, damaging chickens is quite another. I fling open the door instead, hoping to tempt some of them back into their shed. Although why any creature would choose to go back into the black pit of chicken faeces is beyond me.

The moon lights up the scene in the yard beautifully. There are chickens everywhere, some are heading down what looks like a creepy lane, four plump hens have broken into the tractor, and the gate we climbed over earlier is surrounded.

'What the hell are we supposed to do?' Tess asks.

That's when I hear it: a concentrated cluck so familiar it rattles my nerves. It's coming from an overturned wheelbarrow.

Before I've even registered what's happening, I am lifting up the wheelbarrow and heaving it to one side. Underneath is the saddest thing I've ever seen. Lady

Macbeth is lying belly up, with her legs rotating in the air. Her left wing is all battered, as if she has been flinging herself against the rusty sides of the wheelbarrow in an attempt to escape. Her red wattle is bruised and tattered, and she doesn't even smile when she sees me. Her eyes look black and defeated, her expression an echo of the bald chicken who mouthed, *Help*.

'What the— Molly, hurry up!'

'I found Lady Macbeth,' I say.

'Why was she under there?'

'You can't keep a rooster with commercial chickens. I mean, it's chicken rearing 101, but I completely forget because I think of her as one of the girls.'

'Oh my God, let's get out of here, this whole set-up gives me the creeps. It's like turning Claire inside out and finding she's everything I ever imagined and worse,' Tess says.

'Just a minute,' I say, emptying most of the supplies from my backpack.

'I can't put her in the sack – she's too injured. Can we wrap her in your school jumper? It's not like you use it,' I say, pointing at the jumper Tess forced me to pack bundled beneath the other supplies.

'No way, that chicken is not creeping all over my knitwear. Like, I might someday wear it and end up with some foreign chicken cancer growth.'

'You know that's not how cancer works, right?'

I poke Lady Macbeth gently with a finger to try and turn her over, but she's not her usual cooperative self; she feels rooted in place. As I try to figure out what to do, she rocks to and fro on her back.

I give her ample warning.

'I'm going to have to touch you now,' I say, but Lady Macbeth's eyes remain blank.

I've lifted enough traumatized chickens in my time to know the dangers of pecking, scratching and, on occasion, body slamming. I put my hands either side of her rotund body. She looks alarmed, her beady black eyes bulging.

'Tess, hold my bag open.'

'Are you serious?'

'I am *not* putting her in the sack.'

Lady Macbeth squirms in my hands. She is heavy, her once silky feathers feel rough. I'm careful not to touch her broken wing.

Tess reluctantly holds open my bag as I ease Lady Macbeth in, careful of the side of her body with the dodgy wing. I zip the bag slowly, so as not to alarm her. I make sure her head is poking out the side of my bag, so she won't be confined to another small dark space and can get a gulp of fresh air. Lady Macbeth stares at me reproachfully. Chickens are big on dignity.

'So, we've saved one, at least,' I say, as if to reassure myself.

'We're Ballyfert's answer to Gandhi,' Tess says. 'So, can we go now?'

'What about the others?' I ask.

'I don't think we've time,' Tess says.

She's right. The sky is already starting to lighten, and the place is riddled with fleeing chickens. It would be impossible to track down my six missing cluckers. But I can't help feeling all Tess wants is the transgender chicken for her social media war; it's not as if the rest of them matter to her.

As we stand guiltily wondering what to do next, a light flicks on in one of the upstairs windows of the farmhouse, a shadowy outline moving towards the window.

'Claire . . .' Tess says.

'Oh God.'

As soon as Claire opens the curtains she will see the escaping chickens, and then, standing gormlessly in their yard . . .

'Run,' I whisper. 'It's going to be OK,' I add, because Tess's face is all scrunched up like she might cry. I tug her sleeve, and we sprint towards the gate, climbing over it in seconds, Tess deftly pushing a chicken out of her way with the side of her foot. We don't bother closing the shed door or saving any other chickens. I silently hope that some of them make a bid for freedom. But I know it's not likely. It's not like chickens can get very far; they've limited resources.

We don't speak as we run across the fields. Tess dives through hedges and scrambles over walls without hesitation. We endure the sloshy puddles.

Once my house is in sight, we slow.

'This is awful,' Tess says. 'As if I need the complication of a chicken-guilt complex right now.'

I glance back at Lady Macbeth; her head looks limp.

'At least we got Lady Macbeth back,' I say, but we both know that will never be enough for Tess. One look at her expression and I can see she's already plotting.

5

'Molly, Molly, Molly, you have to wake up.'

Tess is sprawled across the bottom of my bed, shaking my foot with one hand and operating her phone with the other. I don't want to open my eyes. It is seven on Monday morning and I only managed three hours of sleep. Three hours that featured countless nightmares about the chickens. I'd woken twice with a start. I try to remember my nightmares, but all that comes back is a dark room and a sea of glinting chicken eyes.

'Attention, Molly . . . A quick memo from reality . . . Time waits for no chicken fighter!' Tess says in her best public-announcement monotone.

'You mean chicken rights activist, otherwise it means I wrestle chickens or something.'

'You know the rules, no pedantic comments before coffee,' Tess says.

I unstick my eyes, fixing them on the drawer I'd left beside my bed. It's lined with pillows and my softest jumper. Inside it Lady Macbeth is resting.

Earlier this morning, I stuck her back together with plasters and Sudocrem. Not exactly chicken-specific medication, but it will do for now. I'm relieved to see she has stopped shuddering, even if she is eyeing the egg I gave her as if it is likely to betray her.

'Well, at least Lady Macbeth has perked up,' I say.

'Oh, yeah, because one fat happy chicken completely eases my conscience. As if I even want a conscience,' Tess says, rolling her eyes. 'Do you think I can trade it in for something more useful, I dunno . . . like abs?'

I know what she means. Rescuing Lady Macbeth simply shone a light on a much bigger problem. And the worst part is, we're in the wrong . . . not only did we steal a chicken, we released three hundred more. What if we were seen? Claire will not hesitate to destroy us. It will be even worse if our families find out. Mum will ignore me completely. That may not sound bad, but her most terrifying line of attack is silence, an icy wall of it. When it's not aimed at me, it's impressive. It has caused grown men to cry (Dad).

I try to reassure myself that the other chickens will be fine, but there is a curdled feeling in my stomach as if it is telling me to climb into my wardrobe and remain there for the foreseeable future.

'It's not like we can do anything,' I say, mostly to myself.

'Well, we can, I'm not sure what . . . but there is no way I can live with bald chicken nightmares for the rest of my life – think of the therapy bills.'

'So, what do we do?'

'For now, we go to school and act normal – how hard can that be?'

'You realize we've got art, right?'

'And what, Molly? You're not capable of acting normal in the vicinity of the illustrious Fiachra?'

'He's not illust— Forget it, that's not what I meant . . . Art isn't ideal for . . . well, acting normal.'

'Because of Fiachra.' Tess grins, enjoying herself far more than is appropriate.

'No, *not* because of Fiachra . . . Some of us can actually function in the presence of cute guys.'

'So, he's cute?'

'You're impossible.'

I'd actually meant Sandra, the art teacher, was a problem. She puts me so on edge that I tend to reveal things I never intended to. Like the day she asked why I painted the sky red and I ended up confiding in her about Dad leaving.

'You really have to get over him,' Tess says,

assuming my silence is Fiachra-focused. She continues to tap on her phone.

'I've never been into him.'

'Oh, right . . .' Tess gives me the eyebrows.

I drop it, concealing my reddening face with the duvet. Suggestive comments always make me blush, but Tess takes the redness as confirmation of whatever she is teasing me about. Usually boys, but all the ones at school are unsuitable. Not only do they specialize in bathroom-themed humour, they also appear to assume girls are objects to kiss behind the bike sheds. There's also a disturbing focus on quantity over quality.

In the duvet's soft embrace, I inhale the stale sleep air.

All that trudging through fields and only one chicken to show for it. What will I do when Mum finds out? Maybe I should march downstairs and show her Lady Macbeth's injuries now. Explain about the state of the Kellys' farm. Surely Mum is opposed to poor chicken conditions?

I've lapsed into my own world, and Tess is jabbing at my feet to get my attention.

'Molly, if you dare say a word to that mother of yours . . .'

'But maybe she won't mind?'

'Eh, she will.'

55

'But—'

'Nothing. Just give me a few hours, I've got a plan formulating.'

'Oh God . . . you remember how your last plan played out? Right?'

'Well, if you come up with a better idea, we can always go with that,' Tess grins.

She knows I am about as strategic as a chicken trying to cross the road.

I don't normally wear make-up, but Tess says I need to look like I've had a decent night's sleep. Making me look well-rested is an intensive operation which involves a lot of dabbing, ten pots of gunk and three different brushes. She lines up the different pots and creams, speaking in comforting tones, stating that we'll go for an effortless natural look. I get frazzled soon after the foundation. We've already spent ages moisturizing, priming and concealing.

'I can't do this any more! My face is effortlessly natural already,' I say, pushing away her hand. She shakes her head solemnly.

'Someday you'll understand,' she says.

As Tess gets ready, I settle Lady Macbeth for the day. She hasn't touched the bowl of food I gave her last night, so there's no need to refill it. I top up her water dish in the bathroom sink and make sure her drawer nest is invisible from the door. I do this by cluttering up the rest of the bedroom, so that if Polly pokes her head in, she will be so disturbed by the clothes strewn everywhere, she won't notice the chicken hiding in plain sight. Any other day, I might have put Lady Macbeth in the wardrobe without thinking, but I don't have the heart to put her back in a small dark space. She still looks strangely unhappy, so I hum a bit of 'Hush, Little Baby' to her. She stuffs her head into the soft jumper in protest.

I don't dare pick her up, but gently run a single finger along the undamaged side of her body. When she doesn't freak out, I add a few more fingers to the mix and give her a proper stroke. The feathers are silky, her body warm and soft. Normally, Lady Macbeth would wiggle about to ensure I was stroking her in just the right places, but now she is motionless under my fingertips. I stop when I notice how hard her heart is hammering.

Seeing her like this makes me feel sad and powerless. I can't help wondering about the others. Are they still in the cold dark shed or wandering about Claire's farm in search of freedom? If only I had glimpsed a few of them.

'At least you're home,' I say to Lady Macbeth. She

s still frozen in place as if the stroking of her feathers has caused her to fear for her life. I'm reluctant to leave her alone for the day, but Tess is right. We need to act normal.

'I'll see you downstairs,' I call to Tess as I walk past the upstairs bathroom. She is busy putting her face on.

I make my way downstairs, taking my time on the steps, and counting the book spines I brush my fingers against. *Act normal, act normal, act normal*, I repeat to myself. I'm a terrible liar and prone to blurting out confessions. Under no circumstances can Mum and Polly find out about the chickens.

I pause outside the kitchen door to get a feel for the atmosphere.

'Our house is a pox on architecture,' Polly is saying, in a syrupy voice. A habit she developed in her early teens. She realized she could use a nice voice to impart terrible truths and get in much less trouble than if she screamed them.

'It's not that bad,' Mum replies in clipped tones.

Monday mornings are hard for Mum: she has to balance her new life as an artist with the few farming chores she still bothers to do. Aside from some half-hearted weeding and the occasional batch of jam, she's pretty much given up on the Leitirmór Farm legacy. I think it's a case of, *If he doesn't have to farm any more, then neither do I.*

I am about to enter and save Mum from Polly's morning wrath, when Polly starts up the sugary voice again. But this time, she is struggling to keep it sounding sweet.

'Really, really? Then what is growing on that wall? It looks like diseased yoghurt. I don't understand how you can live like this. Look, look at this – when was the last time you dusted the skirting boards?' Polly is likely to be advancing across the kitchen, brandishing a feather duster in Mum's face.

'Do people dust their skirting boards?' Mum asks, with genuine curiosity.

I can imagine the scene perfectly. I've seen it enough times. Polly is pacing the floor and stabbing the air as she indicates all the dirt. I wonder whether she is flashing the ring at every available opportunity. Mum will be oblivious, sipping her morning coffee. She tends to retreat inwards in Polly's presence, the lines around her eyes deepening.

Mum is not the only one to age in Polly's presence. The kitchen also tends to look shoddier than usual. It is like Polly's judgement casts a new light on the everyday landscape of our lives. Suddenly the bills seem more unpaid, the curtains more lopsided. The ashes tipping out of the range jig about in all their glory, the heaps of paper on the dresser stare disapprovingly at all the chipped and dirty cups on the table. The jam jars seem stickier and like they need to be put away.

'Everybody does, and they clean the dishes and sort their mail and keep an eye on their kids and remember what night to put the bin out,' Polly's voice is saying in her *I am the master of the adulting* tone. Now that she's marrying BrainDrain, she probably feels like she's powered up on the domestic-goddess front. Kind of like when you get the gold star in Mario Kart and are suddenly invincible.

'It's a wonder they find the time for all that,' Mum muses.

There is a lapse in the exchange. Polly is possibly bleaching the counters violently.

I cough politely before pushing open the door to the kitchen. Nobody appears to notice my presence. Usually I mind when they ignore me, but right now I'm OK with it. Mostly because the thought of what I might burst out with if I had their undivided attention is terrifying.

One half of the table has been made into an example for the other. It is pristine, not so much as a teaspoon obscuring its surface. The other half is the usual mishmash of condiments and half-eaten packets of stale bread.

'There are no vegetables in this kip,' Polly says.

She is at the fridge, pretending to talk to herself, but the sentiment is directed at Mum.

Mum isn't listening. She is busy at the cooker, carefully tipping bowls of berries into the giant saucepan. It's the first batch of jam she's made in weeks, no doubt a way to keep herself busy while Polly lectures her on the fundamentals of kitchen hygiene.

'Oh, Petal of the Morning,' Mum says to me, 'we're having a proper dinner tonight. Gary's coming over – it's Polly's idea.'

'The Hulk?'

'Well, yes . . .' Mum thinks carefully for a moment about whether to scold me for the nickname. 'Polly says it is high time you both get to know *Gary*.'

As she says this, Polly emits a shriek and flings a half-rotted lettuce across the room. It is unclear if the shriek is related to the lettuce or her intentions for the dinner.

Mum is oddly calm.

I'd expected her to go berserk when Polly announced the wedding, but instead Polly seems like the one who is nearing the brink. Maybe Mum is happy to marry Polly off? It could be like the chickens – one less thing to worry about.

I go straight for the kettle. There are some

mornings that can only be solved by coffee. Mum insists my coffee addiction shows wisdom beyond my years, when all it really says is premature caffeine dependency. As I wait for the kettle to boil, I pop two eggs into a saucepan of water then put them on a spare ring to boil. I have a hankering for a proper breakfast as a temporary solution to the lack of sleep.

'Eggs for breakfast?' Mum gives me a confused look. Usually I am way too lazy to eat much beyond digestives on weekday mornings, and, if she comments on my health, maybe an apple.

'In memory of the chickens,' I say, hoping she will drop it.

She does. A look of guilt spreads across her face, and she pops some toast on for me.

'So, um . . . Gary was wondering if he should bring Fiachra . . . Or if that would be too weird,' Mum says, pausing mid-stir as she waits for my answer.

'Too weird,' I say.

'OK, well, feel free to invite anybody you like, you know, if you have—'

'I do *not* have a boyfriend.'

'Well, if you did—'

'Which I don't.'

'You girls are impossible.' Mum turns back to the jam. 'If one of you is throwing a nice family meal, the other is busy impersonating a troll . . . Maybe someday we'll experience twenty-four hours of harmony.'

'Oh, yeah, the Hulk and Brian Doran, just what we need to create one big harmonious family,' I say, hurt that I am considered a troll in a situation where Polly is loudly bleaching the kitchen into submission.

There is a pause after I mention Brian Doran. It's as if his name has wiped the hope from Mum's face. Polly shoots me a dirty look from the fridge. This must mean Mum has no idea about Brian – no wonder she is behaving humanely. Polly must be saving up the news. I glance at Polly's hand: it is clutching the sponge, and, sure enough, it is greeting the morning ringless. Polly catches my eye and gives me a threatening grimace, although she hardly needs to. She trained me from a young age not to reveal her secrets.

'Brian Doran?' Mum says, looking at Polly with confusion. 'Surely you're not still dating that dimwit, are you? Wasn't he some kind of rebound after Dermot? You know he explained profit margins to me like I was a duck with its head on backwards.'

'You said I could invite whoever I wanted, so if you want me to sit politely through a meal with that vibrating muscle of yours, then I will be bringing Brian.' Polly smiles evenly at her.

I retreat to the clean side of the table with the toast and eggs, splitting them between two plates, one for

Tess when she eventually shows up to breakfast. I slosh a load of milk into my cup, then sit dissolving spoon after spoon of sugar into my coffee.

Mum continues stirring the contents of her saucepan. Her jumper is rolled up at the sleeves, and her blue wig sits stiffly on her head. Her lips are pinched together.

'Fine, he can come, but he can leave the damn calculator at home,' she says.

That seems to settle it. Polly returns to her violent scrubbing, no doubt planning a dramatic reveal of her wedding plans at tonight's dinner. I cough to get her attention and perhaps share a knowing look. Instead she looks at me as if I am some sort of toe fungus.

'Yes?' Polly says, in a way that suggests I should get over myself.

Mum looks sideways at Polly, interjecting with a half-hearted, 'Girls . . . It's not . . .' Then she seems to think better of voicing an opinion, because she sighs and turns back to the saucepan.

Polly ignores Mum, focusing on cleaning out the egg tray. Her straight back irks me; destiny has not granted me the same elegant posture. She is wearing jeans and a tight red top that displays her neat midriff. Her hair is flung into a messy bun.

'So, Tess is here,' I offer.

'Oh! What startling news!' Polly says, her head

disappearing further into the fridge as she reaches for some distant speck of dirt.

I give up communicating and swallow more egg.

As I spoon the last bit of yolk into my mouth, Tess enters the kitchen. She is wearing her interpretation of our school uniform. It involves a lot less skirt, and a lot more cleavage than the prescribed version. Even with all the alterations, Tess looks strange in a skirt and blouse. In a long line of imaginative decisions, our principal made the uniform varying shades of grey.

Polly emerges from the fridge, brandishing a lump of fungus in Tess's direction.

'Look at this – isn't it disgusting? It's like a forest of unmentionable growths in here. When was the last time anyone else cleaned this place?'

Polly directs the last question at me, flinging the lump of fungus across the room. It lands with a dull thud beside my morning coffee. I sigh and take a long slow gulp, watching Polly twitch. She wanted the fungus to land in my coffee.

'Eh, nice to see you too.' Tess juts her hip out to one side and folds her arms in mock disgust. She is excellent in tense situations.

'Ah, shut up, Tess – you know I love you,' Polly says.

'OK, let's not get carried away here, we're going to be late,' I say, mostly to stop them flirting. Everyone flirts with Polly.

'Ooh, sassy,' Tess says.

Then she strolls over to the table, demolishing her eggs and toast in under five minutes. She brushes the crumbs from her lap, before giving both Mum and Polly a quick hug goodbye. I don't follow. Hugs don't come naturally to me.

'Have a lovely day,' Mum says.

I feel like Judas walking out the door. I should have told Mum about Polly or the chickens. Or both. Although maybe she won't find out, and *sad that the chickens are gone* hardly suggests I would stage an attack on Claire Kelly's farm. If she figures it out, Mum will go mad. Maybe she'll disown me, lock me up in a boarding school (which I do not have the social skills for). What if she leaves? It would be me and the crumbling farmhouse with brief intermissions where Polly and her husband turn up to clean and do taxes.

'You have really got to quit worrying,' Tess says as we walk down the hill. 'You're doing your resting face absolutely no favours.'

6

The sky is its usual blanket of grey as we trudge into the thick drizzle of the morning. The roads look dull and defeated, grey, potholed and home to various patches of mud. It's no wonder the town is called Ballyfert. Tess looked it up once on some website and apparently it means 'town of the tomb'.

'We're like literally living in a goddamn graveyard,' she'd said with despair. 'How am I ever going to break the internet?'

As we plod along the network of roads between Claire Kelly's house and mine, we only pass one vehicle. It's a car full of schoolchildren with a hassled-looking mother at the wheel. She flies past, forgetting to wave even though we stand in the ditch making extra room for her to get by. There are no hard shoulders down our way. The only other sign of life is a jogger who springs along the road towards us.

'A man that age wearing that much Lycra is just wrong,' Tess says.

'Ugh ... It's the Hulk,' I say.

'So that's why your mum is into him,' Tess whispers, because he is now only about thirty metres from us. 'I mean, if I was totally ancient, I would.'

'Morning, girls,' he says, breezing past us with a friendly grin and quick wave. The Hulk has a remark-ably annoying ability to do the right thing. Other mother-boyfriends might stop us and force us to awkwardly chit-chat, and another breed of terrible boyfriend might pretend we weren't there. But he nails the right amount of friendly.

Tess spins to watch him bound into the distance. 'Yup, he's definitely in shape.'

'Eh ... can we please discuss something other than the shape of my mum's boyfriend?'

After that, the roads are silent. Tess veers on to a boreen that disappears into unruly hedges and has grass sprouting down the centre. It is winding in the opposite direction to our school. We are going to be late for class. Neither of us says anything, but it's obvious we're both scanning for any signs of escapee chickens.

I'm relieved when a flash of colour in the ditch

turns out to be a trapped plastic bag. Tess starts nattering non-stop, as if she can ward off our fears if she simply keeps talking.

'The rain is killing my hair, I'm gonna be a total frizz-ball,' she moans, as if it is her biggest concern.

'Put up your hood.'

We amble along, Tess switching between weather complaints and explaining why her latest Tinder catch is barely up to scratch: 'He wouldn't know how to squeeze a boob if it slapped him in the hand.' I'm busy with my own thoughts, trying to select the least anxious ones and make them override my doubts. I often reconstruct my feelings until they seem normal.

Tess stops dead in her tracks, and stares into the hedge. I let my eye follow her jabbing finger.

'Do you see that?' she whispers. 'Molly, it's . . .'

In the hedge is a bloody feathered lump. It is chicken coloured, but not at all the shape of a chicken.

The body is bludgeoned, its face twisted into a distorted pancake, beak crushed. The stomach is split open and a trail of guts splay out. The blood is crusting into brown and the flies have begun to gather and buzz.

I bend down, willing my breakfast to make a reappearance. Instead my insides tie themselves in an impossible knot as I dry-heave.

'You don't think . . .' Tess's voice drifts towards me.

'It could be anyone's chicken,' I say, still crouching and gagging. An automated part of me is answering; the real me is entirely numb. Roadkill is common enough, but I've never felt responsible for it before. I can't stop staring. My brain soaks up every inch of the smushed chicken body: the jarring angle of the legs, the clump of feathers sitting to one side. It could be Mrs Danvers or Bellatrix. There's no way of knowing.

'I guess . . .' Tess sounds doubtful. 'Should we cover it?'

'What?'

'Like, bury it . . . We can't just leave it like that.'

'Somebody else did,' I say, because the dead chicken has clearly been scraped off the road and left in the ditch.

'Well . . . it's not very dignified,' Tess says.

I stare blankly at the corpse. All my thoughts are shrivelled up and trembling.

'Let's just cover it in grass to minimize the fly access . . .' Tess tugs bits of grass from the roadside and sprinkles them on the chicken.

With all my emotions on pause, I crack thin branches from a nearby tree and criss-cross them over the body, spreading the leaves over any gaps. It is like building a miniature pyre.

When we are done, the chicken is covered in enough sticks, leaves and grass to conceal the body completely.

'Shouldn't we, I dunno, make a tombstone?' Tess says.

We poke about for a flat enough piece of wood. In the end, Tess pulls a long wooden ruler from her bag. The measuring side is covered in graffiti, with layers of Tippex where Tess has blocked out the names of old boyfriends. The back of the ruler is still blank. Tess scribbles on it, 'We won't forget. R. I. P.'

She hands it to me and I stick it into the ground. There's nothing else we can do.

For the rest of the walk to school, I try to forget its flattened face, its one unscathed black eye staring at us in accusation.

As we reach St Martin's, I almost sigh with relief.

The school sits in front of us: fat, concrete and predictable. It is the only place I want to be. All I have to do is slot into my desk and carefully put predetermined answers on paper. I will be either right or wrong, there will be no grey patches appearing in the textbooks to pose troubling questions. I'll never admit it to Tess, because we operate under a *school is hell* policy, but sometimes school is my one sanctuary. Just as I am taking comfort in my vision of an orderly few hours, Tess clears her throat and says, 'What if that's not the only dead chicken?'

We knock on the art-room door, and Sandra's eye appears in the tiny rectangular window. Sandra insists we call her by her first name and doesn't like it when people interrupt the energy of her class. She opens the door, nodding towards our seats. We shuffle in. It's more accurate to say I shuffle. Tess makes a production of taking her seat, smiling at the class as if to say, *Yes, you may begin, I have arrived.*

Sandra ignores Tess and returns to circling the easels and peering at people's work to offer suggestions. Sandra has long white hair, flowery Doc Martens and a limited interest in any of us. The art studio is the only vibrant part of our school. Sandra has pasted the walls with prints by famous artists and the occasional student drawing. There are various skulls, random objects, pieces of fruit and bottles of coloured glass dotted about the place. Everybody perches at an easel, trying to look like they know how to sketch.

The front of the art room is occupied by Barry. He is holding a broom and the class is attempting to capture his portrait. Some of the keener students hold their pencils up in the air, attempting to look as if they are drawing Barry to scale. I'm not sure why they bother. Most of us have given up competing for Sandra's praise. Most days she sighs at our attempts.

'It will get an A, but . . . where is its heart?'

This is her most damning critique, and we've come to learn she doesn't expect an answer. She is bored by our drawings. She has even stopped us using the internet, because one too many students decided to print off and trace the *Girl with a Pearl Earring*.

I sit down, inhaling the smell of paint and charcoal that permeates the art room, glancing around at the disembodied heads floating across most people's pages. There are also a couple of strangely shaped human outlines, and, beside me, Fiachra has given up depicting Barry and has instead committed to drawing a hyperrealistic dragon. Fiachra is the Hulk's only son, and therefore the worst. If Fiachra wasn't related to the Hulk, he would be incredibly handsome. As it stands, I'm not confident he has thoughts.

Fiachra hasn't noticed my arrival and is intently sketching his dragon. This isn't unusual. We tend to work in a quiet haze of mutual scorn. Seeing him reminds me of the dinner tonight – as if I don't have enough to worry about. Maybe Fiachra's silence isn't his usual silence, maybe it's full of disgust. Perhaps he's equally embarrassed that our parents are chaining their souls together. It's hard to tell; his deft pencil strokes give nothing away.

I convince myself that the nervy feeling in my stomach is because we are doing portraits. I like art, but it seems awfully judgey to draw my classmates accurately. Nobody is ever happy with how I render them on paper. It's led me to believe that it's hard to see oneself clearly; either that or the people in my class are deluded. Most of them are happier with a bland portrait, leaving out any wobbly, knobbly or oddly coloured bits. Adjustments like bigger eyes or a slighter waist tend to go down well.

'Well, remember to have some fun with it.' Sandra nudges me as she walks by. I've been staring at the wings of Fiachra's dragon. They are an impressive mix of greens, blues and purples. My page is still empty aside from a straight line drawn hastily down its centre.

Sandra yawns, mimes drawing in the air at me. I pick up my pencil and start sketching as she moves through the chaotic arrangement of easels, delivering essential art tips like, *Yes, yellow and blue do make green.* She barely pauses to remove a pair of sharp scissors from the hands of one of our school's notorious juvenile delinquents (I avoid learning their names and making eye contact).

I try to get emotionally attached to my drawing.

Before Sandra, I'd always been told I was half decent at art, but all her sighing has made me less sure. Still, drawing usually calms me. If only I could just focus on the lines of Barry and pretend nothing monumental is happening inside. Except I can't stop thinking for a second. All I am having are thoughts, and none of them helpful.

As I sketch Barry's head, I realize that the tension between Fiachra and me is about to be multiplied by awkward. If our parents are staging a couple's dinner, then family picnics and holidays will be next on the agenda. Or maybe our tension already has all the awkward a tension can hold; it's not like we are on speaking terms.

And what about Dad, and Lady Macbeth, and the creepy-ass Kelly farm, and the escaping chickens, and the *dead* chicken, and all my other chickens . . . and, and, and . . . chickens, chickens, oh God, the chickens. It's as if my brain is jamming on chickens, it's hard to pull any one thought to the surface and focus.

'Oh my, what? Molly, are you OK?' asks Sandra.

I glance down. I've drawn Barry's body quite well, but in place of his head there is a chicken head.

'Um . . . yeah, why?' I ask. But I can see the drawing: I know why.

'What the hell?' Barry says. He is incredibly vain and has broken from his pose to see what I've drawn.

He stands beside Sandra looking affronted.

'Barry! Language!'

'Is an art form, Miss,' and he winks. Barry gets away with winking at most teachers, even when they're male.

'You know how I feel about your language and your winking. Do you want a comment in your journal?' Sandra threatens to give behaviour comments, but never follows through.

'Nah, Miss, I want to look at this . . . Is that how you see me, Molly?' Barry asks with a mocking tone. Barry is what Ballyfert labels a rebel. His hair is shoulder-length, despite school regulations, he wears a bow tie, and he smokes in the girls' changing room, which explains almost everything about Barry that anybody needs to know.

'Is that a chicken head?' Sandra asks. It's rare that she stops at someone's easel, and so people are beginning to turn in their seats, craning their necks to see what I've done.

'What are you trying to say with this?' Sandra peers closer, tracing the outline of the chicken head with her finger.

'I'm just preoccupied,' I whisper, hoping she will lower her voice or leave me alone. There is no way I need Sandra psychoanalysing my art. I can feel Fiachra regarding me with a furrowed brow.

'It's totally abstract, like a comment on society.' Barry puts his hand up for me to high-five. This isn't an unusual statement for him – about a year ago he became vegan and arty. He's not very good at art, so he tends to lean on concepts quite heavily.

I ignore him, leaving the high five hanging, and look instead at my bulgy-eyed chicken portrait.

'We should probably not get too political with our art,' Sandra says, latching on to Barry's interpretation. 'We wouldn't want to offend the examiners.'

She wafts to the front of the room, fiddles with books on her desk and strokes one of her many beloved sheep skulls as if trying to summon its power. With a sigh, she delivers her well-worn lecture on the importance of making statements in art, but the lack of room for them in a culture intent on a bell-curve grading system.

'I mean you either want an A or you want to make art, and it's my job to direct you towards the A,' she says wistfully. Teaching art has ruined Sandra.

As soon as the bell rings, I skedaddle.

I walk to our main classroom, ahead of the others. Usually I dilly-dally with Tess, letting her fill me in. But I am in no mood today; the sooner I sit down in my next class and switch off the better.

I wish I could just get out. But there are high green fences surrounding the school and it's situated right on the edge of Ballyfert to stop students disturbing the peace. We're not even allowed out of the school grounds at lunch, in case we wander into one of Ballyfert's three shops and buy a packet of gum. Our principal's greatest fear is that someone will get a blot of gum stuck to his pristine tarmac car park.

Inside the school, it is scuffed around the edges – everything from the teachers to the facilities seems jaded. There's only one water fountain in the whole place and rows of faded blue lockers line the walls.

I hurry past the older lads with my head down. I'm not sure if they ever go to class; they seem to spend most of their time leaning against the blue lockers, staring the rest of us down. I ignore the quiet murmurs. If you don't give them any attention, they tend to let you pass without breaking into wolf whistles. Girls that react get it bad, but not as bad as runty boys who blush. They get their bags emptied on the corridor floor, or their shins kicked in. Every now and then the principal gives an uninspired speech on *respecting your fellow students*, but it doesn't do much to change the everyday reality of walking the corridors. As far as the big lads are concerned, it's all part of a tradition, one they were subjected to back in their runty years. For the rest of us, it's a case of drawing as little attention to ourselves as possible. Nobody wants to be the snitch, and if the teachers wanted to see what was going on, they could. Sometimes I wonder if they're just as intimidated as us.

The maths classroom is empty. The whiteboard takes up an entire wall, there's a projector that is rarely used and a TV that is only ever switched on by our Irish teacher. I slip into my prescribed seat and watch as the others filter slowly in, swinging their bags from their shoulders and under their desks.

The chaotic sound of chairs and tables being pulled into position fills the room and people lean back precariously to chat to whoever sits behind them.

Some of the boys snort with laughter as they crumple up paper and blow it through emptied biros into Claire Kelly's perfect blonde hair. She doesn't turn around. She simply shakes her silky locks and lets the paper slip out. The boys give up and thump each other on the shoulders instead. I try to gauge what Claire knows by sneaking sidelong glances at her. I'm still not sure whether she saw us last night. It would be just our luck if she peeped out of the window and recognized our retreating figures. It's hard to know because, as usual, she is perfectly composed. Her pink-painted nails tap expectantly on her desk as she talks, one of her minions giggling beside her. Claire is never without a minion. They are created quite creepily in her image (think Ugg boots and all the pink). Like Tess and Barry, they take advantage of loopholes in the uniform code. I just wear the grey with big clodhopper school shoes because I don't want to draw attention to myself. But Ugg boots are technically brown, as are Tess's thigh-high boots, so they all get away with it. The pink watches, jackets, scrunchies and lip gloss do cause raised eyebrows. But the Kellys are the most powerful farmers in town, so Claire can go where no St Martin's pupil has gone before when putting her own stamp on the uniform. All her minions get immunity by default.

The Ugg Boot Army's only function seems to be to video her and punctuate her sentences with appropriate reactions. I'm not even confident they have names.

Next on the day's schedule is maths, a class in which once again I am seated by Fiachra. All the desks are arranged in pairs and we usually get landed with the same partner. I slump low in my seat, waiting for his arrival, and hope to ignore the chicken-drawing episode. Fiachra hurries in; he's kind of a loner, so nobody pays much attention as he covers the distance between the door and the desk in three strides. He sits down, turning to me and muttering something about 'chicken cruelty' being 'fierce awful'.

I freeze.

Forgetting the chickens for a moment, this is a breach of the Silence.

We've sat beside each other for over three months, and in that time he's said five things. None of them conversation starters, but all memorable because his words are so scarce. Mostly he asks to borrow my protractor, even though he has one himself. I can only assume he doesn't know what a protractor is.

Thankfully, Ms Fitz walks into the classroom and Fiachra stops talking. She is Sandra's opposite. Plump, angry and brutal with a whiteboard pen, she always leans heavily on the board, letting the answers squeak painfully from her hand.

'I'm assuming you've all completed your home-work,' she says, folding her arms in preparation for disappointment. Several hands go up with excuses and the class slogs ahead.

I ignore Fiachra, pretending to be fascinated by algebra, even contributing several answers during the hour.

But questions keep fizzling up inside of me.

What does Fiachra know about chicken cruelty? Is he trying to tell me something?

I shake my head. Impossible. The only person I should be worried about is Claire. And I've more important things to think about than Claire Kelly. Like Polly. How am I going to tell Dad about the wedding? Maybe I should just send an email explaining everything. I try to focus on what I might say to distract myself from thoughts of Fiachra and the dead chicken.

I tidy away my notebook and pens before the bell rings. When the dinging sounds, I am first out of my desk, and I bolt for the door before Fiachra can utter another word.

7

Tess: Meet me in the canteen pronto. This just got real.

Me: As opposed to how incredibly fake it felt before?

Tess: Darling, it would behove you to, like, drop the attitude.

Me: Be there in ten!

Although it's lunchtime when Tess texts, I'm still in the computer lab, composing an email.

'Come on, press Send,' I mutter to myself. Mrs Murphy appears to be fast asleep at her desk (pretty standard), so I'm not under pressure from anyone but Tess to leave.

At last I click Send and watch as my short email disappears from the screen. It's to Dad. I wonder whether he still has the same email address.

I spent our entire computer class drafting it in my head and hung back after the bell to type it and send it off. I couldn't send it during class because the last thing I needed was Claire Kelly peering at my screen and obtaining any further ammunition. She had smiled creepily at me when I took my seat to the left of her in the computer lab. Luckily, she ignored me for the rest of the class. I could just about hear the tail end of her conversation with one of the Ugg Boot Army about appropriate social media platforms, so I tuned out.

I click on my Sent box, glancing at the pathetic words one last time. The email was originally much longer, but I'd slowly deleted most of the sentences, so now (if he gets it) it will say 'FAMILY EMERGENCY' as the subject, followed by: 'SOS! Polly is marrying an accountant on Saturday evening. Mum has no idea.'

After all this time, I barely managed to say anything I wanted to. Not 'Dad', not 'I miss you', and most certainly not 'Love, Molly'.

I take the long route to the canteen. Tess will be tapping away on her phone, so she won't notice if I am a couple of minutes late. Truth be told, I am in no mood to discuss the chickens, but there isn't any way of avoiding it. I trail through the halls, skimming my fingers over the peeling paint of the lockers and trying to switch my mind to the everyday. It is a trick

I use to cope with my family. When they aren't co-operating, I stare at details around the house. Counting books in a line or imagining Mum with new eyebrows. It is hard not to worry about Dad and Polly and the chickens, no matter how many tiles I count or radiators I run my hand along.

The canteen is in the oldest part of the school and is painted an off-white that is so close to grey it almost matches the uniforms. Between the tiled floors and the plastic chairs, it looks and smells like a hospital. There's a tiny telly on a stand in one corner that plays constant reruns of a recording from a music channel. The soundtrack to school lunches invariably includes Beyoncé, One Direction and some golden oldies like Oasis.

I see Tess before she notices me. She is sitting beside Barry, their shoulders touching, as they glare at her phone with matching intensity.

Not Barry! I think. It's typical Tess to use a chicken crisis as boy bait, and for some reason there's no doubt in my mind about that being the situation. There's something about their intensity that suggests a joint purpose. There's no way Barry would be sitting there otherwise. He is Ballyfert's least available boy and has yet to show an interest in anything but making statements.

I won't admit it to Tess, but it might make sense to

enlist Ballyfert's only vegan.

But enlist him to do what?

They are alone in the canteen, except for a gaggle of first years, who are all crammed around one phone giggling. Nobody but first years eat in the canteen during the summer months, because everybody else likes to lurk out by the basketball courts, eyeing each other over their tuna sandwiches and chicken rolls. About once every two or three weeks, a 'new couple' forms and we all pretend not to stare as they make the traditional trip behind the bike sheds. They do this for about three lunches in a row, then quit before things get more serious. If it goes past three lunches, they end up becoming a single life form and no longer need to kiss covertly. They will whip their tongues out right beside your tuna sandwich.

This makes lunch Tess's preferred meeting time. And the canteen Tess's preferred meeting place. She says, *It gives us the kind of privacy that is unheard of in the average prison.*

Tess glances up from her phone and signals for me to join them. There is an urgency to her movements which is frightening. She doesn't even bother explaining the presence of Barry.

'You've got to see the video Claire's gone and posted. She's already got three thousand likes! I mean, does she even have three thousand friends?' I can tell Tess is as upset about the content of the post as the fact that Claire continues to become more and more of a social media superstar by the day. Social-Media Superstar is basically Tess's dream, and instead she's a chicken thief.

'It makes me sick to think what the world is coming to,' Barry sighs, shaking his head and cupping his chin as if that action alone sums up the plight of the world.

Tess tosses the phone to me. Unusual, given that it's more a fifth limb than an object she's willing to detach and hand over. I grapple with the phone, turning it around, and, for the second time in two days, click on a video of Claire talking at me.

The setting for this video is different. Claire has positioned herself in a shed and is taking the video herself. She still manages to capture her face at a flattering angle, and I am momentarily distracted by how flawless her skin looks.

Disgusted with myself, I focus on the shed instead. This isn't the shed we opened. It's mostly empty, with light streaming in and bundles of fresh hay visible behind her. She's shaking her head tragically at the camera.

'So, like, I woke up this morning to this −' she sweeps her arms to draw us into the shed − 'expecting to say good morning to my babies, and they weren't here. That's right, people, somebody opened the shed doors last night.'

She looks deeply into the camera then and makes a major sad face. It's unbelievably fake, but I keep watching.

'And, like, there are chickens everywhere, dead chickens everywhere.'

She pauses, taking a deep breath.

'And the worst thing is, it's all because of me . . .' Then the video cuts to yesterday's video of Lady Macbeth trying to lay eggs, before focusing back on sad-thoughtful Claire.

'I did this: I showed Ballyfert something it wasn't ready for, a transgender chicken, and now Ballyfert has responded with this . . . this . . . hate crime.'

She sighs deeply, looking at the floor, then her eyes flick back to camera.

'You know I love you, guys, and I am asking you a big favour: if anybody knows anything about this . . . horrible crime . . . please contact me. We're going to do everything we can to save as many chickens as possible.'

The video fades away and her contact details appear with a link to a post.

'Did you read the post?' I ask Barry and Tess.

They nod solemnly, waiting for me to catch up.

CARNAGE! LOCAL HOOLIGANS RELEASE 300 CHICKENS IN VIOLENT RESPONSE TO TRANSGENDER ROOSTER

8 May, 11.30 a.m.

Ten chickens found dead and 150 missing, after 300 were released into the wild by vandals overnight. The attack is thought to be a response to a viral video of a transgender rooster released by the farm only hours before.

The alarm was raised at Kelly's Farm at approximately 2.40 a.m. this morning.

Gardaí confirmed to the *Ballyfert Times* that some of the chickens have been recovered, but 150 remain missing.

Sean Kelly, owner of the 300 victims, commented on the situation: 'We want to get as many chickens home as safely as possible. We'll worry about who did what later. It's a dangerous world for chickens out there, and these hens have led a sheltered life.'

Most fatalities have been a result of negligent driving and a couple of chickens fell victim to an open slurry pit.

Claire Kelly, daughter of Sean Kelly, was devastated by the attack: 'I can't believe people are so small-minded in this day and age, it breaks my heart.'

Gardaí attended the scene during the early hours of this morning. An investigation has been launched into the incident.

Anyone with information is encouraged to contact Ballyfert Garda Station.

'Oh God, oh God, oh God . . .' I stare down at the screen, rereading the lines. The more I read them, the less sense they make.

'I thought you'd panic,' said Tess, in a manner which is much too smug for someone who is a renowned mass chicken murderer and small-minded member of the gender police.

'Well, then, why did you show me? You could have let me get through school first.'

'We don't have time to spare you, like, any delicate moments – we need to take control of the narrative ASAP.'

'What you did was incredibly brave. The minute I saw this, I remembered your drawing and just knew,' Barry says, reaching across as if to pat my hand. 'Thank you for sending the signal.'

'It wasn't a signal,' I say, horrified that I'm the one who has attracted him to the cause.

'You're going to have to go public,' he says, his hand still reaching for mine. I draw away.

'How does that make sense?' I ask.

'Oh, shut up, Molly. It hardly makes *no* sense. What do you suggest? We let Claire bloody Kelly start counting dead chickens and shoving them in people's faces? Because very soon that will get ugly.'

I blink, registering her no-nonsense tone.

'But—'

'But what, Molly? Would you rather sit around drawing creepy chicken pictures, as if you need a giant flashing signpost saying, *Hey, guess what, I killed some chickens*, or do I need to remind you that there is a substantial piece of evidence sleeping in your bedroom.'

'We didn't kill any chickens,' I say.

'Well, I'm sorry, Molly, I hate to be the one to make you face your problems, but it sure looks like we killed some chickens.'

She waves the screen in my face. This is unfair. Stealing back the chickens was her idea.

'OK, so what do you suggest?' I ask. There isn't any point bickering with Tess. She is not accustomed to being challenged. Her parents are dead old, by which I mean they're almost dead. After forty years as business tycoons, they retired and gave up arguing.

I slump back in my chair, letting the words from the article sink in: *a couple of chickens fell victim to an open slurry pit*. Tess is right – that means we are chicken murderers. There is no innocence involved in enabling a slurry-drowning. What if Mrs Danvers was one of the chickens that drowned, or Boo Radley has been maimed by a tractor? I stare at the phone screen. Tess places her hand over it, slides it back across the table and pockets it.

'Staring at that is not going to help. We've a video

to shoot,' Tess says.

'What, now? Don't we have double science?'

'We need to get this under control,' Barry says, looking confused by my lack of enthusiasm.

'So, we're going to skip school?'

'Well, look at it this way – it's an institution built to dull your senses and turn you into a—'

'OK, Barry, we get the idea,' Tess says, cutting him short. She heads towards the canteen exit.

I stumble after her.

I've never skipped class before. Rain, sick or father-departing, I have always shown up at my desk and handed in my homework. There is a drawer full of perfect attendance certs in the kitchen dating back to Junior Infants. A horrible prickly feeling blooms in my throat.

The crimes are piling up.

8

It is risky to be seen outside school grounds in uniform, though we do blend into the town's landscape of grey cement. There isn't much uniform happening between Barry's bow tie and Tess's lack of skirt. The two of them eye my buttoned-up shirt and tie with disdain and Tess signals for me to hand over my jumper.

'Think of it as a makeover. You must be the only one that insists on wearing the full uniform, it's a pure embarrassment,' Tess says, stuffing my jumper into my bag and hiking up my skirt. I tug self-consciously at the hem, which is now hovering millimetres below my knicker-line.

We're heading to a shop for more of Tess's infamous 'supplies'. Nobody's given me a chance to ask what the plan is exactly. As we walk, I replay the barn scene from the video in my head: a 'grief-stricken' Claire prances about, waxing lyrical about *her* transgender chicken. As if Lady Macbeth is interested in gender politics. The poor chicken simply wants to mind her eggs, eat the occasional strawberry and avoid Bellatrix's darker moods. *What if Bellatrix is one of the dead chickens?* I try to push the thought to one side. Obsessing over my chickens is clearly bad for the flock's health. I've already done enough harm. Rescuing one out of seven chickens was a complete disaster, especially now that the six others may have had the life squished out of them.

Tess ignores the bigger Ballyfert shop because the woman on the till is fierce gossipy and would have our principal on the phone before we got as far as the aisles. We head straight to the dingy corner shop. It's frequented by people whose staple diet is milk, bread and rashers. Though it's technically called Kavanaghs, the sign is missing most of its letters and has read 'agh' for as long as I can remember, as if the sign itself is a warning. I've never been inside before, because the window display features a tin of biscuits that Dad said has been there since the 1970s.

Inside, an old man is bent over the counter, peering so closely at a crossword that his eyebrows are resting on three across. He doesn't seem to notice our presence and continues to scribble along the margins of his puzzle. Tess bustles among the musty sets of shelves, tossing items to me and Barry to hold for her.

'Lighting,' she says, gathering three torches, some batteries and a candle from a shelf that's also home to three cans of beans, a single loaf of bread and two packets of biscuits. It's as if we're buying supplies from someone's understocked pantry.

'What do chickens eat anyway?' she asks, weighing the bag of custard creams in one hand and the digestives in the other.

'Not that,' I mumble.

'If you're not going to offer solutions, then maybe you can wait outside,' Tess says.

'The custard creams . . .'

'I don't know,' Barry says, 'is that a sustainable choice?'

'You two will be the death of my ingenuity,' Tess says, opting for the digestives with a shrug. 'They're made from grains, right?'

She marches up to the counter and attempts to cajole a few plastic bags out of the old man.

'Knock yerselves out,' he says gruffly, slapping them on the counter. 'I bought those long before the damn taxes.'

Tess grins, indicating the rest of our supplies, and he slowly jabs the prices into his calculator.

'Thanks a million,' Tess says, as we turn to leave. The man grunts before returning sullenly to the crossword. His biro makes inky marks in the margins as he figures out the answers.

'Eh . . . so what are the supplies for?' I ask, outside the shop.

'An exposé, my dear Molly, the likes of which Ballyfert has never seen before.'

'Uh . . . We are not going back there. Do you want to get arrested?'

'What are our lives if we do nothing with them?' Barry asks in a bored voice. He looks as if he's already given up on my capacity for living and is simply tolerating my presence for Tess's sake.

'We're going to get footage of the hellscape that the chickens are being kept in. I am not going down as some kind of chicken terrorist – that is not what my brand is about,' Tess says. 'And if there's time, we can just, like, scoop up a few chickens.'

Barry smiles patronizingly at me. 'This isn't only the beginning of our movement, it's the beginning of—'

'I'm sorry, *movement*? Did I miss something?' I ask.

'Look, Molly,' Tess says, 'we've got a farm to expose!'

My brain is a jumble as the others stride ahead. I reluctantly drag my feet past the five pubs that make up Ballyfert's main street. Stuff like our school and the library were tacked on to the town much later. Tess and Barry natter away. Only some of their words filter back. Thankfully most of it is muffled by the wind, because I don't even want to know what they mean by *vegan sacrifices*.

Claire's lane is right at the edge of Ballyfert, but Tess leads the way to the fields behind the farmhouse. She refuses to use the front entrance in case it's under surveillance. Which proves how out of touch with Ballyfert Tess really is. The only creatures surveying anything around here are cows.

At the back gate, we crouch, taking in the monster shed. If anything, it looks worse in the daylight. Somehow darker and more sinister. There's crime scene tape criss-crossing the yard, but nobody is in sight.

'*I know why the caged bird sings . . .*' Barry says gravely, his eyes fixed on the monster shed.

'Do you ever give it a rest?' I ask.

Tess shoots me a look, whips out her phone, and then swings it around to take the three of us in. She hits Record.

'As many of you know, there's been an attack on some chickens in Ballyfert, and some people are throwing around some pretty nasty accusations,' Tess says, all smooth and buttery. Before I can ask when she had time to script a newscast, Barry chimes in, and I realize this has been rehearsed without me.

'But that attack wasn't what you think. In fact, we're about to expose the real chicken terrorists,' Barry says.

'The truth is, the attack you've heard about was a rescue mission,' Tess says, sounding nothing like herself. It's like she's channelling a weather woman, all polished vowels and enunciation. They must have planned this video while I was emailing Dad.

'And how do we know? Well, because . . . drum roll, please . . . we're those rescuers,' Tess says, flicking the camera back to Barry, who is already breaking out the next line:

'And now we're going to show you just *how* these chickens have been deprived of basic chicken rights.'

'Let's go,' Tess says. 'Prepare yourself for the harrowing reality.'

If the others find it suspicious that the yard is empty, they don't say. Instead they hop over the gate, and waltz towards the shed, stepping over the caution tape as if it's something inconsequential. They're drunk on self-righteousness.

'One small step for chickenkind,' Barry says sincerely.

I reluctantly follow.

In front of the monster shed, Tess trains the camera on Barry, who informs viewers about veganism, chickens rights and some miscellaneous injustices of the modern world that don't seem to be related to the plight of chickens at all. It's an awful pity that Barry is a vegan. People in Ballyfert would respond a lot better to the whole plant-based diet thing if he wasn't the only one pedalling it. Anything I've read about veganism makes it seem really good for the planet. It just seems annoying when someone like Barry talks about it. He's the sort of person that would encourage me to eat meat, despite his obvious intentions.

As Barry's less than inspiring monologue comes to an end, Tess eases open the monster shed door, and shines a torch in. Barry wrinkles his nose in disgust.

'I know you said it was bad, but . . .'

I step into the shed as the other two capture footage. Zooming in on the filthy floor, panning to capture the spot where the torch lights up a medium-sized huddle of chickens near the back of the shed. The reality of how many chickens have escaped hits me. Compared to the sea of glinting eyes last night, there are nowhere near as many birds staring back at me.

'That should be plenty,' Tess says, pocketing her phone and heading back outside. Part of me wants to look for my chickens, but I don't really want to cause any more chicken trauma. It breaks my heart to think they might be shivering in the middle of that chicken huddle, just watching me walk away.

'Did you hear that?' Tess says. Her whole body tenses in concentration. There is complete silence. Barry glances back at me and I shrug, joining them outside and closing the door carefully behind me.

'OK, that is like the height of uncool,' Tess addresses one of the smaller sheds, in a manner which suggests she expects it to respond.

'Um . . .' I say, because if she thinks someone is behind that door, then we should get out of here. Or has Barry brainwashed her so badly that she has forgotten the law. 'Maybe we should—'

I stop speaking as four heads pop out from behind the door. Heads with long blondish hair, perfectly executed eyeliner, matching pink lip-gloss and smug half-smiles. The Ugg Boot Army emerge in a silky line, led by Claire, and file into the yard, approaching like a gathering of clones. One of them takes out a phone and trains it on us.

'So, what do we have here, Tess-kins?' Claire says. She tends to talk like a patronizing aunt. Shockingly, this quirk hasn't put a dent in her popularity.

Her smile is the kind of sugar syrup that flies drown in. The three current members of the Ugg Boot Army follow her and with such swagger.

'Are you getting this?' Barry asks Tess, and she nods, whipping out her phone and focusing the camera on Claire.

Claire seems undeterred by the phone and stands directly in front of Tess and Barry. The other three form a neat row behind her, placing their hands on their tiny hips, then jutting their bodies to one side. I can hear Mum in my head shunning them for bad posture.

'So, like, do you want to explain, or will I interpret this as it looks – trespassing on private property, and . . . Then there's this ruler . . .' Claire speaks deliberately slow, pulling out the wooden ruler that we had left to mark the grave of the roadkill chicken.

'I mean, Tess-kins, surely you know not to leave your name hanging around a dead chicken . . . It's too easy . . . almost like you want to be caught.'

'We're raising awareness, Claire. You of all people should understand that there's no crime in that,' Tess says.

'So, I'm supposed to, like, let you badmouth my family?' Claire's face has a manic glow about it. She hands the wooden ruler to one of her minions, who tucks it away out of sight. Presumably as future collateral.

'Shouldn't you be in school?' Barry asks, as if he doesn't attend the exact same school.

Claire smiles. 'I am the only person who *should* be standing in *my* farmyard.'

'Well, we're doing this for the chickens,' Tess says.

'Oh, Tess-kins, you're such a tiring wannabe. Can you drop the act – I want to ask what's-her-face over there a question.'

Claire fixes her eyes on me.

'I have a name,' I squeak, in a manner that is usually associated with rodents.

'Of course you do . . . but I'm only interested in that chicken you've "saved" – your name is surplus to requirements.'

Claire executes a strange hand movement where she flicks her right hand up in the air and then wiggles her fingers. It must be a signal, because the three girls behind her laugh. She flicks her hand again as if to say, *Enough*. They all stop, their faces settling into a practised sneer.

'The chicken is mine,' I say, realizing I'm admitting to chicken theft on two cameras. I consider flicking my own hand, but Tess is likely to interpret it as some kind of seizure.

'So, you do have the chicken,' Claire says.

'I'm not giving her back,' I say. Tess kicks my shin to try and get me to stop being such a sap. I can't help it. The sticky-sweet smell of their collective perfumes is stifling my thought process.

'This video will suffice for now. What do you think girls – five thousand likes for the chicken terrorists caught on camera?' Claire sneers.

'We'll lower our cameras if you lower yours,' Tess says, aware of how the video the Ugg Boot Army is recording will make us look.

Claire nods, snapping her finger, and the phone disappears. Tess slips her own into her pocket, eyeing Claire warily.

'So, we're going to negotiate?' Tess asks.

'Tess, remember, justice is not negotia—' Barry begins, but Claire speaks over him.

'Oh, no . . . No, I don't think so . . . Not unless you want me to call the guards . . . You will remove yourselves from *my* property and, if I were you, you'll return *my* chicken before I'm forced to make this little video go viral.'

'We've got a video too,' Tess hisses, but it's more panicky than anything, because Claire has an actual following and both sets of footage incriminate us. Keeping chickens in a dirty shed isn't actually against the law. Trespassing and stealing chickens definitely is.

'What do you even want Lady Macbeth for?' I ask. The Ugg Boot Army laugh spontaneously when I say *Lady Macbeth*. I have never witnessed them react spontaneously to anything before; maybe it isn't such a snappy chicken title after all.

'But what about compassion, chicken rights, liberty, justice, global warming, humanity . . .' Barry says, using lots of words but very little direction.

'I don't have time for this. You will give me back my chicken or else . . .' Claire performs an anti-smile – an expression that looks like smiling but is not. The Ugg Boots can't see her face but seem to know from the placement of her hands on her hips what expression they are supposed to be wearing. The effect is a terrifying pyramid of anti-smilers staring us down.

'I . . . eh . . . guess we'll be going,' Tess says. She retreats, trying to climb over the gate with as much dignity as possible. Once we've all piled over, I glance back at the Ugg Boot Army. They're all still frozen in anti-smile formation.

Tess groans. 'That is so impressive, such choreography, such commitment.'

9

Tess and Barry decide we need to move to Plan B, whatever that is. No doubt it's connected to the *vegan sacrifices* they were chatting about earlier. But I'm exhausted and Mum will turn me into a horse sculpture if I miss the family dinner. So I tell Tess to keep me posted and go home alone.

I arrive to the sound of Polly singing, 'How D'Ya Like Your Eggs in the Morning?' I can hear her banging about the kitchen again. So I skip the housewife antics and head straight to my room; Lady Macbeth will need some company. The door to my room is ajar, which is strange because I am not the sort of person that forgets about closing doors. That is every other member of the family. I'm always switching off lights and closing windows and doors behind the others.

Lady Macbeth's nest drawer is empty, as are all the nooks and crannies she could have crawled into. I sigh loudly. Polly must have kidnapped my chicken to force me to have an interaction. I traipse downstairs and stand in the small hall, composing myself at the foot of the stairs.

I swing open the door. Polly has her back to me and is bent over something on the range. She has artfully arranged all Mum's wedding presents on the kitchen table. Mum was given piles of nice tableware for her wedding. She was miffed about it, because she felt Dad's relatives wanted her handcuffed to the range. In a fit of rebellion against domesticity, she locked all the gifts in an old filing cabinet. Judging by the table, Polly has unlocked the filing cabinet and inhaled the luxury. There is a fancy butter dish glinting, Waterford crystal goblets, and an abundance of polished cutlery sitting on silk napkins. An expensive-looking bottle of wine sits front and centre.

The big pasta colander is strangely positioned upside down in the centre of the kitchen floor. As I watch it inch from side to side, I realize that Polly has fashioned a temporary chicken cage. What is up with people putting Lady Macbeth in small dark prisons?

I march over, whipping off the colander, to find that Lady Macbeth is on her back and has resumed her belly-up, legs-to-the-sky stance, as if it's some sort of chicken foetal position. She's rocking back and forth, which must be what caused the colander to move from side to side.

'*Shuk, shuk, shuk,*' I murmur, trying to reassure her. She looks so nonplussed that I lower my voice and my next *shuk, shuk, shuk* comes out more like a question.

Polly hasn't noticed my presence. I scoop Lady Macbeth into my arms, quickly checking for any further damage. The wing looks gummy with Sudocrem, but otherwise improved.

Polly must have worked on the dinner and her 1920s' housewife hair all day. She has on oven gloves, a vintage dress, and a frilly apron. From the smell of the place, she is baking bread and making carrot and orange soup from scratch. She is so busy channelling her inner domestic goddess that she doesn't even notice I have managed to reclaim my chicken.

'We're finally going to be a *real* family,' she gushes at me, somehow still missing the presence of the chicken in my arms. She gestures emphatically at the table, as if using expensive cutlery will finally bring us peace and harmony.

'Um . . . you know Mum gets upset if you use the good goblets.'

'Nonsense – she wants to impress her muscle and we've big news to celebrate.' Polly flashes her hand at me. The big shiny rock has been reinstated.

'Does Mum know?'

'Oh, no . . . I'm saving the news for tonight,' Polly says giddily. As if the prospect of Mum throwing a hissy fit at dinner is enough to get Polly out of bed in the morning. Which to be fair, it is.

A silver banner catches my eye. It is strung above the table and reads WE'RE ENGAGED. Part of me wants to climb up on a chair and cross out the first G, replacing it with a big black R. Because WE'RE ENRAGED is exactly what our get-to-know-the-Hulk dinner will become once Mum takes one look at what Polly has done to her hair and her future.

I imagine Mum and Polly spent a peaceful morning buying up the best of Ballyfert's produce. Bonding over their dream family dinner. Mum blissfully splurging on the organic wine, thinking that the gesture would win Polly over. Polly nodding along happily as they argued over whether crème fraiche or cream was more appropriate for a dinner party.

Meanwhile Polly was secretly plotting an emotional time bomb.

'It looks lovely,' I say, as Polly floats about the kitchen, measuring the distance between items on the table and rearranging an already beautifully arranged vase of Mum's beloved lilies, their pink and white petals stretching towards the ceiling.

Polly is so mesmerized by her own table-setting

skills that she still hasn't noticed I am cradling Lady Macbeth. Should I say something?

There are a lot of ways Polly could react when she finally notices. She might get me to tell her what Lady Macbeth was doing in my room. At the very least, I'm anticipating a lecture on cleanliness. Polly's room might be a mess, but it never stops her lecturing us on the rest of the house. Now that she's found a chicken in my room, she's likely to go to town on hygiene. Polly usually refers to chickens in sentences with words like *ew* and *Dettol*.

But she isn't alarmed at all. She acts like it is the most natural occurrence in the world.

'Oh, Molly, I've been meaning to ask you about that adorable specimen of chicken–hood. Come here to me,' she says, casting her ladle to one side and approaching me with a *Stepford Wives* smile.

'What?' I ask. 'Why?'

'A flower chicken, Molly, for the wedding – isn't that the most romantic thing you've ever heard?' Polly says dreamily.

'Eh . . . not really.'

I glance doubtfully at Lady Macbeth. There are lots of words I'd use to describe chickens, but *romantic* isn't one of them.

'It's fate – I was looking for tulle in your room, and what did I find, but that chicken.'

'Tulle? I hate to break it to you, but coordinating chickens isn't exactly easy. She won't just sashay down the aisle with a mini flower crown.'

'Oh, no, I would never . . . Well, maybe the flower crown . . .' Polly says. 'Now, will you give her here? I don't want anything happening to her before the wedding, and, well, with the condition you left her in, you can hardly be trusted.'

'What? I didn't do that to her, I rescued her.'

'It's better for the chicken if I take it from here. I need her looking radiant for the wedding,' Polly says, her face flickering to annoyance. Nothing irritates Polly more than not getting her own way.

'But you don't know anything about chickens.' I'm defensive. Polly wouldn't recognize chicken feed if she was force-fed it.

'How hard can it be? I can make bread from scratch, sew an apron, clean a kitchen and set a table like royalty is arriving – all while maintaining an air of calm,' Polly says, as if chicken rearing is another basic chore. It's like she makes a list of all the stuff she does all day and then practises reciting it.

'I wouldn't exactly call this an air of calm.'

I glance at the perfectly set table, tightening my grip on Lady Macbeth. Polly is smiling wide enough to break her face, but her eyes are cold steel. She wants me to relinquish control of the chicken immediately. She walks slowly at first, but when she is an arm's length away, she lunges. A vain attempt to catch me off guard. I've spent years observing her lunge-and-grab technique, so I sidestep. This causes Polly to stumble and bump into the table. Bumping into the table has a domino effect.

Polly loses control.

She lunges for Lady Macbeth again, and in doing so, knocks over the crystal water jug, which tips over the bottle of wine, which spills on to the white lace tablecloth. The white lace tablecloth is oddly out of place – a tablecloth is not an item we own.

The wine spillage causes Polly to abandon common sense. She flings herself at the table, and grabs a corner of the white cloth, pulling desperately to salvage the lace. The removal of the lace causes the other items on the table to fall, and the delicate glasses and china to shatter.

The shattering of Mum's wedding trove causes me to throw Lady Macbeth into the air. She sails, momentarily suspended in the air, before falling with a dull thud on to the floorboards. Tasting freedom, or perhaps terrified, Lady Macbeth launches herself forward and zigzags around the kitchen. Polly doesn't even bother with Lady Macbeth. She begins picking up all the broken bits of Mum's wedding loot and chucking them on to the middle of the table.

'I spend all day trying to cook a nice meal for you moronic spinsters and look what happens, you sabotage me.'

Polly continues in this way for a minute or two before sitting in front of the pile of broken crockery and staring at it. I am too busy chasing Lady Macbeth to bother feeling sorry for her. The chicken is surprisingly agile.

During all this commotion, Mum enters the house. Knowing Mum, she has mapped out her whole evening. Perhaps planning a nice long bath, some eyeliner and one of her soft shimmery dresses. Then, she will take us aside and have the *be nice to Gary* talk. Something along the lines of, *It's hard for him too, what with your father and me still being married. The least you can do is laugh at his jokes.* Mum's vision is most likely a simple meal where we all laugh at the Hulk's witticisms before retiring to the sitting room, where we sit around telling embarrassing stories about our childhoods.

Her map of the evening definitely won't involve a pit stop where Polly weeps over a table covered in broken glass and crockery. To make matters worse, Polly is wearing an apron. Mum doesn't believe in aprons.

'What in the name of Betty Crocker happened here?' Mum asks, striding across the kitchen to where

Polly is staring into space. 'I know you miss your father, Polly, but this is a bit much.'

Mum picks up one of Polly's tight curls, rubbing it between her fingers in bafflement. She seems more concerned by Polly's hair than the state of the kitchen.

'This is not about Dad,' Polly says.

'Well, what is it about, then?' Mum asks.

The banner is right there, its tacky message hovering in front of Mum. WE'RE ENGAGED dancing boldly above her eyeline. But she is too focused on Polly's hair to notice it or the giant engagement ring shimmering on Polly's finger.

'It doesn't matter, does it? Why would anyone bother listening to me when Molly has gone and stolen a stupid chicken?'

Polly clutches the table as if it will keep her from spinning off the planet. Mum turns to Lady Macbeth and me. I have successfully cornered the chicken and am shooing her on to a dustpan with the brush. Lady Macbeth is not cooperating. She is almost growling.

'That isn't one of your old chickens, is it? Did you steal it? There was something in the paper about stolen chickens down at the Kellys, Molly . . . Oh God, you know how much that's worth? Right?' Mum asks, as if stealing a cheap animal would be acceptable.

'I found it,' I say.

Mum gives me a funny look. 'Oh, what, it was conveniently lying around . . . And right when we're about to have Gary over for dinner.'

'There are a lot of chickens hanging around right now, actually. It has nothing to do with the Hulk Dinner.'

'What are you planning to do – launch it at Gary's face?' Mum asks.

'Why would I—' I begin.

'Save it!' Mum says, her mouth parted. She utters a few confused throat-clearing noises as she tries to recalibrate the logistics of the evening.

'You're such an attention-seeking chicken thief, it's a stupid chicken, and I'm a real person,' Polly screams at us both. There is never a good reason for Polly to scream, but she does anyway.

'Can you please put that chicken away where I don't have to deal with it?' Mum asks, ignoring Polly. If she could get away with it, I am sure she'd put Polly away where she didn't have to deal with her too.

'I suppose you're going to pretend you don't hate me for ruining your wedding dress,' Polly sobs. That solves the tablecloth mystery.

'Well, I hardly need it again,' Mum says, 'and I could never hate you, don't be silly.'

Considering that Mum doesn't know about

114

BrainDrain, this seems like an incredibly premature pronouncement. Wait till she finds out Brian Doran is about to become a fully fledged member of the family.

I manage to get Lady Macbeth on to the dustpan and am busy easing her into my arms, so I can transfer her out of what is fast becoming a war zone.

'So that's it – you're going to ignore me, and let Molly go around stealing chickens, and pretend, like, there aren't any consequences to all *this*,' Polly says, picking a broken piece of glass from the table and holding it up to the light. She looks deranged, standing there with her robot-lady curls, eyes puffy and red from crying, brandishing a sharp shard of glass.

'I'm sick of the two of you trying to sabotage my happiness.' Mum has found her words and expels them in a flat, controlled voice, which makes it all the more heart-breaking. 'Your dad is gone. I'm seeing Gary, and, quite frankly, I don't care what you think of him. He makes me happy. So you can steal chickens or whatever it is you come up with next in the bid for biggest attention-seeker . . . I don't have the time or energy to deal with this.'

I want to fling Lady Macbeth out of a window and make all the broken crockery disappear.

'Of course, how could we forget that we come last? Why would we expect that to change? It's not

115

like we need your help or anything,' Polly says.

'I'd help you, if I had any bloody clue what you wanted from me. Can't you see I am trying my best?' Mum gestures at the blue wig, as if it alone sums up the extent of her struggles.

I pat Lady Macbeth on the head, because it is overwhelming for a chicken to be in the middle of all this tension.

'I'm going upstairs to get ready. Polly, if you wouldn't mind cleaning up your mess . . . I suppose we'll have to make do with dinner in the big hall,' Mum says.

She doesn't register that Polly's arms are loose by her side or hear her say, 'Nothing is ever good enough for you.'

Mum disappears and the kitchen is quiet, except for the shallow sound of Polly's breathing. After a moment, she tucks her robot-curls behind her ears, dusts down her clothes and gets straight to work. I watch as a smile forces its way across her face, as she pinches her cheeks and wipes under her eyes matter-of-factly.

'By the smell of it, the soup is almost re-ady,' she says, her voice breaking on the word *ready*. She gulps down the emotion.

'Look at me, getting all het up over nothing,' she says, laughing. But her laugh has a narrow sound to it, like she knows well she is missing the mark.

'Do you want to hold the chicken, Polly?' I ask, hopefully.

'No, I do not want to fondle your stupid chicken.'

10

The doorbell rings half an hour early, which is worse than rude. Lady Macbeth is tucked up in her bedside drawer and Mum is still restoring herself in the bath. Polly and I are either end of the kitchen table, trying to manoeuvre it through the kitchen door and into the big hall.

When the doorbell rings, I am on the hall side of the table, which means I have to answer the door. Polly says she has to check on the roasted butternut squash anyway. We abandon the table mid-doorway, and I walk reluctantly towards our first guest. I haven't had a chance to change out of my uniform and am starting to feel as grotty as I am tired.

The doorbell dings for the fourth time, which shows a complete lack of consideration. God forbid they'd have to wait for us to finish moving the furniture.

I swing it open to reveal BrainDrain checking his watch. He has the solid structure of a rugby player, with cauliflower ears and bright pink cheeks. I've met him several times before, but each and every time I am surprised by the size of him.

'Ah, Jaysus . . . I'm afraid I'm early,' he says, looking mildly uncomfortable. 'Mammy was heading into town, so she said she'd drop me off a bit early, and ye know, normally I would insist on calling ahead, but there really is no arguing with her.'

'I thought you had a car?' I say, glancing behind him. The driveway is empty.

'Well, yeah, but I share the car with Mammy. It sounds worse than it is – most of the time we're going to the same place and, as she always says, there's no point wasting money on two cars where one will do the job.'

He rubs his hands together as he speaks. I nod, supressing the desire to yawn, and wordlessly lead him inside. BrainDrain doesn't require encouragement. How can Polly bring herself to marry into the Mammy monologues?

'I was going to bring some wine, but Mammy is after telling me ye can never be too careful, and then there was the bread, but she said there was no telling what Bohemians eat and that ye might turn yer noses up at a bit of sliced pan . . . And didn't I tell her Polly's not like that, but, well, she wasn't having any of it.'

There is no point telling him his mammy is right. Sliced pan is not the way to Polly's heart. It is better to come empty-handed than with bog-standard food fare. I point towards the table which is protruding from the kitchen.

'Polly needs your help,' I say, interrupting whatever fascinating Mammyism he is in the middle of. BrainDrain glances at the table and then back at me, before stepping forward and giving me a brisk hug. He plucks me clean off the ground, crushes my bones together and then plonks me back down.

'I've been meaning to ask ye, I . . . eh, well . . . I'll be proud to have ye as a little sister.' He grins. 'What'll I call ye . . . I was thinking, "lil sis" . . .'

'Eh . . . you can call me Molly,' I say, rubbing my recently squeezed shoulders.

'Oh, right, yeah, Molly.' He looks disappointed. 'Sure, didn't Mammy say I was getting carried away with the "lil sis" stuff, and ye know she's usually right about that kind of thing.'

'Right, well, I've to go,' I say. I've given up count- ing the strikes against BrainDrain. I scoot around the bulk of his frame and shout towards Polly.

'Brain — I mean, Brian — is here.'

'Oh, great. Brian, can you come here a minute? I've a list as long as my arm to get through,' Polly calls.

120

Brian ambles happily in her direction, bouncing back from the 'lil sis' rejection with surprising elasticity. He effortlessly plucks the jammed table out of the doorway and moves it into the big hall. Polly flutters out of the kitchen and disappears into his arms. I can see that they make a strange sort of sense. He is as happy as he is massive, the exact opposite of Dad, something Polly probably yearns for after the past year.

I am about to escape upstairs when the doorbell sounds again. This has to be the Hulk. I groan inwardly, shuffling back to open the door. Sure enough, the Hulk is standing there with a smile on his face, a massive bouquet of flowers spilling from his arms. It is alarming and seems to contain every flower. It is as if he panicked over including Mum's favourites and haphazardly pointed at anything remotely colourful in the shop. The result is an explosion of red roses, fuchsias, lilies, tulips and sunflowers. It's a strange choice for a professional landscaper.

'Molly, it's lovely to see you,' he says, grinning at me over the flowers.

'Wow . . . that's big,' I say, unsure of how else to describe the bouquet.

'Yes, well, there was a very specific request put in for *big* flowers. I think *all the flowers* was the exact terminology used.'

Of course it was. He laughs easily, as if Mum demanding a massive bouquet of all the flowers is perfectly normal.

'Oh! Well, let's hope it's big enough,' I say. 'She's hard to please.'

It sounds polite, but it is a direct warning. I don't want him to be disappointed if she tosses them out of the window or staples them to an art project. You never know with Mum.

'Well, if it doesn't do the job, I can always bulk it out with some twigs and grass.'

Laughing, I usher the Hulk in, noting how different from Dad he looks. They're both tall, but that's where it ends. The Hulk is muscled and fit-looking from all the bounding about in Lycra, whereas Dad used to look like a malnourished sleepwalker. And although it's impossible to remember Dad as much more than a blur, his face was stubble-central, his hair scruffy, and he always looked wrong without at least one coffee stain on his shirt. The Hulk is clean-shaven, wears a neat jumper and tasteful jeans, and he seems to ease into the house. I have a sudden memory of the way Dad would twitch his way through the door, wrinkling his nose at all the musty furniture and longing for a sterilized laboratory.

I am about to close the door when I realize that, lurking behind the Hulk, dressed in a hoodie and baggy jeans, scuffing the step with his school shoes and trying to disappear into the ground, is a mortified-looking Fiachra.

'What are you doing here?' I say, my new-found manners disappearing in the fog of my surprise. Fiachra's cheeks flush, and the Hulk answers for him.

'Oh, I was hoping you wouldn't mind, with all the chicken mania. I mean, who knows what's going on in Ballyfert at the moment? I didn't want to leave him to his own devices – you can't be too careful these days.'

'I see,' I say, feeling a pang. There could be someone specifically abducting fourteen-year-old girls from the Ballyfert area and Mum would just tell me to wear a high-vis vest if I was going to be out after dark.

'Yeah . . . It's a bit overkill,' the Hulk says, 'but, sure, he's the only son I've got.'

He shrugs, clapping Fiachra apologetically on the back. Not that Fiachra is paying his dad one bit of attention. From the look on his face and the intensity with which he is staring at the ground, I suspect Fiachra is envisioning a giant multicoloured dragon swooping down to sweep him away.

I show them into the sitting room. It is the only

semi-respectable room for guests, and the one place the mice don't frequent. It has a red carpet that still retains some sense of vibrancy, and all the half-decent books are displayed in a lovely oak bookcase. There are deep red velvet curtains and an assortment of candles dotting the mantelpiece. The fire isn't lit, but at least old ashes aren't spilling from the grate.

'Well, this is charming,' the Hulk says, easing himself on to the three-seater couch. He doesn't give in to the lure of Mum's cushion collection. She has cushions from every corner of the world spread across the furniture. There are Moroccan ones, African silks and French patchwork. My favourite is a silvery square with embroidered stars.

Fiachra perches beside his dad, managing to sit awkwardly on our most comfortable seating arrangement. BrainDrain sticks his head in the door.

'Polly is after telling me to get out from under her feet, so I hope you don't mind.'

He doesn't wait for a response and approaches the furniture with much less formality than the others. He sighs deeply and sinks into Dad's old blue armchair, which still smells of sandalwood. It sags a bit, crouched in Dad's shape as if it's waiting for him to turn up and settle back into its folds. He used to spend hours there, reading thick science books or disappearing into the internet, where he would chat to fellow scientists and keep up with the latest research. Every now and then he'd read something out loud to us about AI technologies or cancer research. I'd act fascinated, but Mum would always stare off into space and when he'd finished ask him something like, *Have you bothered taking out the compost yet?* Or, *Will one of those robots fix the leaks in the attic?*

'Mammy always says ye can't bate a decent chair with a stick,' BrainDrain says happily.

I leave them to drown in small talk and go to wash my face. I hate small talk; it always feels like gristle between my teeth.

As I rub foam into my face, I realize Fiachra's presence is going to require some adjustment. Not only am I going to have to sit through Mum's reaction to the dramatic reveal of Polly's wedding plans, but I am going to have to do so in front of Fiachra. I rinse off the foam, wondering if I should change out of my uniform. I decide against – it might send the wrong kind of signal, and I can't have Fiachra thinking I am making any special effort on his account.

Before heading back downstairs, I check in on Lady Macbeth. She is still eyeing the egg cagily, so I remove it from the drawer nest, and make sure she has enough food and water to keep her going through the night.

'Don't you worry,' I say, 'everything will go back to normal soon.'

She stares back, as if to say, *Don't be an eejit.*

In the time it took me to wash my face and check on the chicken, Polly has managed to transform the big hall. It is dimly lit by candles, softening some of the shabbiness. She has draped a sheet over the Three Paddys so that their snarls won't ruin the ambience. The table is aglow with candles, and she's mustered up more respectable-looking crockery and glasses from the depths of the house. Anybody looking at her handiwork would assume the big hall was a natural place for us all to gather for dinner. The WE'RE ENGAGED banner is nowhere to be seen, but Polly's rock is determinedly in place.

'I like what you've done with the Paddys,' I say.

'Don't personify the stuffed animals,' Polly says. 'You'll only upset Mum.'

'I don't think it's me that's going to be upsetting Mum tonight,' I say. Polly glares at me.

'There's no need to take that tone with me, I'm only trying to make our lives better.'

She busies herself trying to position the Hulk's flowers so that they are less overpowering. She splits them between two vases but has trouble settling them on the table. Eventually she sighs and puts both vases on the windowsill.

'I don't see what he's trying to prove,' she mutters, fiddling with a rose. She must wish it was her husband-to-be that had turned up with a grand flower gesture. Instead he can be heard waffling away in the sitting room about his mammy, the Hulk quietly encouraging him with a low rumbling laugh.

Mum is still upstairs getting ready.

'I'm going to have to serve the food without her,' Polly says. 'She always has to make a bloody entrance.'

Polly hates a lot of Mum's habits, but the ones she hates the most are usually also her own. Dramatic entrances are the bread and butter of both their personalities. She could be worried that her announcement is going to be upstaged by Mum's entry.

Thankfully, her desire to serve edible food outweighs her desire to thwart Mum. So we call in the lads and sit around the table. BrainDrain takes up one end of the table, as does the Hulk, who sits at the opposite end. The rest of us squeeze in around them, Polly sitting directly across from Mum's empty seat. I have no choice but to sit beside Polly, opposite Fiachra.

We spoon Polly's signature carrot and orange soup into our mouths. BrainDrain isn't eating the soup, much to Polly's agitation. There is a sharp intake of breath from her when he asks why it is orange, and a sharper one when he reveals the lack of vegetables in his diet.

'What do you mean, you don't eat vegetables?' Polly says. I can't help feeling that this is first-date territory and not ground one should be breaking so close to the big day.

'Don't worry about it, Poll-Poll, Mammy says it's all marketing. I get all the nutrients I need.'

'Well, you're a decent-sized lad, you must be doing something right. What do you eat?' the Hulk asks, trying to ease the tension. Seeing Polly's expression, he quickly adds that the soup is divine. This settles Polly a bit. But she stills seems as if, at any moment, she might upend BrainDrain's bowl of soup over his head.

'Same as everyone, really,' BrainDrain muses. 'Yere breakfast roll, yere chicken fillet roll, some Taytos and, well, I'd never say no to some ham sandwiches if they're going.'

Fiachra catches my eye as BrainDrain lists his diet. There is a look in his eye that suggests we are both stuck in this ridiculous situation together and I smile cautiously back at him. You can't be too careful with the spawn of your mother's bit on the side.

Mum misses the entire first course. We look glumly at our empty soup bowls and wait. Polly refuses to move on to the roasted butternut squash without her, and keeps her ring finger tucked under the table, determined to make the reveal with Mum present. The Hulk makes polite conversation.

'And what about this art teacher Fiachra's always going on about . . .'

'I am not always going on about her,' Fiachra mumbles.

'Well, as much as he goes on about anything!' The Hulk laughs. He is about to say something else when Mum finally enters.

It's more accurate to say she floats. Mum floats into the room in silks. Actual silks. She's taken off the wig for the evening, and her naturally dark hair is pinned elegantly to one side. She sort of wafts about the room as if she might take flight. The dress is a midnight green colour that shimmers in the candle-light, and her eyes are lined in black and shining hopefully.

Polly takes in Mum's appearance sulkily. The silk dress makes Polly's robot curls and vintage dress look old-fashioned. Frankly, I don't know what she is so cross about. As the one dressed in a grey uniform and sporting a bald face, I am the only one with any reason to be sulky.

'You look . . . amazing.' The Hulk stands up, look-ing amused by the get-up. BrainDrain grins from Mum to the Hulk in delight, and Fiachra blushes furiously at the table.

Mum smiles coyly and glides towards the Hulk, pecking him on the cheek. Then she seats herself gracefully in the empty seat opposite Polly, blanks BrainDrain completely and turns instead to Fiachra.

'It's so lovely to finally meet you,' she gushes.

'You too,' Fiachra says, sounding less than enthused, his redness deepening.

I can barely eat. The tension in my stomach is a tight knot, and I watch as Polly plays with her ring underneath the table, all through the butternut squash course. I will her to let us sit in peace a few moments longer. Mum is so distracted by the Hulk that she doesn't notice.

I wish I didn't know about the engagement. Without it, this memory of Mum would be one of those stills to hang on to. The happiness is easing the tension that normally sets up home in her face. She is all effortless beauty; for a brief half hour she is rekindled in the candlelight. There are photos from back when she first married Dad where she looks like this.

As Mum glitters, Polly darkens.

It doesn't help that BrainDrain picks at his butternut squash unenthusiastically before announcing it tastes funny. He produces a family-size bag of cheese and onion Taytos from his pocket. I cringe as he opens them. Polly withers.

'I never leave home without them,' BrainDrain confides to the table, showing no shame as the bag bursts open and he spills the contents on to his plate, shovelling a handful of crisps into his mouth. 'Mammy says ye can never be too careful.'

Polly reaches across the table with her fork, stabs at the butternut squash on his plate, stuffs it in her own mouth and chews meaningfully in his direction. Swallowing, she seems to decide it is time. She clears her throat loudly, but Mum and the Hulk are busy giggling over their squash as if it's the world's most entertaining vegetable.

'I've an announcement to make,' Polly says in a high, clear voice. It is right there on the border of a screech.

'What's that, love?' Mum asks, sipping her wine and looking serene.

'I'm getting married on Saturday evening,' Polly says, slowly. As if annunciating each syllable will make it more real.

'Don't be silly, dear, you're only a child,' Mum says, waving her hand at the news as if she is magicking it away.

'I'm not a child. Eighteen is officially an adult. I am getting married. There's nothing you can do to stop us. We've already sent out the invites, and we're having a big bonfire in the yard,' Polly says evenly. She is back in the driving seat. 'Someone needs to take responsibility for this family.'

Her face is set, and she holds her hand across the

table as proof, the giant rock shining in the candle-light. Mum freezes, staring at the ring, then calmly turning towards BrainDrain.

'And I suppose this simpleton is responsible?'

BrainDrain looks deeply wounded, but his mouth is full of crisps, so he is in no position to retaliate. Polly keeps her hand extended, letting the ring cast its frightening spell across the room.

'Congratulations,' the Hulk says. Fiachra coughs awkwardly.

'Maybe we should leave,' the Hulk adds.

'Oh, no, Gary, she's just trying to embarrass me, this is all some sort of joke.'

Mum breathes deeply, centring herself on the seat and swiping Polly's outstretched hand away. 'Now, if you don't mind, I'll have my dessert in the sitting room.'

BrainDrain is swallowing the last of his crisps and seems to be summoning some outrage, but Mum has already walked away. Polly wrings her hands and pinches her lips together.

'I knew she would pretend it wasn't happening,' she says.

'It'll be OK, Poll-Poll,' BrainDrain says, placing a giant paw on her delicate shoulder and pulling her into an embrace.

There's a puzzled expression on the Hulk's face as

he tries to interpret the situation.

I jump up from the table – the last person I need directing pity at me is the Hulk.

'I'm going to get some fresh air,' I volunteer to the room at large.

Fiachra's chin is understandably level with the table, but at the mention of fresh air, he slides easily on to his feet and mutters, 'I'm coming too.'

11

'That was rough,' Fiachra says, continuing his grand tradition of stating the obvious. We are walking down our big wet hill and I am trying to come up with something for us to do. It isn't like we are young enough to play hide-and-seek, or have enough in common to sit and natter. Any attempt at real chat would mean talking about Mum and the Hulk, and I have enough to be worrying about.

'They'll get over it,' I say, kicking at some loose pebbles as I walk. The farm's potential for boredom is magnified in Fiachra's presence. What do you even do with a boy?

'Do you think Polly will marry him?' Fiachra asks, oblivious to my discomfort. I let his sentence hang in the dark. The moon is out and if we look back towards the house, we can see the outline of our parents sitting side by side on the sofa.

I don't want a vision of Mum necking imprinted on my brain, so I stare out across the dark landscape of the farm instead – a blot of shed and tree outlines against a navy-coloured sky. The air is scented with the smell of mud and turf burning in one of the neighbours' houses. The closest neighbour is about a half mile down the hill, but the smell of a turf fire carries.

'I don't really know if she'll marry him. It's hard to imagine,' I say eventually. The only predictable thing about Polly is her lack of predictability. She is as likely to get hitched as she isn't.

'They're not really ... y'know ...' he says, letting his sentence meander into the silence of suggestion.

'Yeah . . . I know,' I say, surprised to land on the same wavelength. I sneak a glance at him. He stoops a little to hide his height and his gaze is fixed on the potholes ahead.

'So, did you see that video?' I say, trying to sound nonchalant. 'The one about the chickens?'

'Yeah ... seems like the usual Claire bullshit to me.' He looks at me curiously, then seems to think better of whatever he was going to say. 'Why?'

'Oh, nothing . . .' It's nice to know he has a low opinion of Claire, but anything else might be too much. I can't exactly admit to being an accidental chicken-murdering thief. Can I?

'Why did you ask, then? It's not like you to ask a question for no reason.' He looks at me even more strangely, as if he knows I'm hiding something.

'I . . . eh . . .' I'm stumped, because he's somehow managed to make it sound as if he kind of gets me.

'Look, if you don't want to tell me, it's fine,' he says. I can't see his expression.

'No, it's not that, I just, well . . . I found one . . .' I say. That's right, I can start small, see how he reacts to the dead chicken before delving into anything else.

'You did?'

'Yeah . . . um . . . it's dead, though.'

'Figures.'

'It's kinda left there, though. I never said anything to it.'

'You never said anything?' he says, then, after a brief pause, 'To the dead chicken?'

'You know, like final words, to give it a bit of dignity back . . . apologize,' I say, wishing the word *apologize* had stayed in my head. But if Fiachra notices, he doesn't say. He stops walking and looks up at the sky. There is a long pause, so I crane my neck too. The sky glitters. The one good bit about living so far from civilization is that the night sky is always awake with starlight.

He turns to face me.

'Why don't we do it now?' he asks with a shrug, as

if inviting me to pay my respects to roadkill is the most natural thing in the world. 'What else are we going to do – sit around watching our parents nuzzle? No thanks.'

I nod, trying not to think about the word *nuzzle*.

Suddenly, all I want to do is give the chicken a proper send-off.

We walk along the roads in the dark. Time slugs by and neither of us says much. It must take us well over an hour to find the right boreen, and the cold has settled around us in a gentle mist. It takes another while to retrace my steps to the pyre, but we eventually find it. Claire may have taken the ruler, but everything else is as we left it.

'So, this is it,' Fiachra says.

'Yeah . . .'

We look at each other over the chicken grave.

I'm not one for speeches and now that I'm here, I feel as if all my thoughts are colliding. There's Mum and Polly arguing in the kitchen, the chickens and all their untimely deaths. Part of me feels like the chickens are just a reflection of everything else. Yet another part of life I can't control. Even saving Lady Macbeth is a disaster – she can barely look me in the eye. And I can't look at her without thinking of the six chickens I left behind. It's as if nothing ever goes back the way you want it, no matter how hard you try to force it.

Which makes it all seem impossibly big. Dad, chickens, Mum, Polly . . . all of them hurtling in different directions.

'What should I say?' I ask. The last thing I want to do is deliver an outpouring that alludes to all the other tragic chicken deaths.

'Something sincere,' Fiachra says.

'Yeah . . .' I say, though sincerity would not be wise. I'll only end up listing all my lost chickens' names and begging forgiveness from all the recently deceased chickens.

'A poem,' he suggests, when it's clear I'm not coming up with anything appropriate. 'A poem for a funeral . . .'

All that comes to mind is Seamus Heaney peeling potatoes with his mother. Which is grand, but not exactly a good fit.

'I know,' Fiachra says. 'That one we're learning in English.'

'The mad depressing baby poem?'

'Yeah.'

'I guess it could work. I didn't learn it yet, though.'

'I've pretty much got the gist of it,' he says sheepishly, before swallowing hard and launching into a practically perfect recital of Sylvia Plath's 'Child' poem. His voice rings out in the mist. The lines are weirdly appropriate. The first line refers to a single clear eye, an uncanny parallel with the dead chicken that had retained one dark piercing eye despite its bludgeoning.

As Fiachra pulls the lines from memory, drawing out the last line, about how Plath sees the world as a dark sky without a single star, I am comforted. He lets silence settle. The mist and the poetry have gone straight to my head, and if I didn't know myself better, I'd say I have a sudden urge to reach out and touch him. My brain seems to be insisting that I need a hug.

Before I completely lose sight of myself, I break the moment.

'We should go back.'

'Yeah . . .' Fiachra says, already walking away.

12

I wake to the tap of Tess's nails on my window. The morning light is streaming in and I can hear the patter of rain on the glass. I crawl out of bed, settling the duvet around my shoulders in a bulky cape, and go to let her in.

It is lashing. Tess stands outside the window, nose pressed to the right-hand pane of glass, as water slides down around her features. Her fingers are drumming the other window pane. Her hair is setting into rag-tails, and mascara is streaming into ugly blots of warpaint down her cheeks. I crack open the window and she quickly jumps inside.

'I've been out there for, like, half my life. What took you so long?'

Tess whips off the top layer of her wet uniform, then goes straight over to the wardrobe and swings open the door. She helps herself to one of the towels hanging on the back of the door.

'I was having a weird nightmare . . . but I can't remember clearly,' I say, shuddering at a half-remembered scene involving Lady Macbeth as a bludgeoned flower chicken with one eye. Worse, Polly and BrainDrain were getting married and I spent the entire nightmare cuddling Fiachra as he tried to claw himself away from me.

'OK . . . Well, meanwhile, Molly, back here in real life, we are having, like, a *real* nightmare.'

Tess paces about the room. Her energy causes Lady Macbeth to stir from the corner. I spent most of the night trying to settle her in the nest drawer, but Lady Macbeth shunned my efforts, opting instead for huddling in the corner on bare floorboards. When she finally did fall asleep, she kept waking us both with painful squawks. I'm starting to think she's mourning her sisters. I miss them, and I couldn't even communicate with them beyond the *shuk, shuk, shuk*. It's so much worse for Lady Macbeth, who has lost her entire chicken community; no wonder she's so closed in on herself. I wish there was some way to just go back to the way things were before. Me and my chickens against the world.

As Tess paces the room, frantically drying herself with the towel, Lady Macbeth clucks and zigzags towards the bed, ducking under it, and settling back down. I tuck the duvet tightly around me. I don't need to ask Tess what the *real* nightmare is. She doesn't require that kind of encouragement.

'Claire has gone and posted another one of those stupid videos saying she will post a video on her channel soon. And, eh, we both know what that means. And if that isn't, like, bad enough, the *Ballyfert Times* ran an actual article. Look, look at this,' Tess's hand emerges from the towel, phone intact.

I scan the article, dread tightening my stomach.

DEAD CHICKENS RAIN DOWN ON BALLYFERT IN LOCAL CHICKEN GENOCIDE

9 May, 6.30 a.m.

Kelly Farm is the victim of what is being referred to locally as the 'chicken genocide': 120 chickens are still reported missing, and the death toll continues to rise.

To date, most of the chicken deaths have been gruesome, including: several chicken carcasses left by the priest's cat at the door of St Enda's Church; slurry-pit drownings; ten known roadkills; and a tragic incident with a baler.

Miriam Ward, a local vet, has seen over twenty victims in the past twenty-four hours and made the following statement:

'We're firefighting down here. People keep calling us out to see some half-dead chicken that's shown up in the garden bed.'

Locals are stepping up to the plate, reporting any chicken sightings, and returning many of the battered birds to their rightful home.

Sean Kelly commented on the dangers of amateurs adopting the chickens: 'It's not as easy as it looks. There's few around these parts who would have the cop on and facilities to give these chickens a life they deserve. I'd urge anyone with notions of keeping them as pets to consider the wellbeing of the chicken.'

Garda said the investigation is ongoing and that locals should respect the privacy of the Kelly Farm.

Anyone with information is encouraged to contact Ballyfert Garda Station on.

'What are we going to do?' I ask. Generally, Tess only shows up after figuring out an emergency plan, so it's best to avoid wasting time by presenting solutions.

'Fight back! I'm not taking this lying down ... Oh, no ... She thinks she can post her stupid videos and accumulate all the likes and followers, and that we're just going to hand a viral superstar over ...'

'Um ... Lady Macbeth is not a viral superstar.'

'She is now. That video Claire made has gone past five thousand likes. She is so much more than a pet – she has a future.' Tess's eyes gleam.

'Well, yes, but that future involves peace, hay and maybe the occasional egg.'

I'm not liking where this conversation is going.

Tess's dreams all include the word *viral*, and it would rankle her to death if Claire got more internet fame from a chicken that has been under Tess's nose for years.

'She's taking total advantage of those vulnerable chickens,' Tess says, 'and it's not like she really truly cares about them.'

'And you do?'

'That hurts, Molly . . . Who was the one who helped you rescue her?' Tess says, and she's right. Without her, Lady Macbeth would still be living under a wheelbarrow.

'OK, so what's the plan?' I ask.

'Well, Barry came up with this vegan idea, but it's, like, a pretty big commitment . . . He thinks we can pull it off.'

'Vegan?'

'Yeah, y'know, use Lady Macbeth for good, or whatever.'

There is a pause as Tess shuffles through her school bag and pulls out some notes. She rifles through them and waves a sheet of paper at me. It has the words *Vegan Movement*, *Vegan Sacrifices*, *Control the Narrative* and *Release the Footage* scrawled across it in random directions.

'How is that a plan?' I ask.

'It's not. We were trying to, like, create a briefing.

Anyway these are, like, Barry's notes. The plan is in here somewhere.'

I slump back down on the bed, tucking the duvet under my chin. I stare up at the criss-crossing fairy lights. How has this happened? I am going to join Barry in the land of no eggs. I wait as Tess tries to locate their master vegan plan.

A crashing noise comes from the kitchen and I can hear Polly's fluent cursing As if we need any further disasters.

Tess, oblivious to the commotion downstairs, holds up a piece of paper.

'Here it is,' she says. I can barely make out the title, but it looks like *The Ballyfert Vegans: A Social Media Movement.*

'Oh, yes, I get it,' I say sulkily. 'We'll take pictures of milk and post them online.'

'My God, Molly, do I have to, like, explain everything? Read it. Not only do we have all that incriminating shed footage, but we have a freaking rescue chicken. Think of the selfies! All we have to do is just go, like, totally vegan and become the face of veganism in Ballyfert.'

'And how does that work?'

'We completely thwart Claire by, like, saying we rescued the chicken because of the substandard conditions on her farm . . . I mean, we can actually take credit for this.'

She hops from foot to foot with unsuppressed glee. Tess has always wanted to be the face of something, and it doesn't really matter what.

'But what if I don't want to take credit?'

'Molly, if we don't do this, she will. I mean, she's posting regardless of what we do so this is our only chance to control the narrative. If we don't, she will just post that video of hers first. And then what?' Tess's eyes are shiny with opportunity. This is becoming less and less about my chickens. I wonder if it has even crossed her mind that some of the murdered chickens might have been mine. Does she notice how trauma-tized Lady Macbeth is, or even care? I lumber out of bed, bringing the duvet with me.

'We have, like, three days tops to make the most of this, before some kid on the internet sticks a raisin up their nose, or a cat learns to, like, hula-hoop, and we are going to make the most of those days.'

Tess's face looks equal parts sinister and excited; the mascara that has made its way down her cheeks gives her a slightly unhinged air.

'Ehm . . . just throwing this out there, but maybe we should back down. Claire might never post that video. She might be all talk,' I say. I am all for Tess becoming a superstar, but not with these stakes. We are, after all, wanted chicken murderers.

'We could simply disappear,' I continue. 'You know, live out our days with Lady Macbeth securely taken care of, and forget . . . Claire.'

'Molly Darling, that's not an option, because Claire won't forget about us, or do I need to remind you . . .'

'I'd sort of thought she mightn't go through with it,' I say.

Tess shakes her head sadly at me, as if she's disappointed by my naivety. She rifles some more, pulling out another piece of paper and waving it triumphantly.

'We'll start with a Vegan Gathering . . . Barry says we need to get a feel for the support base.'

'Right,' I say, 'but you're forgetting one thing . . . Why would anyone come to a Vegan Gathering?'

'Oh, Molly, Molly, Molly, how you underestimate me.' Tess looks smug. 'Do we, or do we not, have Ballyfert's only viral chicken sensation with us in this room?'

'Lady Macbeth is bait?'

'Yep, I would bet my actual life that everyone is going to want to get a decent gawk at the transgender chicken.'

'So . . .'

'There's no point looking for problems where there are none. Now, if you're done with all the *poor me* stuff, we've got an online presence to launch.'

The look on my face must have signalled my acceptance of her terms, because Tess bounds across the room and throws her arms around me. I'm still a duvet mound, so her arms are barely long enough for the hug.

'You won't regret it, Molly. I've got it all under control and Barry's already working on our messaging.'

'I *am* going to regret this,' I say, watching as Lady Macbeth eyes us from under the bed.

Polly sticks her head into the room. Her hair is pinned up, and her cheeks are flushed with excitement.

'Good morning, my cantankerous darling . . . oh, and Tess, of course, how lovely.'

'What do you want?' I snap.

'No need to take that tone, I've made a special breakfast and Mum has agreed to be in attendance.'

Polly looks massively delighted with herself.

My mind is a tumble dryer of thoughts.

'Mum said she'd come? Willingly?' I ask. I'd assumed they might ignore each other for the foreseeable future.

'Not in so many words, but she did say we might as well get this nonsense over with, so, you know, not the height of mothering, but I'll take it.'

'Fine.' I feel glum, like a great big gluey bowl of porridge.

'Polly, we'll be down in ten minutes.' Tess blinks innocently in her direction. 'As you can see, I'm in need of a decent blow-dry.'

'Ten minutes it is.'

Polly's head disappears. I hear her skip away down the hall.

The next five minutes see Tess transform from drowned rat to her usual self. Clothes are discarded, spare uniforms borrowed, then altered, hair tousled, and make-up magically slid back into place. Tess preens and puffs.

'OK, we need to, like, take a chicken-selfie, and get this campaign underway,' she says, turning from the mirror, phone ready.

I am still dressed as Mount Duvet. The duvet will be needed to get through breakfast. Polly often interprets my body language as hostile, which means I get in trouble for my reactions even when I don't speak. Apparently, my body says it all.

Tess has me drag Lady Macbeth out from under the bed. We position her between us and pose. I go with surprised-face, and Tess does sultry.

'Are you putting it online?'

'We'll let the video do its magic first.'

She scrolls through her phone, pulling up the footage from the farm. We wait a few minutes as she uploads it to the internet and types a title to accompany it: 'Ballyfert Vegans Reveal Mass Chicken Abuse'.

Without so much as a deep breath, she presses Post.

13

After the selfie, I change into my uniform and try again to settle Lady Macbeth in the drawer. I leave her a bowl of water, some chicken feed, and reapply her Sudocrem. Her eyes are still defeated, but she at least stays in the drawer. I hope she's slowly starting to feel more chicken again. Every time I look into her eyes, the ghosts of the other chickens are there. I wish some part of Tess's plan was to rescue the flock, but I accept that it won't be possible with Claire on high alert. Now that our video is live, Claire is bound to rage respond with her own. It's only a matter of time. Knowing this doesn't make things any easier.

Downstairs I observe the kitchen table from the doorway. Tess laces a pile of Polly's pancakes with honey, butter, blueberries and a dollop of cream. Polly coughs lightly and points to a round dish full of dark chocolate shavings. Tess puts her hand to her mouth.

'Don't you just think of everything.'

Tess takes a spoon and sprinkles the shavings over her pancakes. The effect is mouth-watering, but not remotely vegan. As if reading my mind, she shrugs in my direction and says, 'One last hurrah.'

Even Mum looks faintly impressed by the pancakes, but her mouth is full, so it is hard to be sure.

'How good of you to join us,' Polly says to me. It sounds polite enough, but the remark has her usual brand of caustic sarcasm attached.

'I was admiring your feast,' I say, hoping the comment will be deemed suitably neutral.

'Molly, what are you doing in that ridiculous duvet?' Mum asks, her tone light. It suggests she thinks the breakfast is going to involve news of the wedding's cancellation. 'Do we not give you enough attention? Have you stumbled out of a cave and forgotten basic etiquette?'

'I'm a bit chilly.'

Both Mum and Polly shrug at this. Tess is thoroughly engrossed in her pancakes. At her house, breakfast is usually toast and eggs or porridge. Her mother insists that people who *only* eat eggs and porridge for breakfast look younger, even though she looks ancient.

I slouch in my seat, eyeing Polly suspiciously. Chocolate flakes mean there's another announcement on the agenda. She tends to dole out the sugar in times of stress. Mum is oblivious, chomping away, asking Polly where she finds the time, and has she ever considered culinary school. Polly remains surprisingly civil. So civil that I find myself quite unable to dig into the pancakes on my plate. My stomach is frowning at the food.

The duvet slips from my shoulders, and I hug it closer. My dread intensifies the sounds and smells around me. Honey and butter cling to the air. The slurp and gurgle of the others eating turns my stomach.

Polly is halfway through her pancake pile when she pushes away her plate and gives a deliberate, listen-to-me-now cough. Tess looks blindly in Polly's direction, but her heart is still seeing pancakes. Mum nods as if to say, *Go ahead, petal, make me proud.* I try not to move. I sit, eyes fixed on Polly, the duvet concealing my statuesque pose. Polly addresses the table, each word flouncing from her mouth.

'There's something I've been meaning to tell you all about the wedding.'

'There's no need to be embarrassed, Polly. We all make rash decisions – at least you didn't go through with it,' Mum says happily, gesturing to the pancakes as if they are enough to fill up all the gaps in our lives.

Polly smiles sweetly at Mum. It is chilling. I need a shield more protective than a duvet. Tess glances down at her plate. She is probably sensing the conversation is taking a turn for the nightmarish and considering how tactful taking another bite would be. Oblivious, as usual, Mum spears a blueberry with her fork and pops it into her mouth before saying, 'Isn't this lovely?'

'I'm *still* getting married this Saturday, and there's one other thing ... Dad is coming. He's staying here – I've done up the spare room. There, I've said it, you know, it's done.' Polly lets the words rush towards us, all bundled up and looking for air.

'Dad?' I mouth. It feels like I am screaming, but I am not confident any actual sound comes out.

'That's nice, dear,' Mum says. She takes a forkful of pancake, cramming it into her mouth and chewing, before lowering her fork, swallowing and looking at Polly. 'What do you mean, Dad is coming?'

'Brian Doran is going to be my husband,' Polly says, 'and Dad is coming to walk me down the aisle ... or, well, the yard in this instance.'

She smiles. I think it is meant to be reassuring.

'Don't be a fool, dear,' Mum says, looking alarmed. Then, without any further comment, she pushes her plate away and gets up from the table. She doesn't even glance at Polly as she strides out the door, saying, 'Well, put your clothes on, Molly. I'll drop you and Tess to school. We can't be distracted by this nonsense.'

154

I am still mouthing the word *Dad*, the tension in my stomach oozy. I have so many questions . . . Is Polly speaking to Dad? How does he know about the wedding? Why is he coming now? Is Polly the only reason he's returning? Did he get my email?

But none of the questions come out. I get up from the table and run after Mum, the duvet and Tess trailing behind me.

Mum is waiting in the car, her hands pressed against the wheel, eyes fixed on the line of grey clouds behind the sheds. We bundle in, avoiding any mention of Polly's breakfast announcement. Tess is typing, her thumbs jabbing furiously as she responds to notifications for the video. I refused to look when she squealed, 'Oh my God, Molly, there are, like, three hundred comments already.' Because Tess is busy on her phone, nobody bothers talking. The first minute of the drive to school is the kind of silence that hope drowns in. I consider the quality of it, to avoid the questions strumming a nasty tune in my head.

There are a lot of questions, none of them formed correctly. *Dad and BrainDrain? Polly?* There are images attached to each of the questions. When Polly passes through my head, there is a puffy wedding gown and a lot of iced cake. Dad is not one clear image, but a mishmash of French seductresses and pie charts.

'Ms Darling?' Tess says.

Mum shakes herself awake at the wheel. Not that she is sleeping – she is simply comatose with thoughts. She is perhaps experiencing a bout of nostalgia.

'Tess, call me Anne, I've told you before.' She smiles at Tess in the rear-view mirror. It is forced. I am sitting in the passenger seat and the pulse in Mum's neck is frightening.

'Sorry, Anne, I was, like, wondering, it's this last-minute emergency, you see . . .'

Tess continues talking at top speed for five minutes, outlining the tininess of the Vegan Gathering, how we lost our venue at the last minute, detailing our requirements, and assuring Mum that everyone will head home by 11 p.m. There are lots of comments thrown in about stress, tough times, and, *If you can't cope, don't worry.*

It is a masterpiece as far as Tess's monologues go. There is no way Mum will admit to not being able to cope, she also doesn't have the energy to listen and highlight problematic parts of the operation, so when Tess reaches her closing statement – 'Is that OK?' – it is obvious that it has to be OK, or Mum will sound unreasonable.

I don't add my voice to the request. Mum finds it easy to shut me down, but she always has trouble saying no to people outside the immediate family. I fiddle with the lock on the door, locking and unlocking it to pass the time.

Tess waits. She doesn't say another word as Mum drives us to the bottom of the lane and turns right towards Ballyfert. The fields smudge by in a slur of greens and I start counting cows to stop myself speaking.

Tess maintains the silence. Mum breathes softly and appears to have forgotten there is a question waiting to be answered. It is a lesson in self-control, as well as highly uncomfortable to be sitting in the middle of.

As Mum drives up to the school gates, a good seven minutes after Tess's speech, she sighs, stops the car, and turns to Tess.

'Of course, Tess, that all sounds fine, I'm not even sure why you bothered asking.'

'Thank you, Ms Darling, and I'm, like, sorry about Polly and Brian and John and all.'

Brian and John. This is a step too familiar. Tess has conjured up the unmentionables. A cloud descends over Mum, one of those thick, dark clouds that it's impossible to see through. I hop out of the car.

'Tess, we're going to be late. Thanks for the lift, Mum,' I say. Tess has what she wants. She needs to scram before Mum changes her mind.

Tess understands immediately. She pats Mum's shoulder, thanks her again, and steps out of the car. We join the stream of grey uniforms and colourful backpacks that mope towards St Martin's. Tess is about to turn and wave Mum off.

'No matter how bad you want to, do not look back,' I say.

The car hasn't moved, and I know that Mum will be staring into the near distance, letting her whole marriage dance before her eyes. I don't want Tess to see Mum like that.

14

I insert myself in my seat, closing my eyes and taking a deep breath. Inhaling the chalk-and-sweat smell of the classroom. I'm trying to tune out the sound of Claire and the Ugg Boot Army, who are hogging the window seats and giggling loud enough to let us all know how much fun they're having. Each high-pitched squeal makes me increasingly anxious. Do they know the video went live this morning? Will everyone think I'm some insane chicken murderer now? I'm almost certain that Claire will post her video soon. Knowing her, there will be a few edits to make the most of the tiny bit of footage they captured.

'Have you ever considered the message your shoes are sending?' Barry's voice interrupts my thoughts. I open my eyes. He's leaning on my desk, one foot nudging my school shoes, a hand running absent-mindedly through his hair.

'Oh, let me guess . . . conformity,' I say. 'I should rock a rainbow pair and let my soul shine, or something along those lines.'

Fiachra, who has just sat down beside me, sniggers.

'There's that,' Barry says, giving us both a solemn look and casting his eyes over Fiachra's school shoes too. 'But there's also the fact they were once, y'know, the skin of a living animal . . . kinda a mixed signal, what with you being part of the *movement* and all.'

He adjusts his bow tie, administers his trademark wink and floats off to judge someone else. Fiachra stares down at his own shoes.

'Ignore him,' I say, 'he's full of it.'

'He has a point,' Fiachra says, sitting his schoolbag on top of his shoes to hide them.

This angers me so much that I take out my Irish book, smooth out a copy book and arrange my pens in a neat row. How does nobody else see through Barry's bow tie and posturing? I can't be the only one who feels like he's reading from a script on *how to be liberal* ninety per cent of the time.

First up is double Irish. I try to focus on the hardship that is conjugating verbs in the *modh coinníollach*, the conditional. We slump over our desks mumbling incoherently as Mrs O'Driscoll, a woman with beige trousers strapped as high as her elbows and a stern haircut, marches up and down saying, '*Arís!*' Her idea of teaching is to get us to repeat Irish phrases infinitely and hope that it will all magically slot into place one day.

This is our third week on the conditional, and as I chant '*Dhéanfainn é dá mbeadh an t-am agam,*' I can't help feeling it is strangely relevant. The English translation fills my head as Mrs O'Driscoll scribbles across the board, chalk squeaking: *I would do it if I had the time . . . if I had the time . . . if I had the time . . . I would do it . . .*

And there lies the conundrum: I'm not even sure what I would do. My entire life seems to be playing out in the conditional tense. If I wasn't sitting in this stupid seat slowly letting my brain turn to mush, if Mum hadn't sold the chickens, if I hadn't released three hundred chickens into the wild, if my sister wasn't getting married, if my dad wasn't coming home, if Fiachra wasn't an additional confusion, if Mum wasn't dating the Hulk, if Tess didn't want to use Lady Macbeth in a stupid social media war, if Barry hadn't suggested a *movement*, if I didn't have to become a vegan . . . The *ifs* are endless. I'm starting to feel as if I've become one of those cantankerous old ladies that go around taking my crankiness out on everyone else.

Mrs O'Driscoll wraps up the class with her idea of a treat. We all play along because it's far better than chanting verbs back at her for ten minutes. She plays what she stresses is a 'real life' conversation in Irish, then grins at us as if listening to people speak in 'real life' is the high point of the school day. The video involves two farmers with thick accents speaking loudly and slowly about *if the rain doesn't come, and if the spuds aren't good this year.* I suspect she makes these videos herself, because she beams whenever anybody guffaws at one of the clumsy jokes.

As we file out of the classroom, groaning over the list of verbs we've been given to put into conditional sentences for homework, Tess runs up to me, panting. She pulls me along the corridor until we are a few steps ahead of the rest of our year. Not that any of them are all that bothered – everyone tries to walk as slowly as humanly possible to their next class, praying it will shave a few seconds of mind-numbing torture off the day. Our next class is maths; usually it's in the same room as Irish, but there are practical exams going on before lunch and they don't want us disturbing the Leaving Certs, so it is taking place in one of the school's two prefabs – sad-looking boxes, with hollow-sounding floors, at the back of the main building. It usually takes us between ten and fifteen minutes to mooch over there. Some kids take the 'short cut' around the pitches, which tacks on another ten minutes.

'Oh my God, we're winning, Molly, we're actually going to go viral, do you know how many people have asked me about Claire's disgusting farm?' Tess says, slapping me on the shoulder. 'It's like the whole school just needed a reason to hate her.'

'Yeah, Tess, I'm not sure this is the best—'

'You realize people want to, like, raise money and stuff?' Tess says, shoving her phone under my nose. I nudge it away. She skips sideways beside me, so she can see my reaction. She looks like she is warming up for soccer. She really has no shame. Half the girls in our year don't even run properly any more – they kind of hold their hands up beside their boobs as they run. As if they're terrified the boobs will detach and make a bid for freedom. It makes them look like running T-Rexes. But not Tess: she will bound anywhere, arms flailing, stuffed-bra bouncing.

'I don't need money.'

'This is not about you, Molly. This is about the movement.' She says the word *movement* with extra relish. 'If we raise enough, we can, I dunno . . . buy back the chickens.'

She falls into step with me. We are halfway to class.

'Just give it a minute to sink in,' she says. 'I'll wait.'

We walk in silence. I consider the prospect of buying back the chickens. I shake my head – I am getting carried away. Even if we somehow did have a fundraiser, we might only raise twenty euro. I'm not even confident my chickens are alive. Imagine going to all that trouble only to find out they met an untimely end. I could be doing something useful, like mourning.

'OK, well, maybe we're not quite there yet, but you'll see, Molly, it's going to be amazeballs.'

'Amazeballs?' Somehow this one word is more disturbing than everything else that's happened recently.

'Oh God, sorry, Barry says that — he must be rubbing off on me,' she says. 'Now excuse me while I—'

But whatever she is about to say is cut short by Claire and the Ugg Boot Army stepping out from behind a row of lockers.

'I've class . . .' I say.

The Ugg boots groan in unison, rolling their eyes theatrically at me.

'A fascinating update, as always. I suppose you think this is all some kind of joke,' Claire says, quirking an ideally shaped eyebrow at me.

Before Claire can add anything else, Tess slaps her hand to her mouth and says, 'Oh, is this about the Vegan Gathering? Chicken-lovers only . . . And I don't know if you've seen the internet lately, but you're, like, chicken enemy number one, soz, babes.'

Claire is not accustomed to being called *babes* so irreverently. She clears her throat, giving Tess the once-over.

'You can't go around spreading rumours about my farm. I told you I'd post that video and I wasn't joking.'

'Soz, babes, truths not rumours, and I think we beat you to the video punch, just saying,' Tess says.

'Whatever . . .' Claire looks at her with disgust, then, almost as an afterthought, says, 'You will be sorry, I'll make damn sure of it.'

This causes Tess to laugh. I don't find it all that funny. Claire is perfectly capable of destroying us. The girl has a gift for doctoring videos. Not to mention that it would only take one of Claire's secret hand flicks for the Ugg Boot Army to unleash the power of their matching manicures. Which is almost exactly how her threat ends: Claire snaps her fingers and the cohort of girls that form her shadow do their spin and waltz down the corridor.

'Who does she even think she is, like?' Tess says.

'Maybe we should be worried,' I say. Tess looks like she is going to pummel me with my own doubt.

We walk the rest of the way to the prefabs in silence. I slide on to my seat, hoping Fiachra will abandon the notion of talking for this class, but when he arrives, he asks one question too many about the

Ballyfert Vegan Gathering, as if Barry has managed to get inside his brain with that one comment about his school shoes. Either that or he thinks the chicken-pyre poetry was a bonding moment. I am in no mood to be dragged back to that weird mist-coated moment. He is still the son of the man stuck in the middle of my parents' marriage. I do my best to put him off.

'It's not really your scene.'

'Oh, and what is my scene?' he asks, with a jaunty side smile.

'I doubt you have one.' I say it so haughtily that I surprise myself.

'Right . . .' he says, looking wounded and turning back to his copy book. I pretend not to notice and spend the rest of maths with a pressure headache, staring at xs and ys and willing them to make sense. Infuriatingly, they make sense to Fiachra, who is scribbling answers down as if they grow in his head.

After class, I catch up with Tess in the corridor to tell her I will head home early to get the shed set up. She is typing on her screen, and grins.

'Oh, Molly, you legend, I'll get there as soon as I can. I have, like, a strategy meeting with Barry, but as soon as that's done, I will be all over that chicken shed,' she says, without glancing up from her phone. No doubt she is causing online bedlam.

'Barry again?' I ask.

'Oh, well, obviously, he's like the only real vegan we know.'

I nod, feeling a growl of resentment. As I turn to leave, the tapping on her screen stops.

'Oh, Molly, there is one detail I meant to ask you about.'

'Yeah.'

'OK, I don't, like, need the attitude.' She gives me her *pull yourself together* eyebrows. 'So, like, the subject of suitable attire – you . . . um . . . you're not wearing your own clothes, are you?'

'What is that supposed to mean?'

'Well, it's just . . .' Tess trails off. She is drumming her fingers on the screen. She looks at the floor and clears her throat before continuing, 'If you like, I could bring you something funky, like vegan funky.'

'Well, if you have something,' I say.

Tess nods enthusiastically. The moment passes, but it is like I'm not enough any more.

15

It takes me hours to clear the chicken shed. It is easier to focus on the task at hand, rather than worry. I let Lady Macbeth join me. She sits sadly in a corner, bewildered by the absence of the other chickens. This is her old home, and gone are the many nests, the warm feathered bodies bustling about. Seeing her skulk in the corner makes me miss the others even more. It's as if neither of us knows who to be without our strange flock of mismatched chickens.

I brush out the remaining straw, hauling the stack of timber into the neighbouring shed. I drag the kitchen chairs down the hill to the shed and arrange them in a perfect circle.

Polly is busy with wedding preparations. I catch her giving a Celtic humanist priest a tour of the yard. I only know because she specifically introduces him that way. As if 'priest' is too ambiguous a term and I'd immediately assume he was tied to the Catholic Church. No fear of that – he is dressed in jeans and a hoodie, and greets me by making the peace symbol with his right hand and saying, 'What up?'

'God . . . I guess,' I reply, but neither Polly nor the priest find it funny.

The priest is also carrying some kind of staff. Perhaps he thinks the knobbly stick gives him a wizardy vibe, which, judging by his beard, is exactly what he's going for. He spends an hour looking for a fertile piece of soil in the yard for the couple to tie the knot on, prodding bits of earth with the staff and nodding earnestly. Polly trails after him, mesmerized. I can hear him asking questions like, *And should we do the turf rubbing before or after the parable of the jar of pebbles? How do you feel about being bound together with rope?* Polly must have picked this priest to rankle Mum. I doubt BrainDrain or his mother have had a say in the matter and Polly wouldn't think to ask. This is definitely *her* wedding.

I shudder, closing the shed door and focusing on what I can control. After speckling the chairs with a few cushions and throws from around the house, it looks homier, and less like a chicken shed. I push Polly's wedding out of my head and glance around. Not too shabby, and the peeling white paint gives everything a rustic air. I consider and abandon the idea of candles. There are people in our school that a candle would be too much responsibility for.

Once I am sure the Celtic humanist priest is gone, I brave the house again. Polly is gazing out of one of the windows and sighing loudly when I enter the kitchen. There is a strong smell of baking. She's probably practising her wedding cake; there's no way Polly would trust anyone else to bake it for her.

I pop on the kettle and am about to forage for edible food when Polly appears at my shoulder with a tight smile.

'Would you like some pear and almond tart?' she asks.

Ah, sure, what's the harm? I think. Even though every sensible bone in my body knows that Polly uses food like a war tactic.

She makes a big show of setting the table, even frolicking out to the garden to get some flowers to decorate our plates with, and sprinkling the tart with icing sugar.

'Wow, Polly, this is amazing,' I say, taking a careful mouthful. This would be an appropriate response to any other baker. Not Polly.

'What do you think of Brian?' she says, slicing her own tart into miniature pieces, but not eating any of it.

'He's . . . uh . . . big,' I say, swallowing the lump of

tart that is starting to feel dry in my mouth.

'Is that all?' Polly asks.

'Yup,' I say through another mouthful of tart, even though I know it is the wrong answer. Polly reaches across and pulls my plate and the remainder of my tart away from me.

'But—' I say.

'You know why,' she says, before walking to the bin and scraping the remainder of the tart from my plate, all while making intense eye contact. Then she leaves the room.

After that, I grab a tattered copy of *Little Women* from the Great Wall of Books and go to sit in the shed to read it. I never really liked it until Dad left, and now it just seems appropriate. Mum has taken to calling it my comfort book. I reread it whenever our new life gets a bit much. I flick through looking for bits where the sisters are happy or hopeful. I always skip the bit where Beth dies, because she's the one that seems most like me. Even though I would much prefer to be feisty like Jo. Maybe I can force myself to be a Jo instead of a Beth. I probably read it for inspiration – like it's offering me some kind of guide on how to handle a Dad-less home. Sometimes even the most old-fashioned books can make the world feel orderly again.

It's hard to focus without getting sidetracked by

thoughts of the chickens or Claire or Polly or Dad. I keep rereading the same lines over and over.

I am relieved when Tess shows up earlier than expected. She says it's to help. But it is for damage control. She takes one look at the shed and starts walking around it in a thoughtful manner.

'My God, Molly Darling, you've outdone yourself – this is like the cutest,' she says while rearranging the chairs so that they are no longer in an obvious circle. She opens the bag she has hauled in and scatters some vegan pamphlets on the floor, then swaps around the cushions and throws, giving them an extra plumping here and there. She even produces some posters with quotes from vegans written in inappropriate fonts. She tacks them to the walls.

'Are they not a bit much?' I ask.

'Oh, no, Barry says they sum up the Ballyfert Vegan Movement.'

There it is, that awful 'm' word again.

On the wall, large jarring red letters announce how eating animals is like eating your granny, bubbly script describes the body as a grave for animals, and romantic-looking cursive compares eating meat to consuming rotting flesh.

'We need to be taken seriously,' Tess says, smoothing out the rotting-flesh poster. I shiver. I don't really want to be a vegan, but everything has happened so fast. I feel as if I owe it to my chickens.

'Um . . . Tess.'

'Yeah?'

'I . . . uh . . . did you manage to be vegan for the rest of the day?'

'Did Barry tell you about the chocolate? Because I wasn't being weak, I seriously didn't know.'

'No . . . I just wondered, that's all.'

'Think of it as a work in progress, Molly – we just fake it till we're, like, vegans with a million followers,' Tess says as she surveys the room. 'We got three thousand new followers today . . . actual followers.'

'That's nice,' I mumble. The thought of three thousand people knowing I'm a chicken murderer makes me feel ill.

By the time Tess finishes her tweaks, the chicken shed looks entirely different: aside from the terrifying posters, it has a much trendier vibe.

'Ehm, so the obvious question,' Tess says, glancing around with a crinkled brow. 'The wine – your mum did OK the wine?'

'What wine?'

'You can't expect teenagers to show up without alcohol – it's all over the online event that we'll have wine,' she says.

'Oh, right.'

'There must be something lying around the house?'

'There might be some in the attic,' I say reluctantly. Mum has been hoarding bottles of home-made wine up there for years.

In the attic, Tess's eyes widen when she sees how much there is. It is quite the stash: fifty bottles of home-made plonk. Some of them must have been fermenting for at least five years, as there is a film of dust over them. After some debate, we grab a decent supply. Six bottles should surely be enough to intoxicate the Ballyfert Vegans.

When we emerge from the house with our booty, Mum is assembling her many milk cartons in the yard. It is starting to look like a horse – or at least some kind of animal.

'Better in our shed than someone else's,' she says.

'Your mum is, like, the shizzle,' Tess whispers. Mum is busy trying to get the horse's tail (a multicoloured assortment of pipe cleaners) to look as if it's blowing in the wind. Her blue wig is scooped into a messy ponytail. *The shizzle* is the least accurate description of her at this moment.

Back in the chicken shed, Tess arranges the wine by scattering the bottles about the place in what she says is an artful manner. Then she nods, draws her hands into a steeple and faces me.

'There will be no arguments,' she says, picking up her bag and emptying its contents on to the floor.

From the pile of clothes, trinkets and make-up, plucks out some colourful craft feathers and bohemian-looking dress.

'Your outfit,' she says grandly. She makes me change and then fixes my hair so that it is clamped solidly in place. There is backcombing and plaits and the weaving of feathers through it. She dabs make-up all over my face, and then shows me the mirror. She has transformed me into some sort of Hippy of the Chicken Shed.

Tess changes into her outfit. It is better suited to a nightclub than a meeting in a shed: a black miniskirt, a sequinned tank top with a lacy bra under it that pushes her boobs into the ideal position.

Our outfits won't help anyone take the Ballyfert Vegans seriously.

We wait in the shed, Tess preening in her hand mirror, adjusting her make-up and layering on the lip gloss.

I sit in the darkest corner with Lady Macbeth, making sure the blanket nest I've assembled conceals her properly. Tess wants to reveal her at some point. I'm just hoping Lady Macbeth doesn't peck anyone in the eye or go completely rogue.

I mentally calculate the reasons people might not show. It seems most likely that Mum will stop them in the yard and insist on showing them her sculpture, or Polly might fling pear and almond tart at them. The other looming possibility is that Tess's online efforts won't translate to people turning up in real life. Liking or commenting is much easier than showing up to someone's shed to make a vegan sacrifice. Which reminds me . . .

'Eh . . . Tess, what exactly is a vegan sacrifice?'

'Oh, that, dear Molly, is a work of genius,' Tess says, 'you'll see.'

By the time the first tentative knock sounds on the chicken-shed door, I am almost crawling towards it with relief. Even if it is Claire and every Ugg-boot-wearing minion this side of the Atlantic, I am ready to welcome them.

But it's the last person I expect. Standing there, with his brown curls flopping over his eyes, is a slightly apologetic-looking Fiachra.

'What are you doing here?' I ask, glancing at the bag in his hand, which for some reason contains a pair of wellies.

'I've come for the vegan yokamabob,' he says. 'Sure, why do you think I was asking about it?'

'This isn't a stable dance,' I say, which is almost the exact information I gave him in class.

'Yeah, I can read, or are you confused?' he says, looking at my dress. 'I mean, is this –' he lowers his voice – 'some kind of hippy commune?'

I don't have time to deal with his impertinence. The shapes of a few other people are moving down the yard. I usher him inside.

Tess greets Fiachra, her eyes narrowing.

'No prizes for guessing your ulterior motive,' she says.

'Well, um . . .' Fiachra blushes. 'I thought I'd give the vegan thing a try.'

'Sure you did,' Tess says, smirking at me.

Four more people file in. Conor and Cillian first – they're basically our class's ditch drinkers.

'Tess . . . what up? Did somebody say something about free drink?' one of them says. I can't tell them apart. They are completely interchangeable.

'You know it,' the other one says, giving the first one a fist bump.

Niamh is the biggest surprise of the evening: she's the class rep. Maybe she's come to monitor us. She adjusts her glasses as she walks towards a seat, clocking the posters on the wall.

A quiet, mousy girl with a name that begins with S is next. She takes a seat and tries to disappear into it. Then comes Barry. He is dressed in a polka-dot shirt and his signature bow tie, his long hair parted slightly to one side. He draws his hands together and bows.

'Namaste,' he says, before entering.

'Na' much t'say either,' Conor and Cillian say in unison. The two of them snort, bump fists and look delighted with themselves. Barry gives them a withering once-over and sits down beside Tess.

Once Barry shows up, it soon becomes clear that Tess will be dedicating her Vegan Gathering time to flirting. Aside from Tess and Barry, who are busy, we are all sitting around, looking glumly at each other, thinking, *Of course no actual cool people showed up.*

That is why I do what I do.

'How about we get our drink onnnnnnnnn-nnnnnnnnnnn?' I say it like that. With a weird half-dance motion, like getting langered is my number-one priority. I pick up one of Mum's bottles of wine, unscrew the lid, pressing it to my lips, gulping. I've never had alcohol before, but it tastes exactly like vinegar. I wince as I swallow and hand it to Fiachra to take a swig.

He sniffs it and looks at me. 'Did you just drink that?'

'Are you trying to be stupid or does it come naturally to you?' I say.

'I'm not the one drinking vinegar,' Fiachra says. He turns and passes the bottle to the next person. It is the S-girl. She doesn't notice his comment about vinegar and downs half of it. The others have the same reaction as her. They take a few gulps, then say, 'That's some good stuff,' and pretend their eyes aren't watering as they pass the bottle to the next victim.

I don't drink another drop. It is vinegar. Of course Mum would be storing home-made vinegar rather than alcohol. She washes her face with diluted cider vinegar each morning and, lord knows, she pickled enough vegetables with it in her farming days.

After Tess drinks her fair share of vinegar, she stands on top of her chair and bangs the glass bottle with a spoon.

'Attention, fellow vegans! We must start proceedings. Molly, take it away . . .'

Tess had not informed me that I would be taking anything away. I remain seated and whisper. I don't mean to whisper. But they are all looking at me and it is like my voice is trying to climb back inside of me.

'I . . . think . . . we should all, um . . . eh,' I say, then look at my feet and wait for Tess to figure out that I have finished speaking.

'I mean the chicken, Molly. Show the people what they came for.'

Everyone perks up and leans forward a bit. There's a feeling of anticipation that wasn't in the room before.

'Oh, right,' I say, walking over to Lady Macbeth. She is still quietly nestled in the blanket. I crouch over her.

'I'm sorry,' I mumble. Apologizing to Lady Macbeth is becoming a habit. I scoop her into my arms, the injured wing facing outwards and turn to face the others. There is a collective intake of breath.

'It's real?' Niamh asks, peering at Lady Macbeth over her glasses and seeming to take extensive mental notes.

'He's so cute,' the S-girl chimes in.

'*She!* Not *it* or *he*,' I snap. People need to start respecting Lady Macbeth's pronouns. 'It' makes her sound like an alien life form, and 'he' is just plain offensive when Lady Macbeth has dedicated her entire life to being accepted as a chicken.

'Sorry . . . she,' Niamh says, having the decency to look ashamed. S-girl just seems confused.

'Of course *she*'s real,' Barry says, 'and so is everything we've posted about the Kelly farm, including that video . . .'

There's a collective sharp intake of breath.

Lady Macbeth buries her head in my chest, suddenly self-conscious.

'But that means those other chickens . . .' The S-girl looks ready to burst into tears.

'But Claire is, like, totally hot,' Conor or Cillian says, looking confused.

'Can we touch the chicken?' whispers the other one.

I give Tess a look and she nods, so I step forward. Everyone rises and takes it in turns to approach Lady Macbeth and run a finger gently along her untarnished feathers. All except Fiachra, whose expression is completely indecipherable.

'Now that we've established this is all true, I want to propose an awareness raiser,' Barry says, adjusting his bow tie. Tess nods, as if they've also rehearsed this, and whips out a spiral-bound notebook and pens in three different colours.

Tess straightens her back, running her pen along a list of potential ideas and tapping one thoughtfully before saying, 'I think we need more animals, preferably rescue animals . . . you know, ones that are scruffy-looking or missing bits and pieces.'

'What?' Niamh says, eyeing her over her glasses.

'Well, as Barry pointed out . . .' Tess says. Barry nods proudly in the background, leaning forward as if he's deep in thought. 'Lady Macbeth is the perfect mascot for our movement, but . . . people get fed up easily, and we need animals that appeal to a wide audience . . . Lady Macbeth isn't for everyone.'

There is a murmur as someone says they hate Shakespeare and someone else explains that Lady Macbeth is the name of the chicken.

'People can only get so invested in one chicken,' Barry interrupts, matter-of-factly. 'Look, I'm not trying to be pushy, but a gathering of more animals is the best way to make a difference.'

'So, we want to, like, gather as many semi-broken animals as possible and basically have a big event to raise awareness − mostly via social,' Tess says. 'And maybe if we make a big enough fuss, the Kellys will have to do something about their torture barn.'

'I see,' Niamh says. 'I might know some animals.'

'Amazeballs,' Barry mutters, rubbing his hands together and grinning at Niamh.

I return Lady Macbeth to the corner and take a seat in the circle. The ditch-drinking buddies volunteer their mother's rescue donkey. And S-girl starts weeping when she realizes her hamster has led a privileged life.

'I mean, he's so fluffy and well adjusted, it makes him useless.'

'We could have one or two well-adjusted animals,' Niamh says reassuringly.

Tess and Barry talk logistics and title.

'I just feel like "The Vegan Zoo" is a snappier title,' Tess argues.

'But it contradicts our purpose . . . a zoo is a tool of oppression against animals; we want to gather the animals and bring them together . . .' Barry says.

Within half an hour he has worn her down and the 'Animal Gathering' is reluctantly agreed upon. But not before Tess lets everyone know that it is 'the exact opposite of clickbait'.

Tess says she will get back to everyone with the details, and the others nod along enthusiastically. It seems everyone but me thinks it's a good idea, so I don't want to be the one person to point out the kinks – like how am I going to conceal a donkey from y family? Maybe there's a tutorial on the internet: *Hiding Donkeys in Plain Sight for Beginners*. I'll just let Tess know it's out of the question if she brings it up again.

'So how do we feel about the *movement*? Can a chicken truly change people?' Barry says as the conversation peters out.

'Oh, Barry, what a fascinating thought,' Tess says, emitting a giggle. Niamh gives them both a patronizing look.

'I live to enlighten,' Barry says with a wink. Maybe the winking is a nervous tick. He doesn't look particularly comfortable about the way Tess is leering at him. Tess is used to getting what she wants, so when she doesn't, her default setting is a leer.

The S-girl lurches into the centre of the shed.

'I PLEDGE MY SHHHPOILT HAMSSSHH-HTERRR,' she slurs at the group. 'Chickensssshh for life!' She careens about for a moment before proclaiming, 'I am shhooooo drrrruunnnk.'

And then, with no further explanation, she grabs the remaining bottle of vinegar and stumbles out into the yard.

'Should someone go after her?' Barry asks.

'She'll be OK – it is vinegar,' Fiachra says.

'We get it, Fiachra . . . it's vinegar. You're like a broken record,' I say.

'You mean a stuck record,' he corrects.

'Ooooh, sexual tension, just what a Vegan Gathering needs,' says Tess, rather unhelpfully.

'I've to go, my dad is picking me up.' Fiachra stands up. 'Oh, and . . . about the vegan sacrifice . . .'

He bends down and unties his school shoes. They are brown leather and sophisticated, with gold stitch marks along the base.

Barry nods appreciatively and says, 'Righteous man.'

Fiachra blushes slightly and slips off the pair of shoes. He places them in the middle of the shed floor, then he pulls out the wellies from the plastic bag and puts them on. He glances at me before he leaves, and his eyes seem to be challenging me.

Flustered, I glance at my watch to try to stop the blush creeping across my face. It is already 10.30 p.m.

The others take Fiachra's departure as permission to double-check their phones, which results in an end to the Ballyfert Vegan Gathering. People conjure up waiting parents and dip out the door. Before each person departs, they leave something on the floor beside Fiachra's shoes, each saying (with varied levels of conviction), 'I pledge allegiance to the vegans.'

All I want to do after everyone has left is curl up in a corner and embrace my inner hermit. But Tess has other ideas. As we make our way back to the house, there is only one thing on her mind: 'So did you see how Barry was looking at me?'

17

I wake with a dull headache. I don't want to rouse Tess, so I slip out of bed, careful not to make any noise. Tess is sleeping perpendicular to me. She is still dressed in sequins and lost to dreams of Barry.

She kept me up past midnight to discuss his relentless charm.

'Do you think he, like, likes me – likes me, though? I mean, you saw the way he was looking at me,' she said again and again.

'I didn't see much – I was blinded by the vinegar.'

'You'd tell me if I was, like, wasting my hormones on him, right?'

'You're wasting your hormones on him,' I said, but Tess chose to ignore me.

I tuck the crumpled duvet around her, then pull my usual giant woolly jumper over my pyjamas, shove my feet into my slippers, and scan the room. Lady

Macbeth isn't in her nest or under the bed. My stomach drops a little; it's hard not to feel panic after everything that happened the last time she went missing. I try to reassure myself that it's irrational to worry — Polly's probably just taking wedding photos with her 'flower chicken'.

I tread softly downstairs, hoping not to disturb anyone. Part of me wonders if Claire has posted her video yet, but I push the thought to one side. There's no point fretting over it until it happens. I've enough to worry about.

It is about 6.30 a.m.; though I haven't slept much, it's the best sleep I've managed all week.

'Molly, is that you?' Polly's voice comes laced with sugar from the kitchen.

'No,' I say, and think about darting back upstairs. But it is too late.

'Your chicken is in here. Brian has a connection with the vet, so she's coming over first thing,' she says. There it is again, the extra sugar. I am not about to admit it, but I am relieved: poor Lady Macbeth needs more help than Sudocrem. The Vegan Gathering has taken it out of her, and last night her night-time squawks were mere shudders of her chicken body.

I begrudgingly enter the kitchen. Brian is sitting at the kitchen table dressed in jeans and a loose T-shirt, looking as if he's always been here. Polly stands beside him, transferring a large omelette on to his plate. There is a Ziploc bag beside him containing a ham sandwich. His cheeks are flushed, as if Polly has already put him to work.

'Brian is after taking the day off work to help out with the wedding prep. He's already put up the marquee and piled up loads of wood for the bonfire. He got up at four . . . But it has to be done if we're ever going to get everything together on time,' Polly says, walking across the kitchen to the sink, as if BrainDrain's achievements are hers by default. She shoves the pan under the tap, running cold water over it.

'Ah, sure, someone has to do it,' he says, grinning proudly. 'We can't have the guests sitting out in the rain.'

I walk over to the kitchen window. Sure enough, a bulky plastic-covered pile that must be the bonfire is just about visible. There is also a massive white tent where the backyard used to be. There's just enough room left to get in and out of the sheds. Puddles are already forming on the marquee roof, as if the clouds of Leitirmór Farm are filing their objections to the wedding.

I sit across from BrainDrain, noticing how cosy the room is. Someone has lit a fire in the range.

'Thanks for the vet,' I say.

'Well, Mammy says you can't be too careful with vets these days. Wasn't there a lad up one of the hills that didn't even have a licence, and didn't he give a sheep a sedative, and sure didn't it put him to sleep for good?' BrainDrain says, slipping his hand into the Ziploc bag and grabbing the sandwich.

'There isn't one vegetable in that omelette, Brian, you could at least try it,' Polly says, appearing at the table and reaching for the ham sandwich. She smiles in a way that could wilt rhubarb. He responds by mashing the entire sandwich into his mouth. His cheeks bulge like a hamster. Polly sighs.

'I've bandaged Lady Macbeth, so that she looks like someone takes care of her,' Polly says to me.

'But the vet won't be able to see her wing,' I say.

'I didn't superglue the bandages to her. Jeez, Molly, what kind of monster do you take me for?'

She points to the corner of the kitchen. Lady Macbeth is a lump of toilet paper penned in by a circle of forks. She is wrapped up like an Egyptian mummy. I stride across the floor, giving Polly my dirtiest look, before shaking my head at the forks, and scooping Lady Macbeth into my arms. She doesn't protest. Her body is limp and heavy.

'What are the forks for?' I ask, knowing even as the words come out of my mouth that I would rather not know.

'She kept wandering around pecking the floor, and she's terrified of forks, so I did that —' Polly gestures at the ring of forks — 'and she has stayed put ever since.'

She shrugs, as if this is the most natural conclusion to arrive at in the world. I have a brief vision of Polly holding up pieces of cutlery to determine which is most likely to control the chicken.

We settle into mutual morning silence, pottering about with cups of tea. Sitting at the table, I position a pillow on my lap, and nestle Lady Macbeth on it, absent-mindedly stroking her.

Polly busies herself with coaxing Brian into eating the omelette. He tries and spits out three mouthfuls.

'I'm sorry Poll-Poll, but I don't eat all this fancy food. Mammy says I'm a simple man with simple tastes.'

Thankfully, Tess arrives downstairs before Polly loses it and cracks an egg over his head. If Tess is alarmed by the presence of BrainDrain, it doesn't show.

'This is perfect,' Tess says, catching sight of Lady Macbeth. She is all sleep-rumpled miniskirt and tousled hair. Her eyes fix on the mummified chicken. 'Like, this is going to be just the promo we need for the Animal Gathering.'

'That hasn't been confirmed,' I say, 'and I don't think it's the best idea right now.'

'Oh, Molly, always with the nitpicking – you don't have to make a big deal out of every tiny thing.'

'She does do that, doesn't she?' Polly says.

There's no point arguing: I'm outnumbered. I'll tell Tess to cop on later.

Tess makes her way to where I am sitting with Lady Macbeth on my lap. She whips out her phone and pouts, attempting to capture the perfect morning-selfie. I scowl from the corner of the image and Lady Macbeth looks equally cheerful.

'Molly, do something with your face – even Lady Macbeth has a better range of expression.' Tess's face is giving me the evils on the phone screen. I summon up my faintly surprised expression, willing the selfies to end.

'OK, this is perfect, let me see . . . Ballyfert Vegans . . . hashtag mummy chicken, hashtag . . . chickens have feelings too . . .' Tess thinks out loud as she types. 'Hashtag . . . vegans4lyf . . . hashtag . . .'

'How about, hashtag night of the living chicken?' BrainDrain volunteers.

'I like what you did there,' Tess says, adding it to her post.

'Enough with the hashtags,' Polly and I say in unison.

'The vet will be here any second now,' Polly adds ominously. It is only ominous because as she says it there is a loud thump at the front door.

The vet is a large bumbling woman with spade hands. She tells Polly how sensible she was to call, and unwraps Lady Macbeth, raising her eyebrows at the makeshift bandaging and Sudocrem. Without comment, she demonstrates how to administer painkillers by stuffing half an aspirin into a piece of corn and placing it on a dish with more corn. As soon as the corn appears, Lady Macbeth charges forward, pecking at it with wild abandon. Within ten minutes, her zigzagging steps are drowsy. She bashes her head off the ground and resumes her foetal position, belly up, legs to the sky.

'Does he often assume that position?' the vet asks.

She accepts the cup of tea that Polly places in front of her but waves away the offer of cake. I'm not sure why Polly is letting the vet know she is a domestic goddess, but there seems to be no end to the number of people she wants to impress.

'It's the only position *she's* comfortable in,' I say with a shrug. 'Is that normal?'

'Well, sure, I wouldn't say I'm a chicken expert — give me a dog or a sheep any day. Not many round these parts with a rooster for a pet . . .' The vet gives me a hard look. 'Where did you say you found him again?'

'Are you sure you won't have a slice?' Polly asks,

hovering near the vet's shoulder, lemon cake at the ready.

The vet slurps her tea, refusing Polly's slab of cake again. 'Ah, no, I've only just had my breakfast, it's too early for cake.'

Polly clutches the plate. 'Too early?'

'Poll-Poll, will ye let her drink her tea in peace,' BrainDrain interrupts. The vet nods gratefully in his direction, stands up abruptly and gulps down the last drop of tea. She clears her throat.

'I'm glad you called. If he wakes up—'

'If *she* wakes up . . .' I mumble.

'And there are any side effects, let me know.' The vet ignores my correction. 'I've seen it with sheep. Post-traumatic stress disorder. It happens.'

'What about a slice to go?' Polly asks.

'What do you mean?' I add, but the vet is already out of the kitchen door and pretending not to hear us.

18

'I need to stay with Lady Macbeth today,' I say to Mum.

'Don't you have school?' Mum asks, tucking blue hair behind her ear as she focuses on the three horse sculptures that line the kitchen floor. There's the life-sized milk-carton sculpture that towers above the others, a hip-height multicoloured one constructed from painted jars, and a knee-height foal that is still missing a head and has been assembled with parsnips and twine. Mum is sorting through a pile of parsnips, trying to decide which one makes the most convincing horse's head.

Mum isn't paying me much attention. She's half-humming Dolly Parton's 'Jolene' under her breath, which is her idea of a happy song. The Hulk has snagged her a meeting with some community outreach group who are looking for someone to

...vel the county teaching art. They asked for a portfolio of her work, and so the horse sculpture assessment began shortly after breakfast.

Mum is taking the parsnip sculpture a little too seriously, especially when she spent most of my life scolding me for playing with my food.

'I mean, I could take a photo, but you really need to look them in the eye, don't you?' Mum asks me, peering deep into the milk carton that is operating as a horse's head.

'How will you fit all that in the car?' I ask, changing the subject to something safer than eye contact with horse sculptures.

'Gary is going to drive them over there with me,' she says.

BrainDrain and the Hulk are still in the attic. There's a hefty-looking horse sculpture up there that Mum soldered out of old metals. They're struggling to get it to give up its territory.

Polly is sulking in the sitting room because BrainDrain is helping Mum with the horse sculptures and not assisting with the wedding preparations. Tess is upstairs putting her face on.

'So . . . as I was saying, I do have school, that's why I'm asking, can I stay home?' I say, trying to break through the horse-sculpture mind fog.

Mum looks up, startled, a parsnip in her hands.

'Sorry, petal, I . . . oh, is this parsnip horsey?' She holds up the parsnip.

'Are there any lumpy ones?' I ask.

Mum groans, pulling a few more identical parsnips from the pile by her side, and lines them up across the table in a straight line.

'They're all so uniform,' she says sadly.

I point to the fattest parsnip. Mum looks at it sceptically, shakes her head and says, 'Never mind.'

'Well, not like that, but maybe you could carve it.'

'Oh, Molly, you may have cracked it.' Mum picks up the fat parsnip, turning it this way and that in her hand. She rushes over to the knife rack, pulling out the smallest knife and weighing it in one hand as she observes the parsnip closely.

'About school today, Mum?' I ask, hoping that the parsnip breakthrough will work in my favour.

'What's wrong with the chicken?'

So, she has been listening all along.

'The vet said she might have post-traumatic stress disorder.'

Mum considers this for a minute before saying, 'I see, so you're not giving the chicken back?'

'What?' I blink. I thought Mum suspected; I had no idea she had concluded.

'Let's not beat about the chicken, Molly. I may not condone the internet, but I have seen it . . . And even if I hadn't — you rob a rooster that thinks it's a chicken one day after I sold yours. How many transgender chickens exist in Ballyfert?'

'Right . . . well, I . . .'

'I'm not asking for an explanation . . . And, quite frankly, given the death toll, the less I know the better. I'm just surprised — I thought you'd give up and send her back.'

'I can't.'

Mum doesn't say anything, but starts to pare the parsnip, taking miniature nicks from the flesh with her knife. She may feel guilty enough over selling my flock to consider one stolen chicken a type of justice. This is the kind of argument central to Mum's idea of living: life is a bartering system of injustices. Like you can trade a divorce for the death of a parent, or cash in a bad Monday for an OK Friday.

'Look, Molly,' she says, her carving gaining fluency as she works. The parsnip is beginning to take on a horsey vibe. 'The last thing I need right now is for you to be skipping school. What kind of mother would I look like? Your dad is arriving tonight . . . and, well . . . we have to look together — you know, a tight unit that has been navigating the world fine without him.' Her shoulders droop and she sighs. 'You get why that's important, right?'

'But Lady Macbeth needs me.'

'And I'm telling you that I need you to do what you're told for a few days. You're going to school and that's final.' She purses her lips and holds the parsnip horse's head up to the light. 'Now, how about that?'

'That's an important question,' I say, which is as kind as you can be regarding a horse's head carved from a parsnip in the space of five minutes.

'It'll have to do,' Mum says, just as a blood-curdling scream fills the house.

'Do you think the metal horse fell on BrainDrain?' I ask, thankful for a distraction.

'Wishful thinking,' Mum mutters.

'MWAAAAAAAAAA.'

In our rush to the hall, Mum knocks the parsnip horse over and I half-trip over its new head. It rolls threateningly beneath my foot. I note that *evil* should be added to the mental list of adjectives concerning parsnips.

The anguished noise is coming from the bathroom. The door is flung open, blocking the light from the upstairs hall window, and casting a shadow down the stairs. We expect Polly to appear, except it isn't Polly who staggers into the upstairs hall.

Tess emerges, phone in one hand, and toothbrush

in the other.

'MWAAAAAAAAAAAAAAAAAAAAAAAAA.'

Tess doesn't see us, or the stairs. She stumbles down with no regard for the glow-in-the-dark star path to safety. Luckily, she is tiny, so she doesn't crash through the rotting bits of the stairs. Instead, she bangs into a turret of books.

The worst happens.

The Great Wall of Books has survived because we carefully slot books in and out. The removal of one of the wall's precious book turrets has a domino effect. Books scatter, thump, and rain down the stairs.

Mum and I are statues in a book avalanche.

When it ends, some books are cracked open at the spine, others are splayed open and crushing their own pages. The small hall and stairs are a carpet of books. A layer of book dust clogs the air, and I can't help thinking of the generations of book-stackers whose efforts have just tumbled down the stairs. Granny must be turning in her grave and muttering about how she knew the farm would go to pot when she died. She had strong opinions about farming – mostly that Mum and Dad weren't cut out for it.

'Tess?' Mum asks calmly.

'I am, like, so sorry. We will clean it up, I swear, we just – I had to show Molly something.' Tess holds up her phone.

'And what is that?' Mum asks.

Tess pauses for so long that we can hear her brain churning. Obviously, whatever is on the phone is not suitable for parents.

'I feel sick.' Tess changes tack and attempts to look frail. 'Incredible cramps, absolutely whopper, it's like my ovaries have fallen out . . .'

'You look OK to me,' Mum says, casting her eye over the book wreckage.

'Oh, no, I can prove it,' Tess says. I hope she is bluffing.

'Uh . . . that won't be necessary,' Mum says. 'Look, girls, I have a lot going on right now. Clean this up . . . John can't see the place like this . . . Now, where are they with that sculpture?'

'Yes, Ms Darling,' Tess chimes.

Mum pauses for a moment, considering Tess.

'You realize that calling me "Ms Darling" conjures up images not only of my failed marriage and the ex-husband that deserted me, but also of my insuffer-able dead mother-in-law. It makes me feel like taking up knitting and wearing tweed. My name is Anne.'

She turns on her heel, striding back into the kitchen.

Tess makes *big* eyes at me, as if to say, *What in the name of hell was that all about?* I shrug back and am about to say something when BrainDrain and the

Hulk appear at the top of the stairs, red in the face, breathing heavily and somehow balancing the metal horse between them.

'She wasn't messing around when she made this lad,' BrainDrain says, as they set it down at the top of the stairs and lean on it, taking a few deep breaths.

'Oh, Jesus, the back is spasming,' the Hulk says, clutching his lower back and wincing.

'Have ye tried the Alexander technique?' BrainDrain says, dropping to the floor and extending his legs up in the air. 'Mammy swears she'd be in a wheelchair without it. See, like this, back flat to the floor . . .'

The Hulk nods. 'And how long do you do that for, then?'

Mum appears in the small hall, hands on hips, as the Hulk drops to the ground and sticks his legs in the air too, so that the view from the bottom of the stairs is of two pairs of legs sticking up on either side of her menacing metal horse. 'Gary, we need to get the sculptures in the car.'

'Right ye are,' BrainDrain says, jumping to his feet, and pulling the Hulk to his. 'I'll show ye again some-time.'

They heave the horse downstairs, the book avalanche adding an extra complication. They move almost as if they're dancing with the sculpture.

Eventually, all the sculptures are loaded into the Hulk's van. Mum hops in the back to reassemble the parsnip horse.

'I expect the stairs to be fixed by the time I get home,' Mum says to us, as the van doors close.

'You got it, gurrrrrrl,' Tess says. How she travelled from Mum saying *don't call me Ms Darling* to thinking Mum would be OK with being addressed as *gurrrrrrl*, I will never know.

As soon as the van pulls away, BrainDrain heads into the sitting room to see Polly.

Tess and I sit on the stairs.

'Well, I guess that means we can "forget" about school,' she says. 'You might want to prepare for the worst. Claire has ... well ... I'm not even sure what I'd call it.'

'The video,' I say. I'm not sure why Tess is so shocked. This is exactly what Claire said she would do.

Tess hits play on a video titled 'Transgender Chicken Used in FAKE VEGAN MEETING'.

The footage starts with a close-up of my face from when Claire confronted us in her yard.

I look sweaty and pink, and Claire has looped the video so that I keep repeating the words *The chicken is mine*. My voice has been distorted and my eyes have been adjusted to red. The voiceover of *The chicken is mine* continues, my face fades, and the scene cuts to the Vegan Gathering. There's Tess in her miniskirt leaning in too close to Barry, and I stand awkwardly beside them, holding out Lady Macbeth as if she's an offering. The video speeds up and shows everyone petting the chicken, making it look like some kind of creepy sacrificial situation where we are about to burn her alive or something. Judging by the angle that the scene has been shot from, the videographer must have been S-girl. Why hadn't I insisted on getting her name? Trust Claire to find the most forgettable person possible to shoot her sneaky footage.

The scene cuts to Claire's face, eyes watery as she gazes into the lens.

'I know what you all think. But it's time for some truth bombs . . . Who is using the transgender chicken for social media likes? Not me! Who is inviting people over to stroke their chicken as if it's some kind of novelty act? Not me! I've learnt my lesson . . . which is more than I can say for Molly Darling.'

And then Claire's face melts away and the red-eyed version of me multiplies across the screen, repeating over and over, *The chicken is mine, I'm not giving her back*.

The many faces of me eventually give way to a black screen, and once again Claire has posted a link to some further reading in the *Ballyfert Times*. I click in.

SCHOOLGIRLS STAGE PHONY VEGAN GATHERING WITH TRANSGENDER CHICKEN IN BID FOR SOCIAL MEDIA FAME

11 May, 7.30 a.m.

Two self-proclaimed vegans took credit for the 'chicken genocide' yesterday, posting a video of themselves trespassing on the Kelly farm and claiming it was a protest against the brutality of factory farming. They revealed the news on social media.

The post was followed by a selfie of Tess Gallagher and Molly Darling with the kidnapped transgender chicken (photo above), who was tagged as 'Lady Macbeth'. The selfie capitalized on people's interest in the chicken by inviting them to a Vegan Gathering, where they were to discuss the future of the 'Ballyfert Vegans'.

The Ballyfert Vegans revealed plans for a gathering of more animals. An anonymous source who was in attendance said, 'I went to make a difference, you know – all those poor chickens – but it seems like they just wanted to get us drunk and get us to pledge our animals.'

A video shown to the Ballyfert Times this morning reveals that 'Lady Macbeth' was in attendance, and used to get members to sign up for the vegans' cause.

Multiple sources confirm that attendees were encouraged to commit to loaning a pet to the Animal Gathering. Seven animals were pledged, with one source stating, 'I mean, it was awkward not to.'

No information was provided about the quality of life

these animals might experience at what another attendee described as 'a pretty run-down farm'.

The *Ballyfert Times* spoke to a representative from Vegan Ireland, who commented, 'We urge anyone that is considering the vegan way of life to stay away from cult-like groups. There is an active support network in Ireland, and any first-time vegans would be encouraged to get in touch through official channels with Irish Vegans.'

'Oh,' I say. 'She's destroyed me.'

'I mean she has and she hasn't. People aren't stupid . . .'

'That's easy for you to say – you're not the red-eyed *the chicken is mine* chanter,' I say.

'OK, well, firstly, like ten people read the *Ballyfert Times* and most of them are already decomposing. And secondly, way more people liked our mummy-chicken post than Claire's video. She got, like, a hundred and fifty views . . . As long as we've got Lady Macbeth, we've got the power.'

'I can't believe this, it must have been S-girl. She seemed so harmless.'

'Uh, you can't believe that a girl who got drunk on vinegar might be a bit suspicious?' Tess says.

'Well, when you put it like that . . .'

I am trembling. I don't even know one hundred and fifty people. And now one hundred and fifty people think I am some kind of red-eyed possessive chicken freak. I need to breathe deep and calm down. My life isn't over, it is just . . . alarming.

'You're taking this completely the wrong way,' Tess says. 'There's no use moping about it – we've got an Animal Gathering to get off the ground. You should see the list of animal pledges Niamh sent over – that girl is impressive.'

'I never agreed to that. We have to cancel it.'

'Let me deal with it,' Tess says, turning back to her phone and clicking into her messages.

'I mean it, Tess. We can't keep doing this, it just keeps getting more and more complicated.'

'Oh, Molly, you've literally nothing to worry about, I have this completely under control.'

'Do you?'

I bend over to pick up one of the books sprawled at my feet. Tess doesn't answer; she taps away on her phone, no doubt replying to online comments as if this is all some kind of game. Like, surely this is peak internet problems. It's time to step back and survey the damage, think about how much more harm than good we're doing. My six missing chickens are never coming back, and going vegan has only given the Ugg Boots more ammunition.

I sit listening to Tess's rhythmic finger taps and wondering if there's any way to get her to stop.

As if in response, the doorbell rings.

There is a muffled conversation at the front door before Polly comes into the small hall. She glances about at the books, hands pressed firmly on her hips. She seems confused.

'I'm not even going to ask,' she says, 'but, eh . . . there's a . . . well, a donkey at the front door.'

'That's for me!' Tess says, leaping to her feet.

19

The donkey has a shaggy grey coat that is shedding in places. It is chewing the flowers that Mum has placed either side of our doorstep. A bright purple pansy is stuck between its giant yellowish front teeth. I wince, imagining Mum's reaction when she comes home to her newly headless flowers, although it will pale in comparison to her reaction if she ever gets wind of the donkey.

This is not ideal; as usual, Tess is three steps ahead and now there's a donkey on my doorstep. I can't turn it away, either, especially after Claire's latest video. That would make me look like a selfish chicken murderer. This way, I'm a semi-altruistic one. The donkey's owner, a plump woman in her fifties, is encouraging the donkey.

'Dere ye go, Síle, dat's a good girl.'

'It is Maire, right?' Tess asks the woman, who nods

gruffly. Maire has a tired face, dry grey hair and sensible clothing.

Tess circles the donkey, oohing and aahing over its fluffy ears.

'Hello,' I say, extending my hand to Maire. There is a bit of a silence as she sizes us up. She seems particularly distracted by Tess's miniskirt.

'Aren't ye awful young to be runnin' a charity?' Maire says. 'Are ye sure ye can handle auld Síle? Have ye no one bigger about?'

'I can assure you, what I lack in stature, I make up for in personality,' Tess says.

'Well, I've no doubt about dat, but Síle is no pet rabbit,' Maire explains.

'Just a sec,' I say, before disappearing inside to the sitting room, where BrainDrain and Polly are sitting on the floor surrounded by Mum's entire chutney collection. From the looks of it, they will be using the surplus Pickled Chilli Carrot Surprise as wedding favours.

Polly has established an assembly line, and they are relabelling them with stickers. Each one is a hand-drawn cartoon of a bride and groom holding a heart that boasts the name of a chutney. Except the names aren't the useful warning labels Mum always pasted on the jars, like 'Chilli Grape Combo'. At least with Mum's labels you knew what you were in for. Polly has instead given each jar a title, like 'The Secret' or 'Passion'.

BrainDrain is labelling the jars quite slapdash, so there are places where the stickers are rumpling, and Polly is eyeing him as if she wants to mash his brains to a pulp. Neither of them looks up when I enter. He seems intent on enjoying the wedding preparations. Which is admirable − ignoring Polly's moods takes extraordinary willpower.

'Um, Brian . . . would you mind, well, standing outside for a minute?' I ask.

'Any reason?' he says. 'I hate to ask, but Mammy didn't raise an eejit.'

'Well, there's a woman with a donkey, and she needs to see someone bigger, you know . . . in case of an emergency.'

'Say no more, say no more,' BrainDrain says, hopping to his feet and pulling himself to his full height. He marches outside, where Tess is still listing her credentials, as if her social media following is a direct reflection of her capacity for responsibility. BrainDrain puffs out his chest and sticks his hand under Maire's plump nose.

'Brian Doran at yere service, missus.' He grins broadly, and Maire looks instantly relieved.

'Well, yere a fine loaf of a man,' she says. 'Dere'll be no fear of Síle with a good strong lad about.'

'Ye can bet yere donkey on it,' he laughs.

'I've to say I'm impressed with what yere doing here. Don't mind the press . . . hacks, de lot of them. I'm telling ye, I don't see dem donating to anything but dere bank balances.' She gives BrainDrain a hefty clap on the arm, as if he is the mastermind behind the operation. Tess folds her arms and bites her lip; she probably has some colourful words in mind for Maire but thinks better of releasing them.

Satisfied that a giant human is in charge, Maire says she will be back Sunday evening for the donkey and that we should avoid startling it. Then, without so much as asking to see where her donkey will be sleeping, she gives BrainDrain the nod, and we watch as her Land Rover and horsebox trailer trundle back down the hill.

'Well, that took care of that,' BrainDrain says happily, before heading back in to regale Polly with the story.

'I heard every word of it, Brian. I was sitting right here − look, the window is open, I am not bloody deaf.'

'Ah now, Poll-Poll, ye'll have to lighten up, y'know what Mammy always says . . .'

'No! I do not know what MAMMY ALWAYS SAYS, but I can bet my engagement ring you're going to tell me.'

Even the donkey flinches.

Tess and I stand looking at Síle the Donkey for ages. She shows no interest in us and continues to chomp through the flowers, her tail swishing back and forth, swatting at invisible flies.

'I'm not that *small*!' Tess says eventually.

'Of course not.'

'I mean, it's like narrow-minded or whatever,' Tess adds, standing up straighter than usual.

'Completely,' I say, then, gesturing at the donkey, 'When were you planning to tell me? What am I meant to do with a feckin' donkey?'

'Like, in this day and age . . . you'd think . . . but no, no, no, let's trust the ham-sandwich wielding oaf – like, seriously?'

I reluctantly reach out a hand to pat Síle the Donkey.

'I guess you probably want to see where you're sleeping,' I say, ignoring Tess.

Síle the Donkey's doleful eyes stare back at me.

No sooner than we've settled the donkey in the old chicken shed – a difficult process as she is more interested in chewing the marquee than walking through it – more animals start arriving. I give up grumbling at Tess and spend my time thanking people and trying to find suitable spots to house the animals. Barry's dad lets Jack (a three-legged dog) out of the car, flinging a bag of dog food angrily in our direction.

'I'm sick to death of this vegan nonsense, like I don't have better places to be,' he says.

He is a balding, suited man with a pot belly. He doesn't match Barry at all. It's the strangest thing when someone doesn't match their parents, like they've played a trick on the universe. I'd always assumed Barry's dad would wear flower shirts and rock a ponytail. His father's tyres screech back down the hill, and to me Barry feels like a true rebel for the first time.

I let Jack into the big hall. He curls up on the faded rug, lying under the Three Paddys whimpering, as if he suspects the end is nigh and he will soon become the fourth.

I take him down to the chicken shed too. Síle the Donkey eyes him cagily but accepts his presence in the shed after seeing that he is minus a leg and only interested in hopping around in a circle trying to bite his own tail. They are soon joined by a scrawny-looking goat called Ted, and a disorientated duck that keeps waddling into the wall. After Tess takes some teaser videos for her social media, we leave the animals to get accustomed to each other's company.

'This is actually perfect, the animals are so decrepit,' she says, gleefully tapping her phone.

'Perfect is not the word I'd use . . .' I say, eyeing the goat, who is attempting to scale the shed wall.

Back in the house, all is quiet. Too quiet. BrainDrain has gone home because his mammy has organized a tux fitting, so Polly has given up residence of the sitting room.

Tess takes one look at the mess of books and says she needs to take care of the social media side of things, disappearing upstairs to edit and post the clips of the new animals. Any other day, I'd have insisted we clean up the books together, but part of me welcomes some time to myself. I'm angry, but in an odd, detached way. Deep down I knew that Tess would do this, if I had just thought about it for ten minutes. But maybe part of me wants this.

I spend a few hours traipsing up and down, arranging the books back into piles. It is a mammoth task and I use the time to decide whether or not I subconsciously brought all this on myself. Lady Macbeth keeps me company by sleeping on top of the giant encyclopaedia.

I am halfway through sorting the books when Polly appears at the top of the stairs. Her face is wet with tears, the skin all red and uneven, and she is wearing a floral nightmare. The dress occupies every inch of her and seems to be gaining further territory by growing up her neck. A net curtain would look better. It has been dip-dyed in technicolour tie-dye and made poufy in irresponsible places. Obnoxious padding accentuates both Polly's bottom and boobs. In Polly's defence, her hair is beautiful. She has achieved an elaborate network of plaits which are scrunched into a messy updo that looks effortless. It is just hard to appreciate with so much dress going on.

'What happened?' I ask, although it is clear that the 1970s has vomited all over her.

'I was . . . well . . . I followed a pattern. I knew it might not be perfect . . . I thought it would look kind of cute and bohemian . . . I needed a dress to get married in. But I . . . I didn't need this.' Polly spreads her arms wide in a defeated gesture.

'What about Mum's old dress?'

'The tablecloth incident.'

'Maybe you could wear something else of Mum's?' I say, trying to be kind, but Polly only seems more distressed by this suggestion. She sits down on the top step and runs her fingers along the books I'd been stacking.

'Look at me – what am I even doing?' she says. 'I've been trying so hard to make everything perfect, but it's not working. I'm a mess.'

'That's hardly fair. It's not like you usually go

around dressed like a radioactive flower,' I say, focusing on the dress, as if it's the real problem. I am shattered – between cleaning up Tess's book mess and dealing with the surprise animals, I could sleep standing up.

Polly scowls at me.

'I've been trying to have a meaningful conversation with Brian all morning,' she sulks, 'but it's just *Mammy this* and *Mammy that*. I don't even know what he wants from life.'

'Maybe he's got everything he wants.'

'Nobody gets everything they want. Don't be stupid, there's always more.'

'Well, maybe he's happy, you know. He's marrying you, after all.'

'He barely even sees me,' Polly says. 'You know I redecorated my entire bedroom and he didn't even notice.'

'Well, maybe interior decoration doesn't matter to him.'

Polly considers this for a moment, fiddling with her fingers, her face still set in a scowl.

'Do you want to see the room?' she asks hopefully. It is impossible for Polly to operate without an audience.

'Sure,' I say, though I would prefer to keep stacking books.

I trail after her. For all Polly's domestic-goddess

tendencies, her room is usually a stale-smelling pit of old clothes, half-drunk cups of tea and biscuit wrappers surrounded by stale crumbs. Mum used to refer to it as the 'rat trap'.

The first change I notice is the smell of fresh paint. Polly must have borrowed a pot from the attic. The room is no longer the faded green hue of her childhood but a bland whitewash of off-white. The bed is made, and the floorboards are visible. I haven't seen those floorboards since the 2000s.

'Oh, wow, Polly, it's so . . . clean.'

Gone are all her trinkets and pictures she collected: family photos, dreamcatchers, and a limbless teddy bear that survived since babyhood. All her posters have been pulled from the walls and the photo by her bedside is missing. She has steamrolled the history of Polly. The new version looks like it walked out of a catalogue. Cream walls, white bedspread. Even the nightstand is covered with a white pillowcase.

'It's not just clean on the surface,' she says, walking proudly to her dresser and pulling out the drawer she uses for underwear (I know from occasionally having to sneak a pair of knickers out when the washing gets backed up).

She signals for me to admire the drawer. The knickers are folded in colour-coded lines.

'Why?' I ask.

'I want him to know I'm ready, that I'm nothing like Mum. I mean, he's seen this house, he knows what it's like. At least my room says something different – our marriage can work if I do things properly.'

I refrain from asking what folding her knickers readies her for, other than a life in a laundrette. When I don't offer any direct praise for the knicker-sorting, Polly shoves the drawer back into place, then takes cream and eyeliner from the top of her dresser and sits down in front of the mirror. It's a floor-length piece of glass that is stuck to the door of her wardrobe, and there's a giant crack down it, which splits her face in two. The imperfection of the crack is comforting, like it is telling me that the real Polly will surface, that it is only a matter of time.

Polly begins rubbing in the cream and frowning at her complexion.

'Oh, I'm all red. I don't know why I bother getting all upset. Molly, hand me that powder. I need to cover this up.'

I hand it to her. She rearranges the colours of her face, softening the skin into a pale canvas, pressing a rosy pink into her cheeks, pencilling her eyebrows darker, and lining her eyes. It is only after she applies the third layer of eyeliner that I worry. There is a hysterical note to the way she is leaning back to survey her handiwork, then crouching back in and applying more dark lines. Her eyes appear to be bulging out of her head.

'Maybe that's enough,' I say. I am sitting on the end of her bed, picking at the white blanket.

'Don't be silly, Molly.'

She turns to me then, with a look that suggests she has had the best idea ever.

'Molly, would you do me a massive favour?' Her tone is pure butterscotch.

I answer with a shrug, 'Maybe . . .'

'Will you be my maid of honour?'

'Um . . .'

'I understand if it's, like, too much. It's . . . well, I want to have my sister there with me, you know, and, well, someone has to hold the flower chicken.'

I fixate on my feet as she says this. Of course, she still expects Lady Macbeth to act as a wedding prop. Polly stares at me, an expectant look in her eyes.

'Sure,' I say, as if this is the most normal request in the world.

She probably wants my chicken more than me, but it's nice to be asked. It's the first time in ages that we've felt like real sisters.

I decide to leave the room before I blurt out something sentimental or throw my arms around her. I need to do something about this hugging impulse. Maybe my whole life has been a lie and I'm really a rampant cuddle-monster in disguise.

I hop up from the bed and make a bid for freedom.

'I'm going to go get tea, would you like some?' I ask.

'I'm grand,' she says, turning back to her eyeliner.

20

The books are almost all sorted now, I've been restacking them by genre and, if a writer has enough books, I've given them their own book turret. Enid Blyton, Agatha Christie and Margaret Atwood's piles all totter dangerously. There are about thirty titles on the floor still requiring my attention.

I follow the glow-in-the-dark stars to the bottom of the steps and bend to pick up a copy of *Rebecca*. It makes me think of the chicken version of poor Mrs Danvers sitting in that giant monster shed. Reminding me that I still owe it to my chickens to keep trying. Lady Macbeth might be nestled soundly on the encyclopaedia, but what about her companions? It's not worth worrying about; I need to remember that there's a high probability they're all dead and stop wondering what has become of them. I'm just going to have to start working my way through the stages of grief. Maybe it's hard to feel much aside from worry at the moment because I'm still in denial. Some part of me still believes they could come home.

I don't really feel like tea – it was simply an excuse to escape Polly's whitewashed new world. The whole room is a shadow of its former self, as if Polly has seen a life in a catalogue and decided it's better than the one she has. As I slot *Emma* into place in the Jane Austen book turret, I imagine Polly's future bungalow. A neat, centrally heated home full of beige furniture and beige children. There will even be a beige poodle, and Polly will scoot about dusting shelves and trying to keep her personality from seeping out.

I am lost in thought when I hear the front door swing open.

'How did it go, Mum? Do you want some tea?' I call.

But Mum doesn't answer. The voice that does is distinctly male.

'Hello,' the voice growls.

I get up from where I'm neatening the last pile of books and go into the big hall. A young man is standing there, his long hair sitting greasily on his leather-clad shoulders, a guitar slung across his back and his spindly legs encased in black skinny jeans.

And not just any young man, though it takes me a moment to recognize him.

It is Dermot, Polly's ex-boyfriend.

'Oh, thank God,' I say, surprising us both.

'I'd love a cuppa, Molly,' he says.

'Oh, right,' I say, and head for the kitchen. I don't suggest he follows me. If I remember correctly, he will make himself right at home without being asked. Sure enough, as I fiddle about making us tea, he mooches into the room and slouches on a kitchen chair. He begins tapping the table rhythmically as if playing the drums, and tossing his head back to keep his fringe out of his eyes.

I hand him the cup of tea and sit across from him at the table.

'So, she's not seriously marrying Brian Doran, is she?' he asks.

'Your guess is as good as mine.'

'I came back from South Korea to see for myself,' he volunteers, eyeing me over the cup to see if that is an acceptable admission to make.

'Well, if I was you, I'd focus on that . . .'

'On what?' he asks.

'The South Korea thing – it's very exotic, she'll like that.'

'But Brian is the opposite of exotic,' he says, slurping down a mouthful of tea.

'Exactly,' I say. 'I'd say Polly is in the mood for something exotic after listening to the mammy monologues for the last week.'

'I see,' Dermot says. 'Anything else that might help?'

I don't even like Dermot, but at this moment he seems like an angel sent from above. Even if she runs off with him for a week, it will be enough to make BrainDrain see sense and go and find someone more appropriate to marry.

'Well, the whole musician vibe and the Korea thing – I'd say you stand a decent chance.'

'I see, I see. Thanks, Molly, I didn't know you cared.' He reaches out as if to touch my hand. I move it out of his reach, tucking it under the table.

'I don't, Dermot. But Polly might.'

'Polly?'

'Come in.'

I push open the door to her room. She is lounging on her white bed in a pale green top and some skinny jeans. The eyeliner doesn't look so ridiculous now that there is a boy in a leather jacket downstairs.

'Dermot just arrived.'

'Dermot?' She jumps up. 'Oh my God.'

'Were you expecting him?'

'What did he say?'

'Eh . . . it's Dermot, about as little as possible.'

225

'What should I do?'

'Say hello?'

'This is so typical – he didn't even tell me he was coming. I thought he was still in Korea,' Polly says, some of the shock disappearing from her voice as she gathers her thoughts.

'Well, he's here.'

'I suppose he thinks there's still a chance.' She grins. 'Well, he'll see what it's like.'

'Um . . . maybe you should . . .'

'I wonder how much he missed me? He has to regret dumping me now, right? There's only one way to find out.' Her face sets into determination.

She is out of the bedroom door and I can hear her bounding down the steps. I run after her.

Dermot isn't in the kitchen where I left him. Polly seems to instinctively know he is in the sitting room. She charges straight through the big hall, pushing open the door and lunging across the room at him.

'How dare you?' she says. 'Do you've any idea what you put me through? And now you show up here in a leather jacket like it was nothing.'

I peep in the room. Polly's wedding favours are lined up on the floor, as if to say, *We're still happening.*

Dermot is slouched on the couch, feet up on the coffee table, and Polly is standing over him, arms folded, foot tapping.

He stands up, ignoring her words, and putting his arms around her. It's a proper hug, a deep-down, *God, I missed you* movement. Dermot seems to squeeze the light back into her. They soften as they hug, pulling each other closer.

Eventually, Polly pulls away, giving him a once-over. As she gathers herself, and drinks him in, I can see her expression change.

'It's not OK, you know.' She pauses, becoming awkward. 'What you did – you just left like we were nothing.'

'I know,' he says, not even breaking out an apology.

Polly shoots me a look: it either says, *Give us some privacy*, or, *Don't leave me alone with him, I can't control myself around a leather jacket, you know that.*

I can't interpret the look, so I invite myself into the room, shrugging at Dermot and seating myself in Dad's blue armchair.

It would be a nice reunion, if they weren't both so intent on impressing each other. Polly drones on about her wedding preparations and Dermot starts talking about his music. They talk around in circles, then Dermot finally asks, 'So, Brian Doran?'

'Do you know him?' Polly asks.

'Enough to know it's surprising.'

'I wouldn't expect you to understand.'

'Try me?' Dermot says. I might as well not be in

the room – they're sitting close together on the couch. The tension keeps fizzling from downright rage (Polly) to a sexy undertone (both). If I wasn't here, the leather jacket would be coming right off.

'He's solid,' she says quietly. 'He'd never hurt me.'

Dermot nods sadly, shifting a few centimetres closer to her. 'I see.'

They are now sitting so close that they are almost touching. It is worse than if they were touching, because it feels like touching is all they are thinking about. It is all I'm thinking about, and I'm not even on the couch.

It's silent. Polly puts a cushion between them for protection. Although, judging by the look on her face – a mess of frustration – the only person she needs protection from is herself.

'So . . . Korea?' she says, and Dermot goes with it, regaling her with anecdotes about his students.

I begin to long for him to leave. Whatever I was hoping his presence might ignite doesn't seem worth it. It seems as if the old fireplace presses in on us, and the curtains are ready to burst from their rail.

A car pulls into the drive, and I jump to my feet. The crunch of tyres on the gravel is a relief. It's as if I've endured the tension for three eternities. I dart into the big hall and open the front door.

In the yard, Mum and the Hulk are in high spirits, laughing away.

'You did it!' the Hulk is saying.

I wave at them, but if Mum is puzzled by my enthusiasm, she doesn't show it. As she approaches the door, I try to signal with my eyebrows that Dermot and Polly are in the sitting room. Unversed in the art of eyebrow communication, Mum babbles away about how they loved her work, and want to take her on as a full-time art instructor. She practically floats into the big hall.

'Just think, Molly,' she says, surveying the hall with a grin, 'we'll finally have some real control over our lives.'

'That's great . . . Mum . . . It's, eh . . .'

'You know the guy said I was so brave, to stick to it, as a single mum, and that most people give up on their dreams,' Mum says quietly, as if she is afraid to destroy the statement's integrity by repeating it aloud. 'It's the nicest thing anyone has ever said to me.'

The Hulk and I exchange guilty looks as we follow her into the kitchen. 'You should have seen her, though, Molly,' says the Hulk. 'She had them in the palm of her hand. I don't think they were expecting an entire van-load of sculptures.'

'It never hurts to be prepared,' Mum says. They busy themselves making tea and filling me in on the horse-sculpture feedback. I can't help noticing how comfortable Mum looks. She seems light and easy and happy. For once, I am glad the Hulk is there, teasing her gently and sipping tea, as if there is no greater joy than being ordinary together. I wish I could pause Mum's life right on this moment, so she wouldn't have to go back to worrying about Dad and Polly and the wedding.

As if sensing Mum's contentment, Polly appears in the kitchen doorway. There is a clearing of the throat. Mum and the Hulk look up from the table, focusing on Polly, who is tapping her foot and itching to pop their joy.

'Have you cancelled that wedding yet?' Mum asks, a sober look settling on her face.

'Not quite. Dermot has come to stay.'

'Dermot?' Mum says. 'Not that leather bag of hormones that dumped you last year?'

Dermot steps out from behind Polly as if they've planned some sort of reveal.

'I wish I could say you've changed,' Mum says, giving him the evils. He is standing in the doorway to the kitchen, leaning against the frame as if he's lost his spine. Polly is now a few footsteps in front of him, radiating bliss. Mum's eyes make their way from the flop of his greasy fringe to Polly's glowing face.

'I see,' Mum says, with enough disdain to rot a

cabbage. 'And what – you're going to run away with the bride and then dump her the next time you get bored?'

'Nice to see you again.' Dermot has the sense to look uncomfortable.

'Really? And what is so nice about it, I wonder?' Mum says.

'Well . . .' Dermot trails off, thinking better of whatever false sentiment he is about to express.

'Mum, that's not very—'

'Very what, Polly?'

'Very kind?'

'*Kind*, is it? Kind like dragging this hormone out to parade in front of your *fiancé*? I'll tell you something for nothing . . . I might not be *kind*, but at least I'm honest. Which is more than I can say for you, and it's not like you picked it up off the floor.'

'What's that supposed to mean?' Polly screeches, advancing across the room until they are centimetres from each other, their delicate features frozen in fury.

'Oh, you know exactly what I mean.'

'No, I don't think I do, maybe you should SAY it . . .'

'You're as selfish as your deserting father,' Mum says, then exhaling as if she's been holding her breath. This a step too far; it's bad enough that Mum pretends we're background characters in her life, but comparing Polly to Dad is only going to escalate things.

'So that's what you think of me! At least I know,' Polly says.

Dermot is quivering – this is most likely more than he bargained for. It's more than I've bargained for. Part of me wants to sit everyone down with a cup of tea and facilitate a reasonable discussion. But mostly I want to crawl into my bed and cry. Polly and Mum used to be so close, and now there is no greater distance than the gulf between them. Sometimes I wonder if Dad leaving should have brought us all closer together rather than pushing us all apart.

Polly's face contorts into a sneer.

'I am getting married, Mother dearest, whether you like it or not.'

'I'm not giving you my blessing,' Mum says.

'Oh! I don't need your blessing. This is not the dark ages. I've already got Daddy's full support. After all, I'm the one he's coming home for,' Polly says smugly, turning on her heel and leaving the room.

'I'll . . . eh . . . um . . .' Dermot begins. Unable to think of anything to say, he flees.

Mum deflates, all the air and anger seeping out of her. She sits back down, glancing at the Hulk and then switching her smile back on. The Hulk looks like he wants to be anywhere else in the world.

'I . . . eh, Molly —' the Hulk smiles weakly at me — 'would you mind if I had a moment alone with your mother?'

I stand in the small hall, my back to the kitchen door, eavesdropping. I don't usually do that sort of thing, but the Hulk's expression had been so conflicted that I want to know what he is about to say.

'Look,' the Hulk says, 'I . . . well . . . those girls don't deserve this and, well, it's heart-breaking to watch.'

'You don't know what it's like,' Mum says. I can hear her revving up to justify what she said to Polly. Except the Hulk is having none of it. His voice is low, and gentle. I imagine him reaching across the table to cup her hand. That is the sort of tone he is using.

'I do, though,' he says. There is a muffled sound, as if Mum is sobbing. His voice stays gentle. 'After she died . . . well . . . it's not the same, but it hurt, you know? And it hurts still — some days it hurts more than I know what to do with.' He seems to think carefully before adding, 'But I can't take that out on Fiachra, it's not his fault . . .'

'So, you blame me?' Mum sounds defensive, her voice brittle.

'No, I don't think it's ever that easy. Sure, isn't there

two of you in it. But you know, if he can't be here, or won't be here, well, that's on him. But you're here. As hard as it seems and as much as it sucks, that's on you.'

There is a silence as Mum absorbs this. I press my index finger and thumb to my tear ducts – now is not the time for crying. I focus on the backs of the books on the stairs, counting them backwards and forwards, slowing my breathing.

'Maybe he'll come back,' Mum says, her voice all sad and lonely. It is as if the Hulk isn't even in the room.

'And what if he doesn't?'

'Well, I hadn't thought of . . .'

'And that's the problem,' he says.

'So, it's just chin up and move on, that's what you're suggesting?'

'Chin up and parent, I think.'

'Excuse me?'

'The girls need you.'

'Oh, well, thank you, Mr Sanctimonious, I'll be sure to take notes. What is it with you men – and all your *suggestions*? Maybe I'm happy with who I am. Ever think that not every woman is destined to be Mother of the Year?'

'Anne, this isn't an attack—'

'Then why does it feel like one?'

'You're not a bad mother, you're a human one.'

'Human – how generous of you! I hardly know how to thank you for such wisdom and insight.' Mum's tone is stone cold. 'I don't think I can do this any more, Gary. My choices are hard enough without having to defend them.'

There is the shuffle of chairs, and it sounds like one of them has stood up from the table.

'I'm always here . . . as a friend . . . if you need one.'

I don't know what either of them says after that.

It is too much for me. I take the stairs two at a time.

21

'irls, I need your help.' Mum is standing in my bedroom doorway. She looks tired, all the joy of her new job erased.

Tess eyes her sympathetically. We've been sitting on the bed discussing the Hulk's hidden depths and wondering how Mum will ever recover from being told how to parent by a man that wears Lycra seriously. And here she is, not even half an hour later, asking for help.

'Sure,' I say. I wonder if this is a hugging moment, but I don't want to alarm her and reactivate the wind-up version of Mum that motors about for hours making sculptures and pretending everything is fine.

'I'm moving to the chicken shed for a few days,' she says. 'I've had enough. Your dad will be home soon, so I'm going to work on my sculptures and you can all just get on with the wedding without me. Tell that sister of yours not to disturb me.'

'But what about—' I begin, thinking of all the lovely wisdom the Hulk imparted. I hadn't expected a miracle, but hiding in the shed?

'What about what?' Mum's voice has an edge to it, as if she is daring me to mention what I know.

'The animals,' Tess jumps in. 'I mean, well, the shed is full for the Animal Gathering.'

'Animal Gathering?'

'It's an awareness-raiser for the Ballyfert Vegans,' Tess says.

Mum blinks, swallowing this latest roadblock on her route to inner peace.

'I swear to God, I cannot keep up with you girls. If it's not leather-clad hormones, it's turning the back-yard into a zoo. We'll have to move them to another shed,' she says, desperation sneaking into her voice. 'I cannot be in the house when your father gets here.'

'We're on it,' we both chime, darting off the bed and slipping into whatever shoes are visible. Tess starts talking about horse sculptures with strange authority and ushers Mum out of the bedroom door, steering her through the upstairs hall.

It is as if we instinctively agree that we need to settle Mum somewhere, anywhere, just to keep her from splitting in two.

Operation Set-Mum-Up-in-the-Shed involves coaxing the animals from their clean, dry surroundings into damp, grotty ones. The upkeep on our other sheds has been minimal and there are holes in most of the roofs, as well as dripping noises, and the smell of mildew and rats. I can't help feeling the new conditions are on par with the Kellys' monster shed, but there's no time to worry about that now.

Síle the Donkey takes one long look at the dark confines of her new shed and starts backing out.

'Tess, can you give her a prod?' I say. I am still struggling to lead both Jack the Three-Legged Dog and the wayward duck across the yard. A feat that is made all the more difficult by the marquee. There are poles everywhere that either the duck insists on walking into or Jack pees on.

'You mean, like, touch her arse?' Tess asks, wrinkling her nose at me. She chose to relocate the donkey because it involved zero body contact. It has gone smoothly up until this point. She manoeuvred Síle across the yard with a makeshift rope rein, but then made the rookie mistake of letting go of the rope, believing the donkey would go into the dark mouldy shed without being led.

'Yes, I mean, like, *touch her arse*,' I say, mimicking her tone.

'I can't believe I've to say this, but I DO NOT touch donkeys' arses.' Tess steps away from Síle the Donkey. 'I have literally no idea what filth might come out of that yoke.'

I end up abandoning the duck and dog, and prodding Síle the Donkey's arse myself. She reluctantly enters the shed, braying loudly in protest.

Jack the Three-Legged Dog follows her, curling up mournfully in a corner. The duck is more enthusiastic and seems quite keen on the general dampness, flapping about while the donkey continues braying in protest. Ted the Goat seems oblivious to his new surroundings and starts gnawing on a piece of discarded wood.

It takes another hour to move Mum into the good shed. The operation involves lugging blankets, sculptures and even furniture down the hill. As well as raiding the cupboards for bread and jam. I leave Lady Macbeth with her for company. I'm not sure Mum appreciates the gesture, but she does show some mild interest in the chicken, petting her absent-mindedly.

Anyway, Lady Macbeth is drowsy from the vet's meds ninety per cent of the time and when she's not, she still doesn't seem to recognize me and cowers under the bed as if I'm keeping her prisoner. Leaving her with Mum is one less reminder of all my other chickens and what I've put them through.

'Now what?' Tess asks as we plant ourselves firmly at the kitchen table, arms splayed outwards in a show of relief.

'That was a lot,' I moan.

'We might even be dead.'

'Should we pinch each other in case?'

'I would, Molly, but I don't have the energy.'

'True that.'

Tess slumps further down in her chair and yawns. 'I can literally not do any more drama.'

For the first time in all our years of friendship, we resign ourselves to silence. The clock fills in the spaces with its monotonous ticking. Polly is bashing about upstairs and the sound of Dermot crooning filters in from the sitting room. He'll probably end up sleeping on the couch. Half the reason Mum hates him is that he practically moved in when the two of them were dating. He ran away to South Korea because he has what Polly likes to describe as a 'volatile family'. Given the state of our family, I can't even imagine what that means.

He has whipped out the guitar and seems to have an endless repertoire of lyrics that he whines while strumming three or four basic chords. The lyrics are loud enough to decipher, and tuneless enough to cause nausea.

You are my baby
Loving me like twenty
Your breath so minty
Your eyes ain't squinty
You, you, you, my baby

So tell me, baby, if I go too far,
Cos you, you, you like a falling star

You are my lady
Loving me like plenty
Your face so pretty
Your lips ain't flaky
You, you, you, my lady

So tell me, lady, if I go too far,
Cos you, you, you like a falling star

Every now and then the lyrics subside into guitar strumming. After each song, there is a brief intermission. Presumably time for him to pen another set of lyrics and arrange the four chords he knows in a different order. The effect is that as soon as I've forgiven him for one terrible song, another one starts up. As if there is no end to the number of clichés occupying his mind.

Tess gazes wistfully out of the window, oblivious to the background soundtrack. I'm too tired to be angry with her about the Animal Gathering. Anyway, the way she handled Mum balances it out. My brain feels like a giant stress-mush right now; it's as if all I can do is try to keep up. There's no way we can quit the Animal Gathering, we've got to make it work – returning the animals would be worse. Like saying, *Oh, yeah, sorry, we've quit our vegan principles, we're just going to go gnaw on some roast chicken and throw darts at sheep.*

I busy myself boiling pasta, chopping some garlic and thyme and frying it off with some vinegar and a tin of tomatoes. I dish it up in bowls, a big spoon placed in each, because bowls and spoons are both shapes that hold despair well. Unlike forks, which poke holes in the sadness.

We have almost finished our pasta binge when there is the sound of a car outside.

'What now?' Tess mutters.

There is a loud screech from upstairs and the sound of footsteps thumping across the landing. The nasally voice of Dermot calls out, 'There's a car out front . . .'

Whatever he says next is lost in the commotion of Polly flying down the stairs, past the kitchen door, limbs flailing as she clatters out into the big hall. Her face is fresh, and she is wearing pyjamas; her hair swishing in a high ponytail makes her look more like an overexcited twelve-year-old than a bride-to-be.

'Daddy!' she cries.

22

Tess and I follow reluctantly. It's not that I don't want to see Dad, it's that I'm not sure how to feel about it. He never emailed me back and I haven't seen him in over a year.

'You made it,' Polly says, standing in the front door and talking into the night. A shadowed figure approaches the door. He walks with his trademark bowed head, a habit he developed to avoid bumping into low-hanging lights or doorframes. Dad has always been tall, but never quite upright, so that his height sometimes feels like a trick if he stands up straight.

As he nears the steps, the light from inside the house spills out, illuminating him. I imagine it's what seeing a ghost is like. There's this person that you love who disappeared for ever, and suddenly they are right there with you again. If I reached out, my hand might go straight through him. It hurts to see that he exists almost exactly as before. He doesn't look malnourished, or grubby, or in need of a trip to the doctor. Maybe it would be easier if Dad stayed as this strange myth about a man and a PowerPoint presentation.

But here he is.

Big kind eyes.

That apologetic smile.

Polly throws herself down the steps and into his arms. And I wish I could, but I know, even as I watch Polly embrace him, that it's only a matter of time before he disappears again.

'Oh, Daddy,' she says.

He pats her head awkwardly. I inherited my aversion to hugging from him. Or at least I thought I did. Maybe I just copied his hatred of hugging. It's one of those quirks that made me feel closer to him. Like, *Oh, well, you know how Dad and I hate hugging.* It gave us more in common. Polly used to try and make art to impress Mum in the same way. It's like we both chose a parent of the family to model ourselves on, and now that we can see their flaws so clearly, it's confusing to figure out who we really are underneath all their borrowed habits.

His hair is still dark and stands upright from his head, he is as narrow as ever, with a slight paunch at the stomach. His thick square-framed glasses slide off his nose in much the same way they did a year ago.

'Girls . . . I can't even begin to tell you . . .' He gulps, his eyes meeting mine over Polly's head.

'It's so good to see you,' Dad says. His whole body seems to vibrate ever so slightly. He glances around, taking in the shadows of the yard and staring up at the house. His eyebrows furrow at the bald flowers by the door. I wonder if he's replaying a bad memory or just confused by the damage the donkey inflicted on the poor flowers.

'So,' he says, 'it hasn't changed much, has it?'

'We've made some improvements,' Polly says.

'I'm sure you have, pet, I'm sure you have.' He nods sadly, and it feels as if we're all thinking of how he used to struggle to do the most basic things. Cutting the grass, fetching fuel, or even just walking across the yard had been impossible for him most days. He would sit in his armchair buried in books, pretending the farm could take care of itself.

'Well, there's plenty of time to show you later,' Polly says, but her quick smile seems forced.

I don't manage to say anything; all my feelings are stuck somewhere between my stomach and my throat.

Dad takes off his glasses and rubs them on his jumper.

'We should have tea,' Polly says grandly, snapping

back into Stepford-mode and striding back into the house. 'I'll give Dermot a shout.'

'Was it not Brian you were planning to marry?' Dad asks.

Polly whips around.

'Dermot is just an old friend. I swear, you old people have no imagination ...'

'What's he doing here, then?' Dad asks.

'He's ... ugh ... I don't think *you* would understand,' Polly says, her composure slipping slightly.

'I don't suppose I would,' Dad says, raising his eyebrows so that they shoot up over his glasses.

Polly marches away. From the set of her shoulders, she's now ready to send Dad straight back to France. She never did like the way he asks questions. Mum tends to fling accusations about, so Polly can fight back. But Dad takes a more scientific approach: stepping back and asking the questions that force Polly to consider her circumstances.

Dad makes his way up the steps and I turn quickly to avoid eye contact. I'm not ready yet. I hurry inside, Tess close on my heels.

In the kitchen, Dad sits at the table while Polly bustles about making tea and cutting up a cake into perfect wedges. Dad takes off his glasses and starts to rub them again, even though they must be clean by now.

Tess appears to be holding her breath beside me,

looking from me to my dad to Polly to the tea things with terror. She has maxed out on drama for one day.

'I missed you,' Dad says then, but it's not clear who he's talking to.

'We missed you too,' Polly says graciously, plonking a slab of cake in front of him.

'Where's your girlfriend?' I blurt out, because I want to remind everyone that this is a passing visit, that he is momentarily sauntering into our lives. He has his French seductress and his Lyons apartment. Why would he ever come back to the farm?

'Ah, Cecilia – she is at home, she had to work, she's joining us for the wedding day, *if* there is one. I thought I'd get here first to ...' He peters off. 'Well ... now is not the time.'

'Home,' I echo, because it is confirmation of what I suspected. His heart is elsewhere now; we're an inconvenient loose end.

'What do you mean, *if* there is a wedding day?' Polly says, her tone suddenly cold.

'Well, pet, we have to discuss it.'

'There's nothing to discuss.'

'Well, we disagree on that,' Dad says, and his tone is reasonable and kind. The only problem is his calmness seems to be causing Polly to implode. She drops the plate of cake on the table and doesn't seem to notice that the slices fall out of position.

As the conversation continues, all the words they are saying blend into a kind of low buzz. I can hear things like, 'You can't change my mind,' and, 'It's for your own good.' But I can't attach any meaning to it other than, *Dad's home is with Cecilia now. He came back for Polly. He was probably only addressing Polly when he said, 'I missed you.' Otherwise he would have said, 'I missed yee' . . . Right? He's already counting down the hours to his departure. And what will he do this time — make a diorama? Or leave us a sample of his DNA to grow a replacement clone Dad? Who cares? He's not even looking at me. He is fixated on Polly.*

Somehow seeing them like this, bickering back and forth, makes me feel completely alone.

Tess pinches me, before getting up from the table and shooting the others a hurried smile. With an apologetic shrug, she announces, 'It's been real, guys . . . but . . . uh, I've got to, like, borrow Molly. We've business to attend to.'

Tess grabs my hand and leads me from the room. Donning the full dazzle, she drags me to my bedroom. For a moment, I think we are on our way to discuss some important part of the vegan move-ment and put the world right.

But as Tess closes the bedroom door firmly behind us, the dazzle fades.

My previous mood creeps in like a thick fog. I

jump straight into bed and tuck the duvet under my chin.

'Wake me up when it's over.' My words are a dull thud.

'Look, I'm sorry . . . I just thought you should get out of there. I'm going home, I need a break,' Tess says. She gathers her clothes from the floor, opens the window and climbs out on to the roof. 'See you tomorrow.'

She leaves the window open and I hear the rattle of the wheelie bin as she eases herself off the bathroom roof. A fuggy breeze fills the room, and the smell of fresh-cut grass reminds me that it is almost summer.

I pull my copy of *Little Women* under the duvet, letting enough light leak in to see the text. I stare down at the words, but I can't concentrate. I would give anything to disappear into the world between these covers right now.

Dad and Polly are still arguing downstairs, their voices ricocheting around the house. As the words of *Little Women* blur before my eyes, I realize that Dad cares much more about what happens to Polly than me. He probably didn't even notice me leave the kitchen. It's as if my presence was not on the agenda. He came to solve Polly's problems. I snap the book shut, pressing the heels of my hands into my eyes. It's all I can do not to cry.

23

'My flower chicken is missing, you need to get up!' Polly says.

I feel as if I only just fell asleep. Before I've time to adjust to the morning, Polly is pulling my covers off.

I scramble to stop her, clamping my legs around the escaping duvet to regain ownership of it, but I am not strong enough. Polly tugs it out from my legs' grasp and heaps it on the floor. I curl up on the bed, hugging my pillow for warmth.

'What do you mean – Lady Macbeth is gone?' I say.

'Gone, vanished, hey presto, the chicken has left the building.' Polly is pacing up and down beside my bed, throwing her hands up dramatically.

'Mum has her in the shed.'

'Mum *had* her, and then apparently the squawks

were too loud, so she put her in the yard, and now, big surprise . . . she is gone.' Polly continues to pace.

'But—'

'Molly, we are minus one flower chicken for my wedding.' She flops on my bed, staring blankly up at the ceiling. 'What am I supposed to do?'

I scooch forward, patting her head gently, knowing the despair has a lot more to do with the wedding than the disappearance of Lady Macbeth. Lady Macbeth has probably just sheltered in an alternative shed. I'll get up and retrieve her as soon as Polly can face the morning sans emotional crutch.

I sit up, keeping my hand in patting motion. It seems to be calming her down.

My phone is buzzing on the floor. It vibrates violently when it wants to be heard, so the vibration can be felt underfoot. I stretch out my leg. My big toe extends far enough, and I use it to slide the phone within reach of both feet. I pad at it with my feet, all the time keeping my hand firmly in comfort-Polly motion. I slowly flip it over, and see that I have six new messages, with new ones accumulating.

I abandon Polly, lunging forward and plucking the phone off the floor, fumbling with the buttons as I try to establish what is going on. I click into the first message.

Tess: Polly just rang and told me to give back

the chicken. She said she would end my actual life if she didn't get her flower chicken back.

Tess: Maybe it's not the right time. But, like, WHAT is a flower chicken?

Tess: Wait, do you think I'd stoop low enough to steal Lady Macbeth? Like, what the hell?

Tess: You don't think Claire and the Ugg Boots, like, stole the chicken back . . . that would be crazy, right?

Tess: I mean, that's exactly what she would do, right? She can't stand that we're, like, famous now.

Tess: Gurl, I've rung you three times, pick that thang up.

Tess: Why even have a phone?

Tess: OK, never mind, when you see this – call me immediately. We need a plan

A quick walk to the kitchen reveals an upended house. Polly must have thrown herself into searching for the chicken. The chaos created by her search is everywhere: cupboards spill their contents on to the floor, plugs, childhood toys and abandoned clothing all joining forces to form waterfalls of mayhem. Every drawer in the kitchen had been pulled open, as if she believes chickens have the dexterity to slide a drawer out, hop in and say, *Wake me up when it's morning.*

The intensity of the search only makes real sense when Polly announces that Dermot is also missing. She makes the announcement while prepping breakfast. She is buttering the toast so violently that the bread is tearing.

'He said he can't stick around for the wedding, it would break his heart.' Polly seems torn between finding this irritating and romantic. 'He left this.'

She hands me a guitar plectrum which has the words *Waiting for My Baby* scrawled across it. It is unclear whether this is how the plec has always been or if it has been customized for the occasion. Dermot is the kind of guy who probably leaves similar plecs with engaged women across the world.

'I bet he went through the field,' Polly muses. 'Maybe he went to confront his family.' Her words sound distracted. I don't know if she means Dermot or Lady Macbeth.

I'm the only one in the kitchen with her. As far as I know, Mum is still in the shed. Dad hasn't come downstairs yet. He is most likely holed up in the guest room preparing a PowerPoint to map the trajectory of Polly's 'infinite despair' if she marries BrainDrain. Dad's natural environment is lab-based and pipette-facing. He thinks his PowerPoints explain everything, and that as soon as Polly sees the Pie Chart of

Predetermined Marital Misery, she will call everything off. He is a man designed for solvable mysteries and not the constant flux of human relationships.

'But . . . Dermot only just got here.' I do my best impersonation of a surprised person. I don't add, *It seems like only yesterday he was going to save you from a life of BrainDrain. You've made your choice, Polly: BrainDrain it is. Think of how balanced your finances will be, how bland your sandwiches. Think of the lifetime of songs you'll be missing out on, the one-chord guitar children you will never give birth to.*

'Mum scared him straight off,' Polly says.

Polly smiles, finding solace in blaming Mum for Dermot's departure. It doesn't occur to her that insisting on marrying a walking bag of Taytos is what sent Dermot packing. She looks dreadful. Yawning, she picks poached eggs out of a saucepan with a slotted spoon. Her skin is drawn, and she wears a brown knitted jumper-sack that swamps her. It looks like it has been woven from the hair of a horse. A possibility, if she 'borrowed' it from Mum's wardrobe.

'I mean, Brian would never do anything so frustrating.' Polly looks sadly at the plate of eggs, before handing them to me.

'There you go,' she says, her smile wavering, as if she isn't sure she has any interest in smiling. It isn't the right time to remind her of my veganism. I've the rest of my life to adhere to the new diet.

A slap of sisterly guilt hits me. Ignoring Polly's issues is doing neither of us any favours. I need to participate in this relationship more actively. After all, she noticed Lady Macbeth is missing and had the foresight to ring Tess about it (even if she did so in quite the incendiary manner). Because of her, we are going to school prepared. Well, Tess will be prepared.

'Are you . . . OK?' I ask.

'Yeah, yeah, I'm grand, I'm sure it's all for the best.'

She looks out of the window wistfully, then turns back to her plate and carries it to the kitchen table. We both pick at the food. The guilt continues to pester me. *Ask, ask, ask* becomes a bizarre chorus in my head.

'This isn't about Mum and Dad, is it?' I say.

'The world does not revolve around Mum and Dad's terrible life choices,' Polly says. 'I am perfectly capable of making my own.'

I didn't know Polly's ability to make poor life choices was in question.

She gets up from her chair and pushes away her plate. 'Anyway, believe it or not, I've more important stuff to be worrying about . . . Like my wedding.'

Dad chooses this exact moment to enter, which saves me from having to ask about the 'important stuff'. As if I have time for the list of chores she is planning for today. Knowing Polly, she will be building a makeshift altar from scrap wood and adding trimmings of lace to every surface in the house.

I have more important matters to take care of: namely, a full-blown missing chicken.

'Pet, did you sleep on it?' Dad says gently to Polly, as if I'm not sitting here too. I stab my poached egg meaningfully, letting the yolk flood the plate. I could smash my plate against the wall and neither of them would even blink. I'm that invisible to them.

'What a treat . . . my knight in crumpled plaid,' Polly says. She surveys Dad's rumpled red check shirt with a look of contempt. 'You've no problem abandoning us to the farm, and then what? When it all goes to shit, you turn up to tell me how to live my life.'

She gives him a once-over that is so hateful I have to avert my eyes.

'Polly, when you've calmed down, we'll . . .'

'We'll – what, Dad? Talk about it? Or fix it? Put a nice big plaster on it and kiss it all better? Is that it?' Polly says. A look of sadness briefly flickers across her face, but she composes herself long before Dad has time to interpret the emotion.

'I'm . . .' Dad trails off. He looks old, his face grey and weary, his eyes rimmed with dark shadows and lines.

'Pathetic,' Polly says, before leaving the room.

Dad looks at his feet and sighs before facing me.

'Molly, I hope . . .'

Ah! He has noticed my existence.

'Nobody likes to be second best,' I say. 'This can wait.'

My tone is cold enough to be Mum's. My stomach lumps. I will have to learn to control my inner Mum. That is not a side of my personality I should be airing regularly.

Behind Dad, Polly is climbing the stairs, her posture defiant, her long hair falling messily from its bun, the brown jumper skirting her knees.

I get up from the table without saying another word. I have animals to feed, a chicken to find and school to attend. Grabbing my coat and bag, I head towards the big hall, glancing back. Dad hasn't moved from the kitchen door. He is standing helplessly, arms dead weights by his side. I have a horrible feeling he is reworking the conversation in his mind and trying to figure out what he said wrong.

As the dust motes dance above him in the early morning light, I feel a pang of pity so immense that I have no choice but to ignore it.

24

Tess is waiting at the school gates with Barry. I'm a bit late because I spent the rest of the morning trying and failing to unearth Lady Macbeth in the sheds. It is starting to seem as if maybe Claire has kidnapped my chicken after all.

They're each holding a thick wad of what look like posters. Tess holds one up as I approach. It's a bit ambiguous: there's the selfie of Tess, Lady Macbeth and me, and the words 'The Ballyfert Vegans are Coming for You' emblazoned across the top. There are no other words . . .

'What do you mean, *The Ballyfert Vegans are Coming for You*? Like a boy band or something?'

'We'll steal back the chicken,' Tess says, 'obviously.'

'Although it's more about the principle of being heard,' Barry says, 'projecting the movement's voice into the atmosphere and—'

'I'll project you into the atmosphere, if you're not careful,' I snap, snatching a poster from his bundle. 'Let me see that.'

In the picture, Lady Macbeth stares beadily at the camera, her head turned towards me. It isn't what I would have chosen. But then – call me old-fashioned – I might have put a phone number or email address on the poster.

Tess presses a sheaf of posters into my hands, saying, 'We'll take the entrance, the main corridor and the basketball courts. You can paper the lunch room, and, like, the backs of the toilet doors.'

And so, my morning tour of the school toilets begins. Tess has assigned them to me because there is only one toilet she's willing to visit in the entire school. That's the one in the new extension, which still manages to retain some semblance of hygiene.

I potter about the school, tacking posters over the graffiti that decorates most of the toilet doors. I squint as I work, trying not to breathe through my nose – that way I barely notice the smell, the cigarette burns on the toilet seats, or the toilet paper strewn across the floor.

After I've Blu-Tacked posters to every available toilet door, I go to find the others. The front of the school features a banner of chicken faces (a metre or so from the ground), staring out into the car park.

How they managed to cover so much space, so quickly, is beyond me. The line of beady chicken eyes is haunting.

'Harrowing,' Barry says. 'Perhaps the most meaningful moment in the history of St Martin's, vegans rising up to—'

'It's a missing-pet poster,' I remind him.

'Oh, no it's not,' Tess says, 'it's a message.'

Tess steers me towards class. It is PE, so it isn't like we have to participate. Mr Hayes blushes easily, so all we have to do is claim to have a period and he points to the bench. We shuffle across the back of the sports hall, trying to avoid being hit by a stray soccer ball, and join some of the other serial PE avoiders on the bench. Tess clutches her side and shakes her head at Mr Hayes and I look sad. You don't even really need to fake it. He would never have the guts to ask, in case 'period' was the answer.

The other girls on the bench are three members of the Ugg Boot Army. Without Claire, they huddle together, tapping on their phones and sniggering, their Ugg boots bobbing up and down in time with their giggles. Occasionally they glance up at the soccer game and cheer Claire on. Claire is one of the few girls who bothers to play sports.

'I hate their faces. Why don't you have WhatsApp? It would make talking so much easier,' Tess whispers to me.

'You can hear what you're saying, right?'

'Oh, shut up, I'm not wrong,' she says, careful to keep her voice low enough not to attract unwanted Ugg Boot attention.

'Would Claire be this obvious?' I whisper back. I feel a bit headachy; the chicken thing has escalated to a weirdly personal level, and I keep replaying everything Dad has said to me so far in my head. Which, to be fair, isn't a whole lot.

'And why not?' Tess asks.

'I mean, like, after the article, she'd hardly want to be found with a kidnapped chicken.'

'She is the only one capable of this,' Tess says quietly.

'I suppose.'

I stare out at the amateur indoor soccer game taking place. As if in answer to my doubts about Claire's abilities, the ball lands at her feet and she belts it so hard that the goalie ducks in fear. Claire runs quickly back to defend her own goal, her face never once breaking into a smile after scoring.

The ball thumps from one end of the PE hall to the other, runners squeaking on the hard floor. Three of the more coordinated girls are playing, but Claire is the only one making a concentrated effort, and her face is semi-red from exertion. She's also the only girl that gets passed to by the lads. They tend to play the game around the other girls, not even passing when they are open to score. I reluctantly admire Claire's ability to go head-to-head with them, and then, remembering she is the enemy, I scowl at her instead.

'I wanted to apologize about the video,' Fiachra says. He is standing in front of us, panting, then he plonks himself between us on the bench. He leans back against the wall, treating us to his stale and salty post-soccer odour. His curls stick slightly to his forehead. 'I mean, so you know, I didn't shoot that video, it had to be someone else. I, well, I should have noticed and stopped them.'

'Shoulda, woulda, coulda.' My tone is clipped.

'Molly, I . . .' He lets his sentence trail off.

'Fiachra, your apology is accepted, but you can probably see that we're in the middle of something right now,' Tess says.

'Oh right, eh, is everything—'

'No, everything is not OK,' I interrupt.

'I . . . if you need help, I can . . . I mean . . .' Fiachra's words are stumbling in several directions at once.

'Well, we'll see.' Tess is giving Fiachra a curious look, and he is staring back at her, the pink in his cheeks growing stronger as the conversation continues.

'Look, Fiachra, if we need you, we'll ask,' I butt in.

'Oh, OK, well, I guess I'll see you in maths.' He gives me what I would define as a dirty look. Interrupting his flirt-fest with Tess is obviously unappreciated.

'What is your problem?' I blurt, feeling inexplicably tense.

'Maybe you should ask yourself that question,' Fiachra says, before striding off.

'I mean, he should just, like, kiss you already, or get out of our lives,' Tess says without missing a beat, trying to distract me from the sparks flying between them.

Fiachra runs up to the soccer ball and slams it towards the goal. He glances over at Tess, sweeping his hair back in a decidedly romantic gesture.

I get up from the bench, pulling my bag on to my back.

'Where are you off to?' Tess asks.

All I know is I need to be alone for a minute. A little jealous monster has sat down in my stomach and started to sulk.

I reluctantly sit at my desk, noticing that Tess hasn't made it to class. I am secretly relieved. It means I won't have to witness how she distracts Fiachra from halfway across the classroom. I'm hoping Fiachra will do the *how are ya* grunt and then stare at his maths problems like he is having an existential crisis. But no, he decides to start a conversation.

'Are you OK?' he asks.

'What do you mean?'

'Um . . . leaving PE early and stuff?'

His brown eyes look more concerned than should be possible. When I don't answer, he adds, 'Tess told me about the missing chicken, and then there's our parents breaking up and all that . . .'

'What?' I say. How dare he bring up my personal crisis, right before I have to sit beside him for an hour? *Did he run over to Tess the minute I left the PE hall? I bet the two of them had a grand old chat.*

'Just . . . cos you know my dad ended it?' He looks uncomfortable.

'It was mutual.'

'Was it? Well, whatever . . . just—'

'Well, whatever? You think *now* is the time to discuss our parents' *meaningless* fling, is it?' I say. 'You're as bad as your dad.'

'It wasn't meaningless . . .'

'Well, whatever,' I sneer.

I stare at the whiteboard. The numbers appear across it in a nonsensical sequence. Ms Fitz solves equation after equation. If only life could be sorted into *x*s and *y*s and solved with a simple formula. Fiachra almost curls in on himself and it isn't clear whether he is angry, embarrassed or trying not to cry.

Good, I think, *serves him right*.

Or that's what I try to think, but there is this feeling in my stomach like I shouldn't be quite so nasty. The feeling gets worse the longer the silence goes on, and the worse it gets, the less I know what to say. It is like a furled fist telling me to pat his shoulder or offer up some sort of remorse. The more intense the feeling gets, the less I can focus.

The classroom blurs into obscure background noise. Barry stages some sort of mathematical farce, prancing about at the whiteboard and winking at the teacher for laughs. The Ugg Boot Army laugh their hideous laughs.

I can hear – magnified – the scratch of Fiachra's pen on paper. Is it my imagination? Are those sad pen strokes?

It might be wise to leave the room at this point, but instead I say, 'Fiachra, I want to say I'm sorry and I didn't mean to hurt your feelings,' in a sort of stage whisper.

It's the kind of sentence that would have been appropriate if we were ten and I'd called him a dimwit. It could have been appropriate at slightly lower decibels, and it might have been semi-appropriate if I hadn't completely lost the run of myself and opened out my arms.

The class is silent. My brain is silent. Fiachra's face is both horrified and silent. A social code is being broken and I can't stop myself.

Some part of me urges, *Get this over with*.

So I wrap my arms around Fiachra and give him a big squeeze. I would say 'hug' – but that tends to be mutual. He stays ramrod straight in my arms. I squeeze him like he is a long-lost teddy bear. I hate hugs. And yet I can't seem to stop hugging the boy.

WHY NOW, ARMS? Why now?

Fiachra does not hug me back.

He won't even look at me.

I get up from my desk and push my books into my bag.

For the first time in my life, I stare down my class. It's as if they represent everything that's wrong with my life: the return of Dad, the confusion of Fiachra, Polly's marriage, Mum's frustration, my possibly dead chickens, and even, somehow, my inability to do anything about all of it.

I clear my throat, glaring into the sea of judgemental eyes. I make a bold announcement to the class. I don't know where it comes from, but all the frustration and anxiety and stress of the last year come barrelling out into the unforgiving silence of bored teenagers.

'I don't expect any of *you* to understand,' I say, before marching out of the room, eyes fixed forward, my last bit of dignity left wilting in my seat.

25

I'm halfway across the school car park when I hear Principal Burke thundering behind me, 'WHAT. IS. THE. MEANING. OF. THIS. MISS DARLING? IS. THIS. YOUR IDEA. OF. A JOKE?'

For a second, I assume he means hugging Fiachra, but he is ripping chicken posters from the wall and gesturing madly in my direction. His pudgy fingers stab at Lady Macbeth's penetrating glare in an agitated manner.

I'm not usually on Principal Burke's radar. He is preoccupied with kids that spit gum on to the tarmac. But today I have all his attention. He's not dense enough to have missed the news about the chicken genocide.

He has the cardiovascular prowess of an overweight sloth, breathing loudly and audibly between words. It makes his speech come out over-punctuated.

He tears the last of the posters from the wall.

'WHAT. IS. THE MEANING. OF THIS. CHICKEN. GIRL?'

I resent the title but think better of saying as much. He is heaving with pent-up rage. This is a far cry from asking people to stop kissing behind the bike sheds or to pick up their empty Coke cans. There is no principal's handbook for dealing with a chicken kidnapping.

'Uhhhh,' I say. That is all the energy I can muster.

'MY OFFICE. THIS MINUTE. SKIPPING SCHOOL. VANDALISM . . . IT'S BEEN A. SPECTACULAR WEEK. FOR YOU.'

I spend the next hour nodding demurely as Principal Burke assures me that lots of kids from broken families go on to live normal lives. When I blandly state that I am not from a broken family, he gives the mandatory *of course you're not* nod, before foisting a pamphlet for a service called 'Counsellingteens.ie' upon me and insisting that my parents need never know. I stare down at the words *adolescent friendly* and shudder.

'You can. Just call up. Those numbers there. And have a chat . . . whenever you feel. It's free.'

'I don't *feel*,' I mumble.

'Well, if. You ever. Do feel . . . It's, well, normal. You know. To have. Feelings.'

I nod as if this is a fascinating insight into human nature, and fold the pamphlet in two, tucking it into my bag.

'So, you're not. Officially. Suspended, but I need you to. Take the rest of. The week off. I've already. Sent Tess home. We have to. Crack down. Or students would. Run rampant.'

'I understand,' I say, although I am puzzled by Tess's lack of communication. Surely a quick text to warn me that the principal was out to get me would have been in order.

Outside his office, I expect to find her waiting. But Tess isn't there. There's no clack of her heels in the background. The hall is empty, aside from a solitary figure slumped against the wall. Standing with his hair in his eyes and hands shoved into his pockets is Fiachra.

'What do you want?' I ask.

'Someone said they saw you go in to Burke and I saw Tess leave earlier,' he says. My brain latches on to his concern for Tess.

'Oh, right . . .'

'About maths—' he begins.

I interrupt with an incoherent speed-mumble:

'ListenFiachraIHaveToDashWhatWithTheChickenAndAllMaybeWeCanDiscussIt SomeOtherTime . . .'

I start walking away, finishing up just as I reach the

school doors, 'WellIGuessI'llSeeYaRoundOrSome-thingIt'sBeenReal.'

I let the door swing closed on my words.

Tess is waiting in the kitchen with Dad. She sits at the table, spooning perfectly presented risotto into her mouth. She chews happily on the mushrooms and rice. Dad is sitting contentedly at the other end of the table reading a fat book about thermodynamics.

'Ah, you're home. I whipped up some food for the two of you. Tess said you had a tough day,' Dad says without glancing up from his book. I'm struck by how well-rested he looks: his shirt is only semi-crumpled, and the dark circles no longer sit under his eyes.

I glare at Tess, striding over to where a plate of risotto waits expectantly on the table for me. I stare at it for a moment – it was always one of my favourite dinners. Not that Dad would remember that, it's most likely a fluke. I pick it up, inhale deeply, and then, with a smile in Dad's direction, walk over to the bin and scrape the food into it. I watch bits of delicious mushroom slide down the black plastic.

'I'm a vegan, which you'd know if you paid any attention,' I state, even though I've so far done a bad job of being a vegan. I want him to know that I could

271

be a vegan and he hasn't even bothered asking before making a risotto with half a block of cheese in it.

Dad sighs. He is probably considering getting on a plane back to Cecilia. No doubt she swoons over his risotto; she probably stuffs her bra with it, so she can eat some later and remember him as she types out documents on *how to steal people's fathers*.

'Tess, I need to see you upstairs,' I say, in a tone that is oddly calm. Tess gets up from the table, thanks Dad for the food and follows me upstairs.

'So . . .' she begins.

'Where were you?'

'Ehm . . . preparing the Great Chicken Rescue, obviously. We don't have time to waste,' she says, 'we can't just leave it at the posters.'

'Oh,' I feel suddenly stupid.

'So, you need to be at mine first thing in the morning.'

'I do?'

'We're going to Claire's to confront her before school.'

'We are?'

'What if she didn't steal Lady Macbeth – it's not like we have proof?'

'For the love of patience, we're not going to get proof – that's not how *she* operates. And anyway, you're the one hosting an Animal Gathering on

Sunday. People are expecting to see Lady Macbeth clucking about, so you might want to show a little commitment to the movement.'

'I've a lot going on right now.'

'In case you haven't noticed, we all do,' Tess says. 'Look, you've done nothing but moan since day one of this mess. It's like trying to motivate a wet blanket. Would you ever just cop on and take a little, I dunno, responsibility for your life?'

'That's not . . .' I trail off, noticing how deflated Tess seems.

'I'm going home to take a nap,' Tess says. 'You know where to find me.'

She walks over to the window, pulling it open and stepping out on to the roof. She looks over her shoulder, shooting me a half-hearted wave. I notice there are dark rings under her eyes and I can't remember the last time I asked her anything important. We've been so focused on saving the chickens. She has worked herself to exhaustion trying to keep my life moving forward.

Climbing out of the window after her is the right thing to do, I know that. We would hug on the roof and distract ourselves with plans for the Great Chicken Rescue.

But I am stuck in place, heavy-limbed and limp-hearted.

I pick up *Little Women* from the bedside table, opening it and wondering what Jo would do. I don't really need to think about it, though. Jo would do something – anything – to take some control of her life. Tess is right: I've been wandering around blaming everyone else for my problems, which is exactly what Mum does. It's easier to feel hard done by when I pretend that everything happens *to* me, rather than because of me. No more Molly-the-Pushover; any decisions from now on are going to be mine and mine only.

26

Dad has been clattering about the kitchen all evening, trying to get one of us to come out of hiding. As far as I know, Mum's still holed up with her art sculptures in the chicken shed and has managed to avoid him completely.

Earlier, I found Dad standing in the attic looking a bit lost at the sight of all the paint splotches and old canvases.

'What's all this, then?' he asked, picking up a paint-brush.

'You're not the only one that has moved on,' I said primly, which was exactly what I'd been sitting in my room planning to say.

'I didn't mean—' Dad began.

'Save it for someone that cares, Dad,' I said, before skedaddling downstairs. I hadn't planned anything else to say, so a retreat was needed.

His problem is that he assumed nothing has changed in his absence, that he would return to Mum pickling vegetables, that Polly would sit down and see sense as soon as he spoke reasonable words. But the truth is much stranger than that. The farm may look similar, and a year may not have aged any of us too much, but our hearts are cautious now. We can never love him the exact same way again, because he left us without explanation. And that means he can't be Daddy Fix-It-All any more. He hasn't earned the right to meddle.

Oh, how I wish I could sit back and watch him meddle! It would be so simple to fling my worries at him and let him sort them into groups, but he is one of my biggest worries, and I can't exactly ask him how to deal with how prickly my tear ducts feel in his presence, how badly I want to scream at him.

The smell of baking wafts upstairs. It is a trap to lure us into the kitchen for a chat — freshly baked goods are sure to draw someone out of hiding. Polly is locked in her room, and, after trying to get into my book, I've given up and am now sitting on my bed mulling over all the things I need to manage. There's so much to do. Between the Animal Gathering and Polly's wedding, there's hardly time to worry about the chickens. But I don't want to give up on them just yet — I haven't been letting myself feel their loss. They were the one reliable part of my day. Whatever happened, they needed me. I owe it to myself to fight for them one last time. Otherwise I'll be just like Mum and Dad: the kind of person that gives up on those I love.

Polly manages to withstand the scent of lemon drizzle cake for a good thirty minutes before I hear her door creak open and her footsteps pad across the upstairs hall.

I take a deep breath. It is now or never: I am going to have to join her.

Solidarity is important. Whatever is happening with Dad isn't right, especially if it involves cake bribery. I know the emotional price attached to a slice of cake in this family.

Downstairs, I find Polly stuffing her face at the table. Dad grins when I enter, ushering me towards the cake. Thankfully his phone rings before he can say anything.

'Ah, it's Cecilia, I must take this.' Dad points apologetically at his phone.

I often wonder what Cecilia is like. We've never met the woman. I've seen a photo where she is peeping out from behind a Christmas tree, but all you can see are her teeth.

Dad retreats from the kitchen, cradling the phone and cooing into the receiver.

'Well, that's disturbing,' I say.

'Tell me about it.' Polly edges the cake closer. It is all moist and lemony and delicious. She cuts a slice and plops it in front of me, shovelling another piece into her own mouth.

'So, are you still marrying Brain — I mean, Brian?' I ask. It's truth time.

Polly lowers her fork and swallows the last bit of cake.

'What are you trying to say, Molly?'

'That there's always . . . I dunno, other options.' I try not to quiver as I say it. Being direct isn't easy.

Polly gives me a long, hard look. It is so long and hard that it starts to crumble. She dissolves into a puddle of tears. If Polly needs any proof that she shouldn't marry BrainDrain, she could simply document the frequency of her crying fits since getting engaged. She is trying to do the right thing, but I don't understand how she can ignore her body screaming, *No, no, no.*

I sit eating cake, saying, 'There, there, it'll all be OK.'

'No, it won't,' Polly says between sobs. 'It's so confusing.'

'What is this all about?' Dad has returned from his cooing session. His arms are folded across his body. 'I leave you alone for two minutes and this . . .'

He quivers with the stress.

'She's having doubts,' I say.

'Well, thank Christ for that,' Dad says, despite Polly's distress.

'No, I am not having doubts,' Polly says, between hiccup-ridden sobs.

'Everything will be OK,' I say. I'm trying to make Polly stop crying, but all I do is cause Dad to scowl at me.

'She's not marrying that boy,' Dad says.

Polly crumples further.

'I'm not allowing it. She can come to France and sort herself out there. I mean, it'd be good to talk to your mum first . . .'

Dad refers to Polly's future in the kind of tone usually reserved for business transactions. It wouldn't surprise me if he dug out a to-do list with *Stop Polly getting married* listed neatly between *Pick up milk* and *Pay the electricity bill*.

I'm all for stopping Polly's marriage, but Dad is not acting like she has a choice. Which is stupid because Polly is all grown up. She can do what she wants.

'There's something I want to show you, girls,' Dad says, plopping himself down at the other side of the table. Which is when I notice the laptop open and waiting on the other chair. He sets it on the table and pulls a USB out of his shirt pocket.

'Dad, I don't think this is—'

'Not now, Molly. I know I'm not the best with words and I'll only end up saying the wrong thing, as always.'

'This isn't one of those stupid PowerPoints?' Polly asks between sobs.

'I've compiled all the data you need to make the right decision,' Dad says, as he turns the computer to face us. The slideshow is titled: *A Comparative Analysis: Premature Marriage Vs Mature.*

'Maybe Polly doesn't want to go to France, maybe she loves Brian?' I say, flinching on the word *loves*.

'We are going to analyse this properly; it's the only way to prevent mistakes,' Dad says.

'Stop discussing me like I'm not even here,' Polly says. She stands up, fumbling for the tray of cake, tucking it under her arm and picking up a stray fork. 'I'll be in my room.'

Then she is gone. I'm left with Dad shaking his head at me as if I don't understand.

'Do you realize how often young marriages end in divorce? Let me find the slide.' He leans forward, flicking through the graphs quickly.

'At least he's reliable,' I say, and, for good measure, add, 'And you know what? Fifteen years from now, I bet he stays.'

Dad straightens up, abandoning his search for the

slide. He is sitting between me and the kitchen door. I can't bring myself to walk past him. He wants to invite Polly back to France. What about me?

I go over to the window instead. Dad watches quietly, observing my sadness as if I'm under a microscope and ready to be labelled. I want him to say something – anything. But he sits there pondering.

It takes a bit of time to wrench open the window, which makes Dad's silence worse. Eventually there is a groan and it loosens a little. Dad starts to explain about work and commitments and Cecilia. But I could not tell you what he's saying. His words are a fog that is hard to breathe in. His calm tone drones on as I struggle. Finally, it opens. Trembling, I heave myself through it and jump down on to the lawn.

A trip to the shed is in order. We need Mum.

The chicken shed is cosy. Mum has lit some incense and set up a mattress with soft cushions and blankets in the corner. The rest of the place is brushed clean, with makeshift shelves (planks of wood balanced on cement blocks) displaying her food supplies. Fairy lights have been threaded along the walls and she is in her art attire, wig in place, working on a sculpture in the middle of the floor.

Mum is attaching a massive horse's head to an even bigger horse sculpture with a staple gun. The horse project is taking up a quarter of her living space. Her face is tired and strained. She must have been up all night constructing the sculpture.

'Did you sleep?' I ask.

'I couldn't . . . We – well, Gary – decided . . .' she pauses, considering her words.

'Mum . . . I . . . I heard what Gary said.'

'I'm going to make some changes, I . . . just need to get through your dad's visit first,' Mum says, a guilty expression clouding her face. 'It's not easy.'

'We could really use your help up there . . . we're no match for him.'

She looks at me carefully over the horse sculpture, thinking for a moment.

'Your dad?' Mum asks, buying herself some time. She doesn't want to face him, and the longer we talk in circles the longer we postpone her decision.

'Don't ask obvious questions, it's not very creative,' I say, half-joking – this is one of her go-to lines.

She shakes her head at me as she continues to staple the horse's head in place.

'You didn't pick that attitude up off the floor,' she says.

'He wants her to go back with him to France.'

The staple gun keeps shooting, but the frequency

slows. It is like a soundtrack to the speed of Mum's thought processing. I wait until she has stopped.

'He's not staying?' she asks.

'No . . .'

'I see.' There is a finality to it.

'Are you coming up?'

She looks at the floor.

'It can't be worse than hiding in a shed,' I say.

'Touché.' She gives me her wateriest eyes. 'Petal, I just want to . . . well, thank you for being so . . . good . . . this year.'

'It's nothing,' I mutter. My entire body lifts a little as if this one tiny compliment is what it has been waiting for.

Mum gives me a soft look, her eyes still watery, and says, 'It's definitely something. Look . . . Can I hang on to you? I just don't know if I'll get all the way up there without you.'

'Of course,' I say. I try to smile convincingly, but I don't feel capable of leading anyone anywhere. My heart is trembling as I reach out a hand. In a voice that's far too confident to be mine, I say, 'Let's show him what we're made of.'

'I can take it from here,' Mum says.

We are standing in the big hall, deep breathing. She clutched my arm the entire walk up the yard, but now she releases her grip, drawing herself to her full height and asking if her wig is on right.

'It looks great,' I say, trying to inject confidence into my voice.

'I wonder what he'll make of the wig?' she says, laughing a little.

'Too weird, I guess.'

'Will you come with me?' Mum asks.

I nod. There is no way I'm abandoning her now.

We stand on the faded carpet as she takes a few more deep breaths. Basic yoga to control her emotions: I can see her straightening her spine, tucking in her stomach and rooting down through her feet.

Dad is clattering about in the kitchen, unaware that his wife is summoning the power of yoga to confront him. When she has gathered herself, she abandons all yogaesque tendencies, and charges at the door, bursting it open.

'You will not march into my house . . . and banish me to the shed . . . and take my baby girl away!' She is shaky but determined.

'Where on earth have you been?' Dad says, clocking the wig with a faint look of horror. He puts down the pan he is scrubbing.

'Exiled to the shed, while you're poncing about *my*

house as if you never left.'

'Now, hold on a minute, have you been in the shed all this time?' Dad looks genuinely puzzled, then walks over to the kettle, switching it on. I stand awkwardly in the kitchen door.

'Yes, I've been in the shed all this time. What do you expect?'

'I don't know – an adult conversation?' Dad says.

'Oh . . . like the one you should have had before you left.'

'Well, there were quite a few of those, if you remember. I recorded the data, if you want to see it.'

I blink. There had been conversations? I wonder if all of them had involved graphs.

'I mean the PowerPoint,' Mum says. 'Did you really think that was an appropriate way to abandon your family?'

'It was weak,' Dad says, looking at his feet. 'I get that, but without it, I don't know if I'd ever have worked up the courage. I needed evidence that I was doing the right thing for us all.'

'Well, we didn't need evidence! Your PowerPoint was nothing but a slap in the face. How were your poor girls meant to deal with their father's projected boredom?'

'Those were the facts, the formulae never lie.' Dad takes off his glasses. 'What could I have done?'

'Included a slide about how much you loved them?' Mum says.

'They know that. I was putting in the stuff they didn't know ...'

'You'd be surprised how little people believe in love unless you tell them,' Mum says. 'You've to say it over and over, and if you're going to leave, you need to say it even more, just so they know it's not their fault.'

'How could it be their fault?' Dad asks. 'There was nothing about that on the PowerPoint.'

'We fill in the bits between the graphs,' Mum says. 'You might see a list of reasons, but if we can't find what we're looking for, we read between the graphs.'

'But everything is on the graph, there's nothing between the graphs.' Dad scratches his head, his face greying at the idea.

'You can build a load of heartbreak out of nothing,' Mum says. 'You never even said ... good ... bye.'

'I'm sorry,' Dad mutters. 'I thought it was all there ... I ...'

There's a long pause as they both absorb everything that has been said. I lean against the door to keep myself from crumpling, my heart thundering.

'Look, Anne, this can't be about us. We need to talk about Polly,' Dad says, eventually.

'Before we talk about Polly, you'll tell me one

thing. I don't care about the evidence, John – I need it without any graphs or whatever . . . Why did you leave?' Mum says, but there's no energy behind it. Her voice is flat.

'We argued non-stop, you know that. Neither of us ever wanted to be farmers, something had to change,' Dad says evenly, giving her solar-system tights a pointed look.

In my head, this encounter played out differently. There were two scenarios. One involved more confetti and romance; the other consisted of a raging argument. This is a bit old and worn out. They both look tired and middle-aged.

'A pretty dramatic change,' Mum says, scowling at the kettle. She is probably having trouble adjusting to the way Dad is making himself at home and assuming she'll have a cup of tea.

'Look, we've more important stuff to be worrying about right now,' Dad says.

'We got married?' Mum asks, out of context. Her question flails about in the dark as if it had been poised for flight all this time. It surprises me. She normally circles that kind of truth from a safe distance, never quite dipping into it. The question hangs in the kitchen, making a desperately sad sound.

'And we're getting divorced. And I don't want Polly making the same mistake we did,' Dad says.

'What about the farm?' Mum asks.

'Oh, come on, Anne, we both know I was a useless farmer. What was it you called me – dead fingers?'

'Well, you did have a magical ability to make all crops die,' Mum says, the shadow of a smile appearing on her lips.

'I'm pretty sure there was one surviving batch of carrots.'

'So that's it – we're over,' Mum says, her face falling.

'That has been it, for a very long time. You know that, Anne. You're the one who kept telling me to leave if I hated it all so much.'

'I didn't think you would.'

She slumps into a chair, her head slightly bowed. Dad walks across the kitchen and crouches to put his arms around her. She sinks her forehead into his shoulder and he tucks some of her hair behind her ear.

'I'm sorry, pet. We tried, you know we tried – we just don't work in that way,' Dad says.

Mum is leaning into his shoulder. He slides a chair over with his foot, sits down beside her and hugs her closer. They look like brother and sister, or two people who have known each other for ever and don't need words any more. It is all so gentle; Dad is gentle.

I have to leave the room to stop my heart from breaking.

27

It's five in the morning. I've barely slept. I'm sitting at the kitchen table, drinking my fifth cup of tea since midnight and agonizing over what is coming later. Part of me wants to confront Claire and get Lady Macbeth and the other chickens back – if they are still alive – but the rest of me doesn't know why it matters any more. Given all the social media attention, Claire will have made a point of setting the chickens up in luxury.

It's not just that, though. Dad is here, and all he cares about is Polly. No matter how hard I try to drum up some chicken-related enthusiasm, my mind wanders back through my recent Dad encounters and I'm left feeling back to front and inside out.

Our conversations seem to be an awkward series of misunderstandings, neither of us quite speaking the same language. And I wonder, is that normal – for the distance between us to seem so much worse when I know it's not only physical? Here he is, under the same roof, and he might as well be back in France. Even if he buried me in a hug and apologized, I would still have more questions than he could answer.

He knocked on my door last night and wandered into my room. I pretended to be sleeping. He walked over to my bed, plopped himself down and shook my leg. Showing no respect for the sanctity of sleep.

'Pet, can we talk?'

I froze. I didn't want to talk. I wanted to scream and throw stuff. He shook my leg a moment longer, then sighed, giving up.

'Whenever you're ready, pet,' he said. 'I am sorry for all of it.'

I lay there stiff and sad and angry. I waited for him to plod back to his room, and spent ages staring at the spot on my bed where he'd been sitting. Unable to sleep, I got up and crept downstairs. A good strong cup of sugary tea would fix it. One cup turned into five.

And now, here I am. I try to bring on the drowsiness by counting the minutes on the clock in fives and threes. If I land on a round number like thirty or fifty, I start again. I climb up the ranks hoping for the clunk of a twenty-seven. I'm in the mood for uneven numbers – they don't split easily in two. They can't be broken in half and turned into two whole numbers, they end up with fractions. Tiny fragments of what they used to be. It seems like marriage is that way: it is meant to be indivisible, solid, but when it finally breaks up, it takes the whole family with it. Nobody is ever really whole again. Sure, they might look whole, but there is always a fraction of their old selves lost to the margins.

Thinking is ruining the simplicity of counting. I pour myself another cuppa, wondering if anything in the world is capable of remaining simple. A brisk knock on the front door interrupts my early morning quiet.

Naturally, I'm imagining it. But wait, there it goes again. Someone is at the door at five in the morning. I've no idea what sort of person shows up at 5 a.m. I glance at the clock to make sure I am right about the time.

I traipse through the house, swinging the door open and expecting Dermot. But it's not him. There, standing on the doorstep, is a multicoloured scarf lady, with a cloud of ginger hair, wearing Doc Martens.

'I am Cecilia,' she says in a voice like a cuddly toy. She has the faintest trace of a French accent.

I'd imagined Mum in pearls with a much sultrier accent. I'd assumed she would be an elegant, slim woman with the kind of hair that sits in place, a voice like a sex-panther and, most importantly, a strong dose of hateability.

She steps forward and gives me a hug. I sink into her arms and feel her squeezing me close. She smells of lavender and soap and she doesn't let go until I do. Something about her makes me feel real again.

'I'm sorry,' she says, then, stepping back, 'but you look like you really need a hug.'

'Thanks,' I say, embarrassed. It's odd to be seen so clearly by a stranger.

Over the next hour, we talk and talk and, somehow, she makes everything seem OKish. I end up updating her on Dermot's reappearance and disappearance, the chicken rescue mission, and the exhaustion of the last week. She nods sympathetically and doesn't once look bored.

'Your dad struggled, because he loves you, but I think he hated the farm. He woke up every day feeling like a horrible failure. When I met him, oh my, he was living in this basement, eating only toast, and working so, so hard. Maybe twenty hours a day. His eyes were bloodshot and, it looked like he had broken his own heart. There is no escape from this condition, even with all the working.'

'I thought he ran away with you.'

'Oh, no, no, no,' she laughs. 'I just can't resist the broken men – I want to fix them.'

'Mum was always the one that kept things going,' I say. It's odd how easy it is to talk to Cecilia about all this – she cuts straight to the heart of the matter, no wishy-washy false sentiments. It's as if she knows I need an explanation. 'I knew he didn't like the farm ...'

'That was part of it ... he had no purpose, and as you got older, well, you don't need him so much. He had to find some new purpose.'

'He didn't have to go to France,' I say.

'It was the only job he was offered after three years of applications. He was out of work so long, the company had to take a big risk, you know. It wasn't so easy for him – I've made him go to therapy, because there's not so much I can do. I don't think he meant to stay away.'

'But he did.'

'Sometimes life is a little funny. You know, as long as I've known him, he talks about you every day. Always texting you pictures, but they never go through – he assumed you changed your number because you didn't want to hear from him.'

'My phone doesn't do pictures,' I say, silently cursing it. All this time he's been trying to stay in touch.

'Well, he should have remembered, but you know what he is like ...'

It's just like Dad to give up too easily. I mean, look at his marriage. Any normal person would have called or sent a barrage of texts, but he sends a few pictures and then gives up.

Cecilia nods gently as she speaks, soothing the tension that is unravelling in my stomach. She asks questions as if she really wants to know the answers, and listens effortlessly. She has brought French chocolate, which we share. It's handmade from her local chocolatier and wrapped up in gold, with a delicate ribbon.

She doesn't share Dad's weird obsession with stopping the wedding.

'I even brought a dress,' she says, 'but don't tell your father. He will come around,' she says cheerfully, as if Polly's big day is not the end of the world and simply an occasion to be enjoyed.

I feel Mum before I see her. It is a kind of prickly sensation on the back of my neck.

I stop making eye contact with Cecilia. Noticing this, Cecilia spins around. And then, before Mum hurls a chair at her or screams about her lost husband, Cecilia makes the first move. She lunges across the room, scarves flying. Mum looks alarmed, but before she can come to her senses and batter Cecilia with a cookbook, Cecilia flings her arms wide and envelops Mum in a hug.

There are few situations worse than having a hug forced upon you, and I imagine one of them is having it forced upon you by your ex-husband's new slice of pie.

In fairness to Mum, she doesn't melt down. She nods curtly at Cecilia.

Cecilia prattles on about wedding preparations and I slide the chocolate away from me. Nobody needs to know I've eaten *her* chocolate. I'd stuff some in my pockets for later if I didn't think Mum would notice.

'So where is John?' Cecilia says.

Mum doesn't answer. She is hardly expected to, given the circumstances. I tell Cecilia that he is probably down the yard. There are a lot of places Dad might be, but the yard is not one of them. It is now six in the morning; he is most likely asleep. All I know is that the yard has enough sheds and animals that it will take Cecilia at least half an hour to search it and return, giving Mum some time to adjust to the latest home invasion.

Cecilia bobs out of the kitchen like a plump apple.

'She's not what I expected,' Mum says.

'What did you expect?' I ask.

'The person she ate,' Mum says, her voice a bitter hole. She busies herself making breakfast, whisking together eggs and chives, heating a frying pan.

It isn't long before Dad wanders into the kitchen in a robe. He is probably wearing it in an effort to appear more casual, but it looks like he is forcing the fluffiness. He has dark circles under his eyes and nods at us both.

'Something smells good,' he says, stretching his arms out and yawning.

Before he has a chance to settle into the rhythm of the morning, we all hear the sound of Cecilia in the big hall. There is a loud squeak. Cecilia sticks her head into the kitchen, rosy-cheeked and beaming.

'There you are,' she says.

Dad gives us such a look of terror that I have to resist laughing.

'*Chéri*, I came to Ireland to say you can't make Polly's choices for her,' she says.

'Well, Cecilia, I can't say I'm happy to see you. Don't you trust me to handle this?' Dad's brows are pressed close together in irritation.

'Cut the crap, John, you're trying to control Polly,' Mum says, reverting to the least helpful version of herself. 'What? You can just march out of here without so much as a goodbye and expect me to let you be their father? If the last year has taught me anything, it's that they're better off without you. I've tossed every one of your stupid postcards, and as for the *boohoo, let me explain* phone calls, I haven't mentioned them, because they're an insult to your daughters. You can't just have everything go back to normal, that's not how this works.'

He sent postcards! This is news to me.

'How could you?' I all but whisper at Mum.

'It was for your own good,' Mum says, glowering at Dad. 'You saw that PowerPoint – there's no coming back from that.'

Does she know I read that PowerPoint over and over again? That I traced the line graph of predicted misery repeatedly, each time hoping it might change. I thought there was only the PowerPoint, but all along, there were postcards, texts and phone calls. It's just like Mum to focus on the PowerPoint and pretend none of the rest of it happened.

'Maybe we should have a little coffee or tea?' Cecilia suggests.

'Tea will not solve this,' Mum says. In the grand tradition of Mum being Mum.

'Polly . . . Polly thanked me for the postcards on Skype,' Dad says. I am sure he is going somewhere with this sentence. Its mere existence surprises me.

'She must have dug them out of the bin, because that is where I put them and, more importantly, where they belonged,' Mum says.

'You Skyped Polly?' I say.

'She always said you were too busy,' Dad says.

'So, all this time you've been talking to Polly?'

'Ah, pet, it isn't like that,' Dad says. There should be more to that sentence, but there isn't.

'I . . . told her to leave you out of it,' Mum admits reluctantly. 'You were so heartbroken, and spending all that time with the chickens, the last thing you needed was more confusion.'

'And what – I couldn't decide for myself?'

'Well, I mean,' Mum says, 'it was for the best.'

'Maybe it was,' Dad says gently.

'OH! ARE YOU ACTUALLY JOKING ME? YOU FINALLY AGREE ON SOMETHING,' I say, not sure where to go with this new information. Dad hasn't been ignoring me all this time; Mum has been protecting me from the one thing I wanted.

'Don't speak to your mother—' Dad says.

'You don't get to tell me how to speak to *my* mother,' I all but hiss.

There is a long silence as they all exchange *the teenager is volatile* glances.

'I have to go,' I say. 'I've a chicken to rescue.'

I don't wait for anyone to try and stop me. No doubt they'll need a secret Skype session with Polly to come up with some sort of a plan. I stalk past Cecilia into the small hall. The gloom and cold are welcoming. I momentarily consider picking up some cookbooks or wellies and flinging them around. Instead, I lumber through the big hall and out into the yard.

The others follow, congregating at the front door

in a dishevelled family portrait: Cecilia in front, with Mum and Dad looking lost on either side.

When I'm halfway across the drive, I hear Mum shouting. It sounds like *Wait, Molly!*

But I'm not interested. The Great Chicken Rescue will be a welcome distraction. I might as well help Tess on her way to social media greatness. Going viral will be a lot easier than trying to understand the shower of eejits I call family.

28

Tess lives in Ballyfert's only housing estate. It's where most of the townies live. The houses are matching detached two-storey homes with neat lawns and rose beds. The only difference is that everyone has a different colour door. Tess's parents chose a yellow door, so naturally she wishes it was red. There are ten houses in total. Tess's house is right at the very end, surrounded by a low hedge.

Tess's mum answers the door, dressed for the day in her pink jogging suit. She looks out of breath and like getting out of her chair has strained her hip. Her hair is brick grey and when she smiles she has no teeth, because she insists that dentures are too exhausting.

'Oh, Molly, so nice to see you,' she says.

'Is Tess up?'

'She sure is, you know where to find her.'

Tess's mum steps to the side in what feels like slow

motion, gesturing towards the stairs. I've always loved Tess's home. There are glass cabinets with china, framed family photos, and a soft, clean carpet. It always smells of vanilla soap. I inhale deeply in the hall, sticking my head in the living-room door to say hello to Tess's dad. He is watching Mass on the TV and looks at me as if he can't remember who I am. I wave anyway, then head upstairs.

Tess's room looks like it is cut out of a magazine for teenagers: cute lamps, bedspreads, and the miracle of coordinated furniture. Barry lounges on a beanbag in one corner and barely acknowledges my presence. Tess must have snuck him in – not difficult when your parents are semi-blind.

Tess is lying on her bed texting, surrounded by cushions. I'm always overwhelmed by the number of them occupying her bed – they look randomly tossed on, but there's a very specific way to pile them. Although, looking at them now, I can't be sure what it is. She waves me into the room, and pats the empty space beside her.

She hits Send on a message. 'Fiachra is the answer to our prayers,' she says.

'Fiachra?' I hug a zebra-print cushion to my chest, stroking it for strength.

'Yeah, he's providing the wheels, said he wouldn't dream of letting us face Claire without him.'

'Seems the *movement* has really changed him,' Barry says smugly.

'I don't really want Fiachra involved,' I say.

'Well, you don't have a choice in the matter – I didn't even ask, the poor sap offered,' Tess says. 'I guess that's what a bad case of the crush does to boys.'

'Or perhaps it's what a higher calling does to boys,' Barry says evenly.

I try to keep my face neutral. Not only am I going to have to watch Tess make moon eyes at Barry while Fiachra makes moon eyes at her; I will also have to pretend to be happy for her when she realizes Fiachra is the only one interested in her and they form a nauseating couple. I'll have to eat lunch alone on Monday as they disappear behind the bike sheds together.

Tess moves on to the next item on her agenda.

'Now, as this is the showdown and, let's face it, could end up online . . . we are going to need outfits,' she says. 'And I have just the thing.'

I sit on her bed pretending to care about our outfits. Tess digs around in her wardrobe before pulling out a crisp shopping bag full of black Lycra items. She must be the only person in the universe that dresses up to visit a chicken. She throws items at both Barry and me. Barry refuses to wear any of it.

'Unless you can guarantee me it's fair trade, I'm

afraid it would compromise my integrity.'

'Whatever . . . suit yourself,' she says, ordering me to try on my outfit.

'Cover your eyes,' I say to Barry.

'As if I'd even want to look,' he says, taking out his phone.

That stings a bit. I tug off my hoodie and jeans, pulling on black leggings and a tight short top that squeezes me all over. It is like a second skin.

'I feel a bit . . . naked?' I say, poking at the bit of my midriff that is on display.

'You look HOT!' Tess says. She pulls on her own leggings and sticks her bum out, looking in the floor-length mirror. 'Correction . . . *we* look HOT.'

She wiggles about, dabbing make-up on her face and asking if I want smoky eyes. I do not.

'You people are impossible,' she says, smoothing sparkling grey eyeshadow into place. In fairness, with the dramatic make-up, she does look a bit like a superhero. 'What do you think, Barry?'

'You look as if you're wearing the blood and tears of sweatshop children,' he says.

Tess refuses to take the bait. Slapping me on the bum, she says, 'Well, personally, I don't think our arses have ever looked so perky.'

'What exactly are we meant to look like?'

Tess is too busy folding down the top of her

leggings to answer.

'Why do you even have sports clothes?' I ask, trying to tug the top down over my midriff and wondering if there is any way to tuck it in.

'I got some after the overall incident . . . no way am I going to risk going viral dressed as a farmer.' She admires her figure in the mirror: she has teamed the Lycra with a pair of stilettos.

'You don't think the shoes are a bit much?' I ask, glancing down at my own beaten-up trainers.

'I don't even know if they're enough,' Tess says. 'I mean, I cannot wait to show Claire exactly—' She is cut short as her phone buzzes to life. *Fiach* flashes across the screen.

Oh, so they have pet names now, I think.

'He's here, it's time,' Tess says, adjusting her eyeshadow with a quick finger-smear and swaggering out of the door. Stilettos are debilitating in that they only allow for tottering, staggering or swaggering. And although she's swaggering, there's a ninety-nine per cent chance of staggering before the rescue is over.

'What do you think he drives?' Tess calls from the bottom of the stairs.

Barry strides ahead of me out of the door, saying, 'Something that pumps toxic fumes into the atmosphere.'

'A bike, he's not even old enough to borrow a tractor,' I say.

'But sure, like, who will check a licence around here?' Tess yells. 'I've dated loads of lads that shouldn't have been driving.'

'Just a minute,' I shout after them.

I've just caught sight of myself in the mirror. There's no way I'm wearing this outfit. That's it — no more Molly-the-Walkover. I'm on board for the chicken stuff, but the Lycra is making me self-conscious. I pull my jeans and hoodie on over the Lycra nightmare, before traipsing after the others.

Tess waves her parents goodbye. They smile politely in our direction. I can only assume they are too blind to notice that there's a boy among us and that their daughter is dressed as Catwoman, not a schoolgirl. Tess is too busy fiddling with her phone to notice I've abandoned the costume.

Tess and Barry are first out of the door.

'Well, it's not a tractor,' Tess calls back. 'And . . . eh . . . we may be slightly overdressed.'

I step outside. Tess clocks my new outfit.

'If you want to go viral dressed like a sack of po-tatoes, that's your funeral,' she says. But I'm too busy staring at what is behind her to bother retorting.

There, sitting at the end of her drive, Fiachra is perched on top of our ride. It is red, battered and, most importantly, a ride-on lawnmower.

'Don't you have, like, an actual car?' Tess asks, switching her scorn for my clothing to the lawnmower.

'Well, no, I'm not old enough,' Fiachra says, looking confused.

'Eh, so you expect us to all, like, fit on a lawnmower?' Tess asks.

'It's all I've got,' Fiachra says with a shrug. He is blushing, suddenly aware that Tess is used to cars with actual seating.

'We could walk,' I say, and we all look at Tess's stilettos.

'Never mind, it'll have to do,' Tess says. 'I'm not prepared to sacrifice the footwear. I mean, these babies say so much more than the lawnmower ever will.'

'It's a nice outfit,' Fiachra says.

'I tried to tell her – it does nothing for the *movement*,' Barry says, sitting himself on the back of the lawnmower.

I glare at them all. Part of me wishes I hadn't covered up the Lycra outfit so Fiachra would notice me too. I squish the thought immediately – it's a bit too dangerous.

'Don't be so negative, Barry,' Tess says, striking a ninja pose. Fiachra laughs, taking more interest in her

Lycra-clad body than I'm comfortable with.

We pile on top of the lawnmower, elbows and knees bumping. Tess squeezes in beside Fiachra, their thighs touching, and I sort of straddle the back of it beside Barry, clutching Tess for support.

'So, Claire's, yeah?' Fiachra says.

'CHAAARGE!' cries Tess, expecting the lawn-mower to shoot forward. The mower isn't having any of it. The engine grunts and dies.

After five minutes of false starts, it groans and splutters to life, heaving under our weight.

Tess is not to be deterred. 'Charge!' she cries again, as we chug forward.

29

We drive excruciatingly slowly to Claire's house. This time Tess wants to take the front entrance. I've never approached it from the front before and it looks entirely different. From the back, it's just monster sheds and bleak farmyard. From the front, it's about as posh as a farmhouse can be, on one of those lanes where all the houses try to outdo each other with fancy lawn furniture and manicured lawns. Claire's house is the biggest, with a conservatory and a pond visible from the road.

Tess insists we park the lawnmower at the bottom of Claire's drive where nobody can see it. Even though there's tons of room in Claire's yard, Fiachra parks it awkwardly behind the hedge to conceal it.

'You're going to get us killed,' I say, agitated. So far, the Great Chicken Rescue has been a lot of watching Tess cosy up to Fiachra on the lawnmower as I cling on for dear life and Barry regales us all with 'interesting' vegan facts. If he mentions the life-changing power of chia seeds one more time, I'll probably shove him off the lawnmower.

'Ah, would you calm down, there's hardly ever cars down here, the lawnmower will be grand,' Fiachra says, which doesn't reassure me.

'You can't just park in the middle of the lane,' I say.

'It's the side, not the middle.'

I am all set to rant about the rules of road safety when the others hop off the lawnmower and start walking up Claire's drive, laughing at the collection of gnomes that edge the lawn. The gnomes are all sorts of colours and sizes. It is no wonder Claire is evil.

I follow reluctantly, catching up with the others, who are peering at a particularly ugly gnome. It has a ladybird painted on its red nose and holds a sign up that says, *Home Is Where the Heart Is.*

'So cringe,' Tess says, a note of pity entering her voice. This is any teenager's worst nightmare. Claire probably can't even invite friends over.

We approach the door in silence. It is stately-looking. You would hardly believe that the kind of people who live here have a monstrous chicken shed out back. There's a gold letter flap, with *Kellys' Residence* engraved in a swirling font. Latticed windows flank the door and two round rose trees stand to attention either side of it. Underneath our feet is a sprawling doormat that reads, *Hi, I'm Mat!*

'Oh God,' I groan, pointing at it.

'Doormats have a responsibility to say more,' Barry says.

'It's kind of funny,' Fiachra says.

'Eh . . . just no,' Tess says, bracing herself to knock. 'How's my face?'

Before we can answer, the door swings open. Claire's mother stands there in all her powdered glory. She is wearing a knobbly grey jumper and big fluffy slippers. She is older and blonder than I expected, her hair scraped back in a ponytail.

'Are you looking for donations? Because I don't give my details to charities,' Claire's mum says, giving us the once-over.

'Eh . . . we're here to see Claire,' Fiachra says, because Tess has momentarily lost her voice and is gaping.

'Claire needs plenty of rest now, the poor girl is recovering . . . Anyway, shouldn't you be on the way to school?' Claire's mum says with a sniff. She looks genuinely confused by our appearance in her life.

'We're suspended,' I say, internally kicking myself for divulging that titbit. In the world of highly strung parents, *suspended* equates to *juvenile delinquents*. Claire's mother sniffs again, as if this information confirms everything she suspected about us.

'What do you mean, she's recovering?' Tess asks.

'We're in Claire's class, and she borrowed our pet chicken,' I interrupt with a sugary smile. I'm sick of people like Claire and her mother verbally disabling me. 'We want it back.'

'So, you're gathered here because of a chicken?' Claire's mum says.

'We're standing up to the man,' Barry says triumphantly.

'Do I strike you as a man?' Claire's mother says, eyeing Barry with disdain.

'The misunderstanding is that your daughter stole *my* chicken,' I say, stepping into the hall.

Claire's mum shuffles backwards in her fluffy-slippered feet and stares at my trainers planted on her pristine floor.

'If this is about that ridiculous rooster . . . I'll have you know it turned a bunch of chickens against us and escaped, and not before they destroyed Claire's back and ransacked the chicken feed.'

'Uh . . . the transgender chicken?' I splutter.

'I don't subscribe to labels, but Claire brought it home and tried to settle it with the others, but it was having none of it, she went to check on it and, from what I understand, there were claws and beaks coming at her from every direction.'

'Are you sure?' I ask, alarmed at the thought of Lady Macbeth forming some sort of violent chicken gang.

'Do I look like the sort of person who would make things up?' Claire's mum purses her lips.

'And we're just meant to believe this?' Tess asks.

'They broke free, and good riddance,' Claire's mum says. 'I wouldn't go looking for them either — you should have a look at what they did to poor Claire. Wait here a second.'

'A likely story,' Tess says, narrowing her eyes as Claire's mum turns, her ponytail swishing as she disappears down the hall. There are framed quotes lining the wall and the hall is entirely beige.

'It's, like, so devoid of heart in there,' Tess says.

'That's what happens when you trade in your soul for corporate—'

'Honestly, Barry, can you say anything neutral?' I ask.

'Guys, I don't think she's lying,' Fiachra says nervously.

'I appreciate all you've done for us,' Tess says, 'but if you're going to fall to pieces, can you please do it back on the lawnmower, where you won't make this operation look like some kind of joke.'

Fiachra looks hurt and is about to say something else when a door opens and Claire walks slowly towards us in a pair of leggings and a tank top.

'This is totally sad, Tess, even for you,' Claire says as she approaches. One hand covers half her face and her movements are almost reluctant.

'Just give us back the chicken,' Tess states. She is at the end of her Claire tolerance, which was pretty low to begin with.

'Ehm . . . I have no idea where the chickens are,' Claire says, and then she lowers the hand covering her face to reveal three raw-looking scrapes down her cheek. She turns round and shows us her shoulder blades: they're a mess of scratches and Sudocrem. I gasp.

'What did you do to them?' I say. I know Bellatrix gets angry, but even she's never done anything like this before.

'I was trying to get some footage, but that stupid rooster wouldn't act like a chicken . . . so I . . . well, it doesn't matter.'

'Of course it matters—' Tess begins.

'When will you get over yourself, Tess-kins?' Claire asks, turning back to face us. 'You'd do the exact same thing if you thought it would get you more followers.'

'For all I know, this is some elaborate joke and you've painted those scratches on, or got your mother to do them,' Tess hisses. 'I'm not leaving until I know where *our* chicken is.'

Claire sighs, taking out her phone and flipping through it, pulling up a video.

'Here you go. And you know what? I couldn't care less if they do drown in a slurry pit – I am so done with chickens right now.'

On screen the chickens are huddled in a corner, and a light shines on them. The shed is unfamiliar. Lady Macbeth and Bellatrix glower at the camera. Boo Radley peeks out from behind Scarlett O'Hara. And there is The White Witch looking as aloof as ever. Flanking the group on either side are Miss Trunchbull and Mrs Danvers, the set of their beaks spelling trouble. There is no mistaking my chickens, not when they're all clumped together like that. They're not dead after all.

One of the Ugg Boots must have held the camera, because Claire approaches the chickens. Lady Macbeth gives the signal – it's the subtlest nod of her head, but as soon as she does it, Bellatrix emits a loud squawk. The chickens rise up as one, launching themselves at Claire. There's a loud squeal from Claire or the Ugg Boot – it's hard to tell, because the camera is dropped and all that can be heard after that is muffled squawks and then Claire's voice screeching, 'My face, my face, my face.'

'Oh my God—' I begin.

'So, you just let them go? After all this, you let the

viral chicken flee?' Tess can't even contain her rage.

'Uh . . . have you seen what they've done to my face?'

'Claire, darling, kindly get those people to leave and close the door.' Claire's mother, who is listening in the other room, steps into the hall. 'I don't want you hanging out with these sorts. It might be contagious.'

'Don't worry, Mum, I am way ahead of you.' Claire pushes me towards the door. I stumble out. *My chickens are alive.* I want to see the footage again.

Claire swipes her phone and takes a picture of us before swinging the door shut. It bangs in our faces.

Tess spins on her heel and starts advancing across the yard.

'JESUS H. CHRIST,' she shrieks. 'After all I've been through, she just releases the damn chicken to the wild.'

'Maybe we should go,' I say. Fiachra and Barry both nod.

Claire and her mother are peering out of the window by the door, arms folded, as we make a show of ourselves in the garden.

Claire's mother pushes open the letter flap and calls out, 'If you don't mind having your fit on your own property, that would be much appreciated.'

The letter flap clangs closed, and Tess glares at it.

'I'll show that smug little face of hers exactly what I'm capable of.'

Before there's time to stop her, she is moving faster than a girl in stilettos should be capable of.

She lunges straight at the first gnome, plucks it from the ground and turns it upside down, jamming its peaked hat into the lawn.

She darts down the drive, tipping over every gnome within reach.

Barry, not to be outdone, rushes forward and tips over the gnomes she misses. They don't stop until the lawn is dotted with gnome bottoms sticking up in the air.

'That'll show them,' Barry says darkly. We're at the gate, surveying the damage.

'Oh, yes, I don't know how they'll recover from the mass gnome tipping,' I say.

'Let's just go,' Fiachra says sadly, as if the whole expedition has disappointed him.

'What about my chickens?' I ask.

There's a silence as the others exchange meaningful looks.

'They're long gone Molly,' Fiachra says.

'But—'

'But nothing Molly,' Tess interrupts. 'Gone, as in out there in the wilderness like ravaging sheep or something, if the state of Claire's face is anything to go by.'

'But—'

'There will be no buts,' Tess says. 'The chickens have spoken loud and clear. Let's just go home.'

Barry pipes up, 'They're free to live their best lives and set an example for—'

'How reassuring,' I say, cutting him short. I'm too fed up to argue.

We pile back on the lawnmower. Nobody says another word as Fiachra revs the engine. It splutters to life more energetically than before. The only problem is that the lane is fairly tight for space and we need to reverse out. Fiachra spends five minutes trying to turn the lawnmower around.

'Didn't you say you knew how to drive this?' I say.

'Yeah, didn't you say you, like, drove it all the time?' Tess asks. Fiachra turns a shade of aubergine that makes it clear how much he loves her. I let out one of those long disappointed breaths.

'When will it end?' I say.

'Um . . . isn't the Animal Gathering on Sunday?' Fiachra asks.

'I really don't want to think about that right now,' Tess says. Her phone starts vibrating, so she pulls it out. Whatever it is mustn't be that important, because she stuffs it back in her pocket abruptly.

'We still have more than enough animals for the gathering,' Barry says. 'Fiachra's right, the fundraiser has to be our focus – we can't let the movement get sidetracked by personal disappointments.'

Tess's phone continues buzzing as we trundle down the road. At first she ignores it, listening to Barry wax lyrical about how we can't let this get in the way of our ultimate goal. I'm not sure what that goal is, now that my chickens have run away and nobody cares about finding them, but it momentarily soothes Tess.

'Maybe you should just check, in case it's about the Animal Gathering or something?' I say.

Tess reluctantly looks at her phone, subsiding into silence as she thumbs through the notifications.

'I don't believe it,' she mutters, all the colour draining from her face. Her anger seems to have completely died away.

'What?' I ask.

'Looks like Claire filmed me tipping the gnomes and posted it already. Drive us into a ditch there, Fiach, while you're at it.'

'There's no need to be so dramatic,' Fiachra says quietly. 'You love that internet stuff.'

'Eh . . . when I'm a svelte animal rights activist . . . not a freaking gnome-tipper . . .'

She replays the video of her outburst as it accumulates more and more likes. I watch in horror: Claire has edited the video so that there are scenes where

Tess tips the gnomes in slow motion, her face a picture of rage.

Her phone buzzes with texts and notifications as strangers add their two cents. By the time we're home, Tess won't even click in to see what they say. Judging by the number of notifications she has received, she has finally gone viral.

She hops off the lawnmower, tottering and on the verge of tears. She hands me the phone.

'I want you to deal with this. I can't watch that video one more time. What have I become? I'm done.'

30

Fiachra lets me off at the bottom of the big wet hill. He says he doesn't know if the lawnmower can handle the climb, but personally I think he is so heartbroken over Tess that he needs to crawl into a dark corner and have a cry. I hop off, happy to have a few minutes to walk off the embarrassment. Not only did we manage to make complete fools of ourselves, but we are finally the face of something — though I'm pretty sure not even Tess bargained for being Ballyfert's gnome-tipping sensation.

As I scroll through the messages, most people are supportive of the stand Tess has taken against the creepy ornaments. It's easier for people to get behind gnome vandalism than veganism. It's not like they go home to a dinner of baked gnome. The chicken thing is harder, because people don't want to have to make uncomfortable decisions about what's on their dinner plates.

I pocket the phone and try to figure out how I feel about my chickens rescuing themselves. Surely they can't survive in the wild? This means I've lost them for good. I could search for them, but chickens are faster than they look, and it didn't do us much good last time. They could be anywhere. If I was younger, maybe it would be easier to believe that they'd survive or that I could find them. I'm too old for that now, I have to accept the obvious. My heart sinks – they're destined to get trampled by a cow or drown in a slurry pit. If the last week has taught me anything, it's that the world is a dangerous place for a chicken. I'll have to make a memorial for them; it's about time I gave up and mourned them properly. At least this way they will die free.

Leitirmór House looks tired, and there is a gathering of trailers and cars in the drive. As I round a crock of a white van, BrainDrain's voice sounds loud and clear: he is issuing commands.

'Back that goat up there . . . We'll have to put the sheep in the marquee . . . We've more animals than we know what to do with, so, as Mammy always says, ye'll have to love us and leave us. It's an awful pity, but . . . well, there's only so many animals one marquee can handle.'

'We will *not* be putting creatures in the marquee,' Polly says pointedly. She sounds as if she's ready to dismantle BrainDrain once and for all.

There are about ten farmers standing about, some with an animal by their side and others pointing at their trailers. There's a proud peacock strutting about, ruffling its feathers, and a grumpy miniature pony on a leash. Polly is looking harassed in the midst of the chaos, as BrainDrain deals with the small crowd. He gives a woman with a guinea pig in her arms a giant clap on the shoulder, and turns to wave at another woman, who is getting back into a car with a haughty-looking cat. She nods back, driving away. It seems some of the animals haven't made the cut. One after the other, the farmers get back in their vehicles, leaving their animals behind.

BrainDrain clocks me first and gives me a friendly nod. Polly is busy scribbling furiously on a clipboard and muttering, 'Is it too much to give me a phone number that has enough numbers in it to actually be callable? Oh, no, God forbid anything happens to your bloody peacock – and what? I'll resort to tele-pathy, or try to guess the missing digit . . .'

'What's all this?' I ask. Even though it looks like the animal donations have escalated, I need confirmation. After what happened with Claire, there is no point jumping to any more conclusions, at least for one day.

'*What's this?* she asks.' Polly looks up from the

clipboard with a brittle laugh. 'Oh, I don't know, Molly – I'd call it sabotage. But then again, I'm the one with a wedding nobody cares about, so what do I know?'

'Polly, didn't I tell you what Mammy said about the positive thinking? Ye've got to look on the bright side . . . Sure, don't they add a splash of colour to proceedings? Look at this one, how can ye not want to adopt the wee baby?' BrainDrain says, crouching down to nuzzle the pony. It bleats back, baring its impressive teeth.

'I want to walk down an aisle, not a yard full of cow manure,' Polly says.

'Well, lucky for ye, there's not a cow in sight.' BrainDrain grins at me as he says this.

'How many animals are there?' I ask, unsure I have the energy to match him.

'I'd say about fifteen at the last count. I've had to start turning away some of the smaller ones – can't be having anyone trampled.'

'Where are you putting them all?'

'Well, I've spent the morning clearing the sheds up, so there's plenty of room.'

'Not to mention *my* marquee,' Polly huffs. 'Seriously, Molly, you couldn't have picked a worse time for all this.'

'I told ye I'd put them in the sheds while we eat,'

BrainDrain says, looking puzzled by Polly's relentless negativity.

'But did you think to ask what I want?'

'Jaysus, are we back there again? Look, Poll–Poll, ye've got the jitters.'

'I have no such thing!' Polly's voice is reaching a new pitch, so I nip past them both and make my way up the front steps. I catch BrainDrain's eye and give him what I hope is an encouraging smile.

The front door is open to let the fresh air in and liven up the dampness.

Mum is sitting under the Three Paddys, cross-legged on the floor, a production line of vases spanning the faded rug. She is filling one with an assortment of flowers.

'Mum ... are you OK?' I begin. I'm not sure where the directness comes from, but for some reason I need to make sure.

'I know, I know ... You were expecting me to sabotage the wedding, not make the bouquets ...'

'I meant about the Hul— I mean, about Gary? And Dad? And everything ...'

'Petal ... with Gary, well, we're just friends. He's happy to help out is all – single parents unite and all that. And everything else, well, sure, what can you do? It is what it is.'

'And you're OK?' As much as I wish she had told

me about Dad, I understand why she didn't. She was done with it all. Which is pretty much how I feel right now.

'It's for the best. Anyway, I'm having a lovely morning, your father has taken that woman for a stroll, and I've had some time to myself,' Mum says. 'So, how did the rescue mission go?'

'How did you—'

'Oh, I know you think we were all born a century ago, but Tess's parents and I text each other updates. I know you don't think I pay any attention, but there's no point ruining your freedom either.'

'You're keeping tabs?'

'How could I not keep tabs? You're still my little girl – I just play it cooler than most parents.' Mum grins up at me. I'm so surprised that I hug her. Mum squirms a bit, but then settles down and hugs me back. 'So, did you get your chickens back?'

'They escaped . . .'

'Oh, petal, I'm sorry. That's a pity,' Mum says, and I can tell she means it. I consider this for a moment as I watch her artfully arranging branches, roses, giant daisies and long grass to create a natural-looking bouquet. She winds ivy around the vase and places it to one side, getting started on the next one.

'Wedding flowers,' she says. 'Chickens and flowers . . . I couldn't have raised you girls more differently.'

'I'm sorry, Mum, for everything.'

'Molly, I'm the one who should be apologizing. It's been a tough year. All we can do is make the best of things.' She shrugs. 'And don't we have a wedding to put on?'

'We do.'

'And, if I'm not mistaken, an Animal Gathering . . .'

We laugh. BrainDrain pops his head in the door, a mad grin on his face.

'Lads, we've landed a cow. I know we're at full capacity, but we can hardly say no to such a fine specimen. Should I give her the spiel?'

Mum smiles calmly up at him. 'If you would, Brian, that would be lovely.'

I listen as BrainDrain speaks to the cow's owner. Every now and then there's an audible sigh from Polly. BrainDrain seems to have an intimate knowledge of cow maintenance, as told by his mammy. Mum laughs quietly as he says, 'My mammy says they need a good firm hand . . .'

I settle down beside Mum, helping her arrange the flowers. We work steadily until BrainDrain pops his head in the door a second time, a bemused look on his face this time.

'Well, lads, it's not often I'm taken by surprise, but it would appear there are chickens on the horizon.'

31

BrainDrain points down the hill, right where the patchwork of sheds breaks into fields. I squint, unsure of what I'm looking at – are they chickens, or just a cluster of brown dots, making a beeline for our farm?

As the cluster gets closer, it clearly becomes seven chickens waddling across the field. Lady Macbeth is leading the others. We stand around in awed silence as the chickens march towards their shed. Taking no notice of the other animals or the marquee, they start throwing themselves at the door of their home with wild abandon.

'Homing chickens . . .' I say softly.

'Violent chickens,' Mum says, watching Lady Macbeth headbutt the door with determination. There's a worried look on her face.

I'm about to run towards them, but BrainDrain

327

grasps me by the shoulder. 'I don't mean to be Mr-Boring-Chicken-Safety, but I'd ... eh ... put a bit of protective clothing on first.'

As if to illustrate his point, Miss Trunchbull lets out an almighty cry and battle-rams the shed door with her entire body. Even Polly looks concerned. Remembering the scratches on Claire's face, I remain rooted to the spot, unable to take my eyes off the chickens.

Mum disappears into the house, then calls, 'Some-one bring her in here.' BrainDrain obliges, steering me inside to where I find Mum ready and waiting with some DIY safety gear. She's dug out old roller-skating pads, some bubble wrap and a bike helmet covered in spiderwebs. First, she wraps every visible part of my body in the bubble wrap.

'Do you really think this is necessary?'

'Petal of the Earth, Polly will murder you in your sleep if you end up hospitalized over a bunch of chickens the day before her wedding,' Mum says as she secures the helmet under my chin and begins strapping on the knee and elbow pads. She takes some wire mesh out of her pocket and Sellotapes it to the front of the helmet as a sort of face guard.

'Voila,' she says, stepping back and surveying her work. I lift my arms with difficulty – the costume is not exactly mobility-friendly.

'And the finishing touch,' Mum says, handing me a tennis racket.

'What's this for?'

'If the worst happens, you have a weapon. I'm telling you, Molly, I've never seen such demented chickens.'

I leave Mum to arrange her flowers.

Outside, I see the chicken-shed door is ajar. I'll ask Polly how the chickens opened it later. For now, all I want to do is cuddle my chickens.

The walk down the yard takes for ever. The padding means I move slowly, each step a stiff and robotic movement. I'm nervous. What if, just like the return of Dad, the return of the chickens is disappointing? What if they attack me too? What if they only came home to make us suffer for all they've been through?

As I waddle past Polly, she sighs.

'Is there no end to the things I've to put up with?' she says, her eyes narrowing as she clocks the face guard.

'I think it's class,' BrainDrain says, joining her. 'Don't she look like something right out of the future?'

'Why on earth would we regress in the future?' Polly says, forgetting all about me as she looks at BrainDrain with disgust.

'Sure, maybe we'll need protection from the sun – Mammy's always saying we don't take sun protection seriously enough.'

I waddle away, leaving them to their bickering.

I can hear clucking coming from the shed. I shut my eyes, pull the door open and stand waiting. I'm prepared for a burst of feathers, or for a load of chickens to fly, claws-first, at my face. Instead there is silence. The clucking has subsided and, as my eyes adjust to the gloom, I see my chickens sitting in an orderly row, gazing up at the last person I would expect to find in a chicken shed.

Dad is crouched among them. He is petting the closest birds and muttering, '*Shuk, shuk, shuk*,' quietly under his breath. There are red scratches on his face and his shirt looks like it has seen better days.

'Hello,' I say, my voice for some reason cracking with emotion. The chickens and Dad all turn to look at me, their eyes shining in the dark. 'I thought you said *shuk, shuk, shuk* was nonsense.'

'I realized the error of my ways soon after the first gash,' he says, eyeing me over his glasses but holding his body still so as not to disturb the chickens. 'I, eh . . . they were trying to get into the shed, so I thought I'd help.'

'You're taming them . . .' I say.

'Well, in a roundabout sort of a way.'

'Are you hurt?'

'It's not as bad as it looks – they calmed down once they realized my pockets were full of chicken feed and I got down closer to their level. Come in – they won't scratch, I don't think.'

I step in, mimicking Dad's posture by crouching down. The bubble wrap makes it a bit difficult.

'Call them,' Dad urges.

I nervously start calling them by name.

'*Shuk, shuk, shuk*, Mrs Danvers. *Shuk, shuk, shuk*, Miss Trunchbull. *Shuk, shuk, shuk*, Lady Macbeth . . .'

They begin to stir. Dad slowly stretches out a cupped hand towards me, gesturing for me to do the same. Once my hand is cupped under his, he tips his handful of seeds into it.

'*Shuk, shuk, shuk*, Bellatrix. *Shuk, shuk, shuk*, Miss Trunchbull. *Shuk, shuk, shuk*, Lady Macbeth. *Shuk, shuk, shuk*, Boo Radley . . .'

I lower myself further, sitting instead of crouching, the bubble wrap popping a bit as I do so. I place the tennis racket to one side and take off my helmet with my free hand.

'*Shuk, shuk, shuk*, The White Witch. *Shuk, shuk, shuk*, Scarlett O'Hara. *Shuk, shuk, shuk* . . .'

The chickens look at each other, as if weighing their options.

I wait. Dad nods encouragingly.

Lady Macbeth steps forward first. She climbs on to my lap and nestles there as the others get to their feet and bob towards me. They circle me, pecking affectionately at my bubble wrap.

'I'll leave you to it,' Dad says, rising up and walking towards the door.

'Dad . . .'

'Yeah?'

'Thanks,' I say, even though there are a billion other words that would be better. Dad pauses in the doorway.

'I want to say I'm sorry. I kind of feel responsible,' he says.

'For what?'

'For everything – not making more effort, leaving you, Polly, your mum . . . It's all so much, you know.' He stands taller, waiting for me to interject.

I stroke Lady Macbeth as the words sink in. I need to occupy my hands. I don't know what to say.

Dad stands silently for a minute or two. He is building up to something, I can feel it.

'I . . . well, we . . . I mean, Cecilia . . .' He pauses, taking a deep breath before continuing. 'We'd like you to come and visit this summer.'

'What?' I say, unable to come up with anything more inspiring.

'I understand if that's not what you—'

But before he finishes his sentence, I've placed Lady Macbeth to one side and am waddling towards him.

'All you had to do was ask,' I say, throwing myself into his arms. The bubble wrap crinkles and pops as he wraps his arms around me and squeezes tight. We stand there hugging and popping, the chickens pecking happily at our feet.

Me: Hey, Mrs Gallagher, sorry! Tess gave up her phone, can you get her to text me back on this?

Mrs Gallagher's Phone: K. Will get her nw! BRB.

Me: Thanks!

Mrs Gallagher's Phone: No prob, TTYL.

Mrs Gallagher's Phone (clearly Tess): Dear God, she texts like a brick. Look, gurl, I am not doing the phone thing any more – too painful, Claire wins . . .

Me: Confirmation RETURN OF THE CHICKENS. And there's a load of new animals at our house, the Animal Gathering is a go . . . And you saw Claire's face. That's hardly winning.

Tess: Whatever . . . The Animal Gathering was old me. Look, I'll see you at the wedding.

Me: BTW people are completely into the gnome tipping. You're viral for all the right reasons.

There's like two negative comments and about 10,000 wishing they could have been there.

Tess: Whatever . . . I'm holistic now.

Me: OK, well, meditate on it, or whatever . . .
xxx

Tess: Totes, babes, I'm like Buddha-central right now.

Tess: Did you say 10,000????

32

I spend the rest of the day with the chickens and by the evening, I'm so exhausted that I crawl straight into bed. I've only just got snug when Polly decides to haul me out of my bedroom.

'I don't care what you've got planned, those animals are ruining my wedding, so you'll at least make yourself useful in the kitchen,' she shrieks. Her hair is greasy and thrown back in a bun, she smells of animals and bleach, and the whites of her eyes are bloodshot. Mum stands placidly in the hall nodding, as if she's tuned out of reality and decided to let Polly have her way.

As Polly charges into the kitchen, muttering obscenities to herself, I glance at Mum.

'She just got a text from Dermot saying he's leaving for Dublin Saturday morning and he's going to miss the wedding. He's got some squat and says it's where the music is carrying him.'

'He didn't—' I ask.

'Yup, asked her to join him.'

'And?'

'Well, she's insisting on getting married with or without the leather jacket in attendance.' Mum smiles weakly. 'All we can do is be there for her, Molly. She'll make her own mistakes.'

That is an understatement. So I nod, and we follow Polly into the kitchen, where she's already established an assembly line for cupcake production. Dad and Cecilia are both mixing up giant batches of icing. Cecilia seems to have managed to create three different bowls of colourful icing, and Dad is still labouring over his first bowl, squinting at the recipe and slowly adding cocoa powder in tiny increments.

'All right, ladies, aprons on!'

To my utter surprise, Mum picks up the apron without protest and wraps it around her thin frame.

The first batch of chocolate cupcakes burns to a crisp. Polly begins weeping and saying it's an omen. She sits at the kitchen table pummelling one into crumbs with her fist. Mum and I air the kitchen, while Dad and Cecilia clean up the mess and set up the assembly line again. Mum coaxes Polly back on to her feet and round two of the cupcakes begins.

It is already the early hours of Saturday morning by

the time the second batch of cupcakes comes out of the oven. The kitchen smells like sugar and warm butter.

Polly cheers up, teaching us how to do the more elaborate designs, and only some of the cupcakes end up gloopy. They are dotted with colourful sweets, crushed Oreos, sprinkles, diced nuts and whatever else falls into the edible-and-sugary category.

The adults abandon us early on in the decorating phase, but Polly sticks on some 1990s' hits. We pipe and sprinkle to her Bootylicious Playlist until long after the sun has crept back into the kitchen.

It is almost 7 a.m. by the time Cecilia comes back downstairs to do some morning yoga.

'It's a bit chilly in here,' she says.

I check the range – we have let the fire die out. I open the fuel chest, but there is nothing but a thin coating of turf crumbs at the bottom.

'We'll have to fill it later,' I say.

'Oh, no, I'm not complaining. I love a bit of cold, it gets me moving,' Cecilia says, rolling out her mat and beginning to stretch her limbs. She is dressed in mismatching luminous Lycra. She rolls around on the kitchen floor, clutching her knees to her chest and heaving deeply.

Polly takes this as our cue to leave, and piles the completed cupcakes into a tower display.

'We better get some sleep before the wedding,' she says to Cecilia, and leaves the room.

I follow suit and we hear Cecilia's motherly tones behind us: 'I'll wake you before the guests arrive.'

On our way up to bed, we pass Mum and whisper that Cecilia is turning the kitchen into yoga-town. Mum looks bemused and alarmed simultaneously, and follows us back up the stairs. We all go into my room and lie across the bed. It is kind of nice. We fall asleep to Mum recounting her own wedding day.

'I was just madly in love . . . I didn't think about the farm or anything, I thought it wouldn't matter as long as we had each other . . . But you can't force someone to be something they're not, even if that person is yourself . . .'

The last thing I see before I fall asleep is Polly nodding gently, a determined look in her eyes.

We must have been exhausted, because the next thing I know is that Cecilia is standing in the door-way, chuckling at us.

'Adorable,' she says. 'I hate to disturb you, but, well, the guests are arriving in a few hours . . . and . . . nobody has seen Polly.'

Mum's leg is weighted across me, her body sprawled in every possible direction. Polly is nowhere to be seen. The sky outside looks grey and eveningish.

I shake Mum awake. She rolls off the bed and on to her feet.

'I guess it's time,' she says, yawning and stretching.

'Polly's missing.' I say.

Mum processes this for a moment, smoothing her hair into a knot at the nape of her neck.

'Why am I not surprised?' Mum says. She pauses, rubbing sleep from her eyes. 'You know, this is as shocking to me as it will be to you, but we owe it to Brian to try and find her.'

'Actually, now that you mention it, Brian's downstairs,' Cecilia says.

We file sleepily downstairs. BrainDrain is sitting at the kitchen table with Dad. There is a pot of tea between them and a plate of digestives.

'There, there, she'll turn up,' BrainDrain says.

'I'm so embarrassed,' Dad says. 'I mean, if she'd just run away when we had time to cancel . . . This is all my fault.' He rubs his temples in despair; his hair has turned to static and he is wearing a rumpled shirt.

The jilted groom smooths the lapels on his tux.

'It's nobody's fault. Sure, Mammy says it's better to find out sooner rather than later.'

We all gawp at BrainDrain: he is radiating calm.

'Are you OK, Brian?' Mum says. 'It must be an awful shock?'

'Ah, it's not too bad. Sure, she left me a note and

339

the ring on the table. And sure, I should get a decent refund. I only paid a deposit on the honeymoon, because, well, Mammy always says you can never be too careful.'

'Note?' Mum says. 'Well, at least she's learning from her father's mistakes.'

'Unless the note is an equation or something,' I say.

'I'm afraid that's personal,' BrainDrain says. 'What happened between Polly and me-self is nobody's business but ours.'

The adults all nod understandingly, as if they would never dream of reading the note. Mum's fingers are practically twitching with curiosity.

BrainDrain makes us all a cup of tea, a pile of toast and jam, and has one last meal with us. He natters on about all the refunds he will get and then, with an air of finality, stands up.

'I hope you don't mind, but Mammy's outside. I'd, eh . . . rather not be around when the guests arrive. If you see Polly, well, tell her I'm thankful – she's after doing us both a favour.'

We follow him out into the hall, gathering in a clump to wave him off. We're all craning to catch a glimpse of his infamous mammy. But she's just a shadow in the front seat and parked too far down the drive to get a proper visual. She throws open the door for her beloved son as he ambles towards her. He doesn't seem remotely scarred by the situation. I wish I could be that serene in the face of disaster.

We watch as the car drives away, the tail lights disappearing down the hill.

'Maybe we should keep him?' I say, and everyone nods.

We shut the front door behind us and return to the kitchen, wondering what to do about the bonfire. We settle around the table and there's a collective sigh.

Suddenly, the fuel chest beside the fireplace starts knocking. I stare at the wooden box; as far as I'm aware, it is still completely empty. Has someone put one of the animals in there?

'Did you hear that?' Mum asks, looking at it. The banging continues. Cecilia gets up and goes to open it, hauling up the lid and revealing a soot-covered Polly.

'My God, I thought he'd never leave,' she says, uncurling herself and standing up. 'If he didn't shut up about his mammy, I was going to show myself.'

Polly steps out of the fuel box as if it is an entirely normal place to be hiding. Or as if hiding is a normal thing to be doing in the first place.

We all blink. There is not much else we can do.

Polly has soot in her hair, streaked across her face and all over the floral nightmare dress, which for some reason she is wearing.

Seeing the scandalized looks on our faces, Polly decides to explain.

'I couldn't, I just couldn't – I put on the dress and panicked. I mean, he's lovely and reliable and boring,' she says. 'And though I long to be boring, it does not come naturally to me.'

Standing there in her ruined wedding dress, she is a perfect illustration of her reasoning. Boring she most certainly is not.

'I still have so much to figure out,' she says grandly, sweeping her arms wide.

'Yes, yes . . . well . . .' Dad says, unsure how best to tackle his sooty daughter.

'This isn't because of Dermot?' Mum says, looking worried.

'Oh God, no . . . Believe it or not, dear Mother, this is about me.'

'Well, that's a relief,' Mum says.

'Do you know what I think we should do?' Cecilia interrupts.

We all stare at her – now is the time for some sort of raging argument, or tearful screaming. That is how our family operates. Mum and Polly are warming up, and here is Cecilia grinning at us all.

'Um . . . not really,' Mum says.

'Why don't we throw the party anyway? We've got the marquee and the cupcakes, we've got a bonfire and guests. I don't see why not.'

We all think about it. Dad scratches his head, Mum shrugs, and I watch Polly carefully. She turns the idea backwards and forwards, looking for holes in it. No doubt Polly had imagined dramatically standing in the drive, shooing away our guests and explaining that she was setting forth on a journey of self-discovery. But I can see her warming to the idea of a bonfire.

'That's a lovely idea,' Polly says, surprising us all.

As we all nod, I realize it's the second time this evening we've all been in agreement.

33

I slip into jeans and a warm jumper before making
my way out to the party.

The bonfire is massive. I glance around at the
weird ensemble: there are Mum's hippy friends; Tess,
Barry, Fiachra; and a load of interestingly pierced
young people that belong to Polly. Cecilia and Dad
are sitting on a log by themselves, and Mum is on the
other side of the fire chatting to somebody dressed
like a dreamcatcher. Every now and then, there is the
sound of an animal grunting or groaning in the sheds,
but nobody seems to mind the *baas* and squawks all
that much.

Barry is busy charming some of Polly's pierced
people with anti-government sentiments, so Tess and
Fiachra are sitting alone together on a log. Tess is glaring in Barry's direction, and Fiachra is trying to
distract her. I sit down beside them, listening to them

mumble and watching the embers from the fire spark outwards and shimmer, before dimming and disappearing into the ground. Fiachra's adoration of Tess is probably intensifying in the moonlight.

Polly comes down looking radiant. She has opted to wear one of Mum's old gowns, a silky emerald number that skims her shoulders and skirts romantically down towards her knees. Her hair is tousled and swept to one side and she's left her face free of makeup. Her cheeks flush pink in the firelight. She is carrying a cardboard box labelled BRIAN DORAN, DERMOT AND OTHERS.

She hugs the guests and sits around chatting, before deciding to empty the box on the fire. People cheer, and Polly laughs along.

Mum joins in the fun and tries to burn an old metal horse sculpture to cleanse *men* from her life, but the metal is resilient, and it sort of sits in the flames, triumphantly glowering at her. It is a bit awkward for Dad, but he copes.

'It's a new beginning,' Polly says. She sits down on a log beside Mum and the two of them lapse into contented silence. I'm not sure how content Polly really is, though, because by the end of the night she is surrounded by empty cupcake wrappers.

Tess shows us her new phone – which is a dinosaur.

'So, you're serious,' I say. Her old phone is hidden in a drawer upstairs in my room for when she finally breaks.

'I mean, it's, like, helping me define what really matters,' she says. One of her hands subconsciously types the air, as if her old phone is still within reach.

'Well, that's good. There's a group dedicated to gnome-tippers now . . .' I say.

'What does it matter? What even is a group in real life? It means nothing.'

'Yeah . . .'

'I mean, at our age it's essential to find yourself,' she says, 'not to be, like, promoting yourself . . . Like, what are you even promoting?'

'Right,' Fiachra says half-heartedly. Because Fiachra is possibly distraught that she hasn't really taken her eyes off Barry all evening. Even as Tess talks about finding herself, half her attention is fixed on the group of older teenagers laughing at whatever Barry's saying.

As far as *I'm not getting married* parties go, it is pretty good. Mum drinks some lethal home-made alcohol that one of Polly's pierced people brought and ends up passing out on a log. One of Mum's friends plaits grass into Mum's hair and hums to herself, while the others laugh hysterically at their own shadows. The laughing at the shadows is too much for Polly, and she goes to bed; this may also be because she has run out of chocolate cupcakes and nobody is paying her any attention.

Cecilia potters about being lovely to anyone that makes eye contact, and Dad gets drunk. He gives me a long speech about how I'll always be his little girl and talks about all the stuff we'll do in France this summer.

Tess leaves early enough. She says she needs to do yoga. Something about a thirty-day challenge on the internet, which doesn't sound all that holistic. She agrees reluctantly to still help with the Animal Gathering, though I suspect it has more to do with monitoring Barry than any real interest in the actual event.

'We can, like, take the vegan movement offline,' she says, 'to real life, where I am not some weird-ass gnome-tipper.'

'That didn't happen in real life?' Fiachra asks mockingly.

'Not if you want to remain friends,' she says, before leaving. As she walks away, she gives Barry one last lingering look.

I sit with Fiachra. He is wearing an actual shirt and his runners are only slightly dirty. It is a bit too quiet. I know how he must feel – losing Tess to someone as pretentious as Barry isn't ideal.

'Don't worry about Tess, she'll come around,' I say. There is no point begrudging them.

'What?' Fiachra looks horrified. He is staring at me with buggy eyes.

'I know you like Tess – don't worry, she'll come around,' I say. 'She'll see through Barry eventually.'

'Eh . . . OK . . .' He looks at his feet, and blushes.

I glance at Mum to distract myself from Fiachra's blushing. She is scratching her face in her sleep. Her friends are cradling her head and singing 'Hakuna Matata' to the moon.

'That alcohol is pretty lethal,' Fiachra says, which is his way of changing the subject and not coping with his feelings. 'Fancy some vinegar?'

'Very funny,' I say. It is so quiet that I can hear my eyelids move. Poor Fiachra seems heartbroken.

'Remember when you hugged me in maths?' he says.

'Nah, I like to forget certain days, and that is one of them.'

I'm antsy. I stand up to go over to Mum, but her friend is stroking her nose, so I change my mind and face the bonfire instead. I'm annoyed. Why is Fiachra trying to rehash the *time a girl inappropriately hugged him* moment, as if I'm not that girl?

As I gaze at the bonfire, Fiachra jumps to his feet. He positions himself close to me. His brow is all wrinkled.

'I wanted to hug you back – I just didn't know

how to,' he says.

'That's nice,' I say. Because the words haven't registered yet, and I'm fixating on a burning piece of log to avoid eye contact.

'I really like you,' he says. 'I like you, like you.'

I refuse to acknowledge this. I'm *not* some sort of poor man's compromise. He really likes Tess. This is the worst conversation in the history of my life. He is looking at his feet again, and I go to step around him, but he puts his arm out to stop me.

'Look, Fiachra, I have a lot going on right now.'

I gesture vaguely at each of my visible family members; as both of them are inebriated or unconscious, it illustrates my point quite nicely. 'I don't have time for all this nonsense, and I don't care that Tess isn't interested in you – you can't use that as an excuse to decide you like me, that's not OK ...'

Fiachra loses patience then. He steps even closer – our toes are almost touching. I stare at his shirt. The plaid squares are all joining up together and he smells all boy-nice, like a Lynx advert, but not the kind of Lynx advert that would kill your cat. I don't know how it happens, but his lips are suddenly soft and warm on mine.

He breaks away, reaches for my hand and places it in his, before saying, 'I like *you*, I always liked you ... Can I?'

I nod, trying to stay calm and collected. But I'm attempting to think of any hints he might have given me. How did I miss the evidence? Why was I so sure he liked Tess? Maybe I should map out all our encounters on a graph . . . I'm feeling giddy and illogical – surely this can't be wise? I haven't even listed the pros and cons of Fiachra yet; I don't know enough about him to feel this fluttery at the touch of his lips.

'We don't have to overthink this,' he says, leaning in to kiss me again.

I'm just getting the hang of this kissing thing when a cough sounds incredibly close to my shoulder.

Fiachra jumps away from me, as if he has been scalded. I open my eyes. Dad is standing within an arm's length of us, swaying slightly on the spot and trying to look stern. His eyebrows are pulled together, and he tuts as he extends a hand to Fiachra.

'I hope, hope you don't mind mmmme, no, I ammmm asking about intennntions,' he half-slurs.

'Dad,' I say, stepping between him and Fiachra and willing time to rewind. 'This is not the time.'

'JOHN!'

Dad's name sounds like a shrill battle cry from the other side of the bonfire. Within seconds, Cecilia is bobbing towards us.

'You better not be – oh, this is so embarrassing, I

am so sorry, Molly,' she says, her eyes darting from me to Fiachra. She grabs Dad by the shoulders, steering him back towards the other side of the bonfire. As they depart, their conversation fills the silence between Fiachra and me.

'This is not better parenting. What were you thinking?' Cecilia says.

'But I . . . I . . . wassss . . . ssssupporting—'

'That is not suppor . . .' Cecilia interrupts, getting him as far away from us as possible.

And that's all I hear, because Fiachra is pulling me back towards him.

Me: Tess, you there?

Mrs Gallagher's Phone (clearly Tess): END MY LIFE. Just spent an hour trying to knit a freakin' chicken jumper with Mum's wool.

Me: WHY?

Tess: My hands were twitchy. Screw being holistic! These hands were made for swiping right, not the goddamn purl stitch.

Me: Well, then, you'll be happy to know I've got your old phone right here.

Tess: Eh . . . so much for believing in me.

Me: I one hundred per cent believed you would come to your senses.

Tess: Ugh. I could do it if I lived in a town with actual people. So why the 2 a.m. text? Not another chicken-related emergency?

Me: Nah . . . So this thing happened with Fiachra.

Tess: OMG . . . Did he finally put his tongue in your face?

Me: Trust you to ruin it.

Tess: HE DID. I KNEW IT. There is a God. I expect details tomorrow.

Me: I shouldn't have told you

Tess: Whatever . . . As the parentals would say, C U L8R! x

34

Luckily Polly is in a helpful mood, whereas Tess has been huddled over her phone chuckling maniacally to herself all morning. There were over a thousand notifications on her various apps when I handed back the phone, and she's busy responding to her new community of gnome-tipping fanatics, as the rest of us put the final touches on the Animal Gathering.

The Hulk came by earlier and dumped a load of hay in the marquee.

'So, you're sure you're not a thing any more?' I asked Mum, as he drove away.

'Oh God, no, I can't even remember who I was back then,' she said, smoothing out her solar-system tights.

'Eh . . . it was just a few days ago?'

'A few days can be a lifetime, petal.'

We spent the rest of the morning spreading out the hay in the marquee and speckling it with wheelbarrows, buckets, watering cans, and other props. Polly is all about accentuating the animals; it's like they're a table she is trying to arrange perfectly. And, to be fair, she has outdone herself. It's the picture of a rustic farmyard.

It's weird – out of all of this, it feels as if the vegan movement is the one good thing we've done lately. As I look around me at the Animal Gathering, I realize that it might have been for all the wrong reasons, but maybe there's something in it? I'm not sure exactly what, but the farm is strangely peaceful. Maybe it's because we're all united for a cause. Or perhaps it's because the wedding preparations are finally over.

The five sheep are penned in using old washing line. Lady Macbeth nestles idyllically in one corner of the marquee, finally a content chicken again. Most of the chickens bustle about. Síle the Donkey wanders aimlessly around in a circle as Bellatrix and Miss Trunchbull take turns pecking angrily at her hooves (the violence may never leave their systems). The goat alternates between sitting in a rusty wheelbarrow and nibbling the corners of the marquee.

The chickens make me hopeful for the future. Tess sees me gazing at them and tells me not to get too attached. I ignore her. Nobody understands my chickens like I do.

Polly has even put an old paddling pool in the centre of proceedings and the duck has spent most of its morning eyeing it warily. Any minute now, he'll take the plunge. Jack the Three-Legged Dog has peed on every pole several times, but none of the other animals seem to mind much. The cow is a bit big for the marquee, so Polly suggests we use her and the pony at the farm entrance to lure people in. She fashions makeshift leads for them and plans to let the children ride them both.

Dad is trying to figure out the appropriate value for a cow ride.

'It's less prestigious than a horse ride, but more unique . . . So if you make y a variable . . .' he says, mumbling to himself as he considers the sign he's making. So far it says COW RIDES €.

'What if someone falls off?' Cecilia asks.

'Oh, we've got a helmet,' Polly says, waving the old bike helmet in the air.

'Do you have insurance?'

'We have bubble wrap,' Mum says. Clearly my chicken-confrontation suit was a prototype.

'I mean, it doesn't matter if we don't have insur-ance – nobody around here can afford to sue us anyway,' Polly says, causing Cecilia to frown.

'It would literally end Ballyfert's morale,' Tess adds, before resuming her texting.

Cecilia nods, and goes back to sorting the donations table. She is planning to man it, and there's an impressive number of home-made vegan cookies on display. She whipped them up using peanut butter and some coconut oil. Polly sniffs at them suspiciously.

'Why don't you try one?' Cecilia asks. Polly reluctantly picks one up and weighs it in her hand. She takes a bite, her eyes widening.

'It tastes like a real cookie,' she says, crumbling the remainder in her hand and examining it. This prompts the rest of us to shuffle over and try one. We stand around, baffled by the soft crumbly goodness of the cookies. The coconut and brown sugar melt in my mouth.

'I always imagined a vegan cookie would be like glorified sawdust,' Mum says, before wandering off to rearrange her horse sculptures for the fourth time. She is using the petting zoo as a chance to try and sell a few. The parsnip sculpture looks like it has begun to rot: the edges are browning and wilted.

'I'll call it "Impermanence",' Mum says, as she cuts off a section that is sprouting blue mould. Her wig has been firmly in place all morning, and Dad has barely bothered her. It's like her spirits have grown ten feet over the course of the night and she's ready to take on the world.

A huge gleaming LandRover pulls into the yard

and Mum glances up. I can't help feel that she's been expecting it.

'Ah, yes, that will be the Kellys.' She says it off-handishly, as if the last week hasn't been spent in a chicken-feud with that very family.

'Wh-what are they doing here?' I splutter.

'Well, we're not in the business of ruining people's livelihood. The money raised will go towards the Kelly farm. They're promising to go free-range and organic, because the whole chicken thing has been very bad press. And there was something about donating gnomes to charity ... She was quite emotional on the phone, I didn't quite catch it ...'

'But—' I begin.

'But nothing,' Mum says. 'We have the chickens, don't we?'

'Hold up —' Tess is on her feet, her phone cast to one side for the first time this morning – 'is that—'

Before any of us can fully form a protest, the Kellys are in front of us. Mrs Kelly's platinum-blonde head is air-kissing with Mum's blue one. They hug like old friends, and Mr Kelly (a giant ginger man) slaps my dad so hard on the back it looks like Dad might have slipped a disc. There's a prolonged silence as Claire hovers behind her parents, staring sheepishly at her feet. The scratches on her face still look raw and sore.

'Claire, honey . . . What is it you wanted to say to these girls?'

'I . . . uh . . .'

'Sweetheart, we talked about this.' Claire's mum is icing-sugar friendly. There's a sickly feel to how she's coaxing her daughter along.

'I . . . well, I'm sorry . . . about all the videos . . .' she mumbles. 'And, eh . . . well . . .' Gone is her finger-snapping elegance; she's not even wearing Ugg boots, just a pair of bog-standard wellies, and zero make-up.

Her mum coughs, handing Claire a plastic bag containing something bulky.

'Oh, yeah.' Claire hands the bag to Tess reluctantly.

'What's that?' I ask. Tess gasps.

'My Ugg boots,' Claire says softly. There's another cough from her mother. 'I pledge allegiance to the vegans . . . And I'm . . . well, I really am sorry.'

Tess pulls an Ugg boot from the bag, holding it up almost like a trophy for everyone to see.

'We're sorry too,' I say, elbowing Tess.

'There are literally no words,' Tess says, somehow avoiding an apology, but managing to sound like she's giving one anyway. She strokes the Ugg boot before placing it back in the plastic bag. Her expression is all innocence, but somewhere deep inside she's doing a cancan. In Tess-land, this means she is now Claire's leader.

The parents all nod, as if we've reached a new plateau of existence. Cecilia ushers the adults over to the donations table, and they nervously bite into the vegan cookies. Their cautious nibbles give way to enthusiastic chomping when they realize the cookies don't taste like sanctimonious sawdust.

Other people start to arrive, and so, thankfully, we're not forced to manufacture common ground with Claire. We all work hard, glad of a distraction. It's an exhausting few hours – it seems as if the entire town has shown up, with loads of people from school signing up to be vegans.

Fiachra turns up midway through the day and reveals he's some sort of animal whisperer. He manages to get Síle the Donkey to cooperate. Before long, kids are doubling their donations for a chance to be led about the yard by Fiachra and his scruffy steed.

The yard is bedlam, people milling about, munching on cookies and gawking at the strange collection of animals. The chickens enjoy the attention, fluffing their feathers, even though most people are more interested in the peacock, who has stage fright and is cowering in the corner. At first, I'm worried that people might prod Lady Macbeth, but the crowd is content with watching her cluck away on her little mound of eggs.

Barry arrives late, but then takes to waltzing about

the donations table as if he did all the work. It turns out to be for the best, because nobody else seems to know much about veganism and Cecilia's expertise extends no further than the recipe for her cookies. Tess sulks at the number of girls preening for Barry's attention. Her face darkens as a gaggle of thirteen-year-olds giggle helplessly at his jokes.

'I'd forget him if I was you,' Claire says, wandering past with a bag of poo. Tess assigned her poop-scooping duties and, because her mum was hovering nearby, Claire agreed.

'Did I ask you?' Tess says, haughtily.

'Well, no – but, like, count how often he checks his own reflection.' Claire nods in his direction, and then, as if to illustrate her point, Barry slips his phone from his pocket and uses the screen to rearrange his hair.

'That's one,' Claire says, as Barry pockets the phone. He laughs at something a girl says to him, but while she's speaking, he picks up a spoon from the donations table and quickly glances at himself in it, before spinning it about as if it's an idle prop.

'That'll be two,' Claire says. 'Oh, and this is too much – look, he's gone for the phone again.'

We stare in horror as Barry checks his reflection again, stroking his eyebrows while maintaining a monologue on animal rights.

'It's like he doesn't even know he's doing it,' Tess says.

'Second nature at this stage,' Claire says. 'Worst thing is, he does it so casually nobody much notices.'

'How did you?'

'We went out for a week. He spent more time checking himself out than me,' Claire says.

'Rough,' Tess says. They smile at each other as if Barry's vanity has cleansed some deep wound. Claire walks away to dispose of the poop, and I realize she doesn't scare me any more.

At this moment, I'm not sure anything does.

'So, you're friends now?' I ask, as we watch Claire shovelling more poo into a bag.

'Let's not get carried away,' Tess says. 'I'm not even convinced she's human.'

Tess: I've been mapping out the next six months of the vegan strategy and . . . we need to talk about your priorities.

Me: Hello to you too . . . I hereby swear to stop eating cheese.

Tess: Uh, this is a little less about cheese and a bit more about a certain boy whisking you away on a lawnmower. We need some, like, proper rules.

Me: Um . . . what? Like . . . thou shalt spend Saturday stroking chickens?

Tess: You laugh, but boys are distracting. This is for the sake of the movement.

Me: Chickens are more distracting. I'd know.

Tess: First rule: lunch is Sacred Strategy Hour for the Ballyfert Vegans. No bike-shed shenanigans.

Me: Bike sheds, seriously? Have you even met me?

Tess: Two: you need to use your new-found boy-control powers to make Fiachra dress up as a giant chicken for next week's video.

Me: Boy-control? Video? Tess! Why???

Tess: It may be my finest work yet.

Me: Your finest work involves a giant chicken? Can we just be normal for a week?

Tess: Gurl, nobody maintains viral superstar-status by eating porridge.

Me: Let me guess . . . Someone else needs to dress up as a giant sheep?

Tess: Look at you – all grown up and having ideas . . .

Acknowledgements

There were so many people involved in the journey of this book. It's embarrassing that only my name is on the cover. My first thank you is to the Chicken House Coop – you've been amazing from start to finish. Sorry about my mini-freak-outs and rambling emails. You've been nothing short of understanding, patient and supportive every step of the way. So, Barry, Jazz, Rachel L, Rachel H, Laura, Elinor, Kesia, and anyone else secretly involved behind the scenes – a HUGE thank you!

Of all the lovely chickens, I am most thankful for Rachel Leyshon, who is the queen of asking exactly the right question. Thank you for having faith in this book when it was clearly not a book and coaxing the real story into existence. You're a novel whisperer and plot-fixer extraordinaire. I will try to be more coherent in future.

Thank you to Daphne. Your copy-edits required the patience of a saint. I'm astounded by your attention to detail and horrified by my lack of it. To Victoria Walters, for reaching out and letting me know she read a rough version of this back in its ugly-child phase. She pitched it to Chicken House – for which I am eternally grateful.

To Rachel Hickman and the team at Studio Helen — thank you for a beautiful cover and for being so understanding. I'm sorry about my aversion to the colour pink. I will get over myself eventually.

There's also thanks due to the Dublin Writers' Forum, particularly Anne Tannam and Fiona Bolger, who were unwavering in their support and kind with their critiques. Nobody could ask for wiser friends. Thanks also to Lia for rolling her eyes and keeping me grounded!

There are plenty of other people who saw horrible versions of this book and were kind when they could (should) have been cruel. So, Siobhán Parkinson, Grainne Clear and Claire Hennessey — thank you! Also, to Tom Rowley, Sarah Griff, and Deirdre Sullivan, who've all said encouraging things somewhere along the line (even if they didn't know it or even intend to encourage such madness!).

I owe another debt of gratitude to Mike McCormack — who told me to be patient and focus on the funny bits a long time ago. I sort-of listened.

Thanks also to my writing friends for sporadic emails, words of encouragement and shared despair. I'm looking at you, Lynn Harding, Sarah Miller, Ronan Daly, Sean Scully, Keith Bohan, Diarmaid Blehein, Méabh Brown, Alice Kinsella, Gemma Creagh and Phil Lynch. A special thanks to Kathy Deady for moral support during the last edit of this book and for casting an expert eye over my pigeon Irish.

And thank you to my family (immediate and otherwise) for providing the sort of endless inspiring madness needed to develop such characters. Mum, Nancy, Lucy, JP, Peter, Dad, Ellie and Anne . . . it's all entirely fictional, I promise. To Caroline, PJ, Aideen, and Bronagh – for being the best second family I could possibly ask for.

For believing in me and sending messages of support over the years – Rachelle le Dukee, Tori Zirul, Ola, Cammy, Julie Naughton, Laura Brady and Emmylou. An extra big thank you to Gaz – who told me to sit down and stop wasting my time on a rather awful short story and write a novel (although he was kinder than that). Sound advice as always!

Thank you to Stephen Murphy. Without you, I'd be a bumbling mess and incapable of finding my keys let alone writing anything close to a novel. You're the kindest man I know, and you've supported this book from start to finish. I fully intend to stop talking about chickens now.

And finally, the reader, I will always be grateful for the time you spent reading this book. It's strange to think of you, out there in the world reading this, so thank you – whoever you are and wherever you're from.

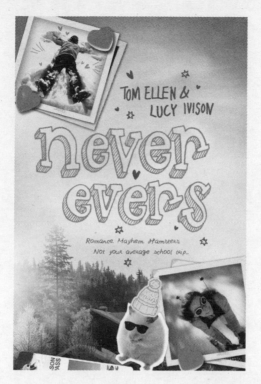

NEVER EVERS by TOM ELLEN & LUCY IVISON

The school ski trip isn't going to plan. Mouse has fallen out with her friends and Jack's totally clueless about girls. But when a French pop star – who Jack's a dead ringer for – arrives in the resort, the snowy slopes begin to get a bit more interesting . . .

> This book perfectly captures the highs and lows of the early teenage years.
> THE SUN

> I gobbled it whole in a day. Everyone who likes enjoying life should read it.
> HOLLY BOURNE

Paperback, ISBN: 978-1-910002-36-0, £6.99 • ebook, ISBN 978-1-910655-36-8, £6.99

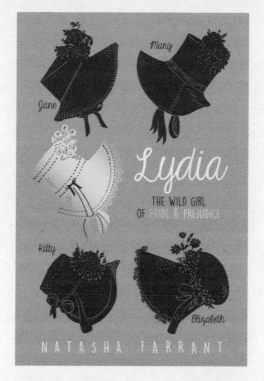

LYDIA by NATASHA FARRANT

Vain, ignorant, idle, and absolutely uncontrolled.

That is what my family think of me. They want to keep me in the countryside to improve my mind, but if I stay here I WILL DIE. Oh, I will go to Brighton if it is the last thing I do, and show my sisters what I am capable of. I shall probably come back with a husband. I'd come back with two if I could . . .

I'm reading [Lydia] and LOVE it. It's like being hugged by a book.
HOLLY BOURNE, AUTHOR OF *AM I NORMAL YET?*

Paperback, ISBN 978-1-910002-97-1, £7.99 • ebook, 978-1-910655-59-7, £7.99

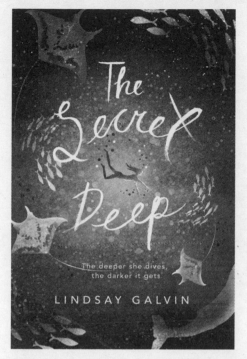

THE SECRET DEEP by LINDSAY GALVIN

When Aster wakes on a tropical island, she has no idea how she got there.

Where's her aunt – and the teenagers from the ecovillage she was part of?

Most importantly, where's her little sister, Poppy?

As Aster frantically searches her surroundings, everything points to the sea and to a deep-water secret that's both important – and impossible . . .

Lindsay Galvin is a creative new voice in science fiction. Real science is used to create mind-blowing magic, in an underwater world that will take your breath away — and give you gills instead.
LAUREN JAMES, AUTHOR OF *THE NEXT TOGETHER*